Gigolos

Gigolos

Steve Poultney

Disclaimer

This is a work of fiction. Names, characters, places, businesses and incidents are either products of the author's imagination or are used fictitiously. Any resemblance to actual events , locales or any person, living or dead, is entirely coincidental.

Copyright © 2022 Steve Poultney

ISBN: 9798353490012
All rights reserved

Bidets and Broken Dreams

The Cortina eased between the faded white lines of the wet car park. It was brown - that out-of-date brown reminiscent of flared trousers in the 70s. It took the passenger two shoves to open the door as it dropped slightly with a dull thud. Slamming it shut with some effort, he stepped into the grey drizzle and out of the foggy haze of smoke seeping its way from the car into the thickening mist.

There was a fumbling from inside as the taller man, cigarette in mouth, leaned over and emerged slowly from the other door, straightening himself up to his full height.

Armed with snap tins and flasks, the two men walked down towards the river and the yard, picking up other stragglers on the way. The Clyde, barely perceptible in the mist, was a cold grey river on which men of steel had built ships of iron for nigh on two hundred years. But this was the eighties and soon, just like many of the other great industries, the shipyards would be all but consigned to history.

On entering the gates they could see a throng of men, soaked by the persistent drizzle, massing around the notice pinned to the board. Simmo, the shorter of the two, was reminded of an experiment they'd done once at school when he'd looked through a microscope, one of the few pieces of equipment the other buggers hadn't managed to break. *Brownian Motion* - at least that's what he thought he recalled

Gigolos

the teacher said – consisted of random particles moving seemingly as if by magic...

His companion, Ally, broke his train of thought – "Aye, I reckon this is it then; looks like we'll be getting our cards".

Simmo looked up with an "uh?" as his companion, like an icebreaker, pushed his way through the crowd. The smaller man hastily followed in his wake toward the board at the front to view the notice, pinned cockeyed and written on an old fashioned typewriter with the ink running down the page like grey tears. Bizarrely, Simmo thought that he could see little holes in the paper where the dots of the 'i's had been punctured by the worn key, and the drizzle, gathered in globules, reflected the arc lights back like the eyes of a scared cat. The words swam in his head but three seemed to stand out above the rest: closure, redundancy and volunteers. The rest were as meaningless as the rain.

"Feck it!" said the big man, slapping him on the shoulders, "they can weld their own fecking ship today. I could do with a drink."

Simmo nodded abstractedly and they turned and pushed their way back through the murmuring crowd, wandering distractedly over to the Cortina. Ally opened the door and climbed in, followed by Simmo who, on his third attempt, finally managed to get the passenger door closed with its usual clunk.

"I think it's time we opened that bottle of whiskey you've been saving," Ally quipped.

"Oh", said Simmo, feeling a wrench in the pit of his stomach.

"Aye, you've had it long enough."

Simmo just turned his face and looked out of the window.

The radio crackled, hissing static, and Ally mumbled "fecking shite," before wrenching the knob to the other side and cutting the newsreader off instantly. They drove on in relative silence, the brakes emitting a gentle squeal in the heavy traffic. Simmo was still amazed that Ally could roll a cigarette whilst guiding the car as though it were on auto pilot. Surreally, everyone else went about their daily business as the car edged its way in and out of the late morning rush.
"Have you still got the builders at your house?" asked Ally, waking Simmo from his morbid musings.
"No, thank Christ, they've gone but they've left their shite strewn everywhere. It's the bathroom fitters' turn now."
Ally started to laugh, "All that for a fecking bidet!"
Simmo shuffled and smiled uneasily. "If it keeps her happy..."
Ally looked at him in puzzlement. "I never quite understood what you use one for..." Simmo rolled his eyes to the sky and thought "here we go".
"Well," he answered, "some people wash their feet in them; others water their aspidistra in them, and others –
"Aye," Ally interjected, "I imagine it's good if you've got a hairy crack. Does Mrs C have a hairy...?"
But before he could finish Simmo screeched "don't even go there!!"
"It was just a thought..."
"Yeah; well keep it to yourself..."

Gigolos

They drove on, easing their way out of the busy traffic into the quieter suburbs. Although Simmo's postcode was that of the posh part of town, they lived on the wrong side of the road to the people who really had the money. Turning off into the street they could see a white sign-written van parked outside Simmo's house. In front of it was a smart looking Mercedes. They found a parking space a few doors down and the ritual of closing the battered Cortina's passenger door was repeated. Walking back up toward the house they could see two men in overalls, presumably the bathroom fitters, sitting in the van.

"Not much getting done today then," said Ally.
"Must be the rain."
"What, in the fecking bathroom?"
Simmo just grunted.
"See what you mean about the mess", said Ally.

There was builders' rubble all over the usually neat and tidy front garden. Simmo grunted again; he would get around to sorting it eventually.

The two men in the van eyed each other. "Do you think we ought to warn them?" one of them said. "Nah," said the other one, "been waiting for something like this to happen for a long time."

Simmo lifted the gate and gave it a heave. It was another one of those things he'd get around to fixing one day. And there, sat in the middle of the lawn on a small wooden pallet like the centrepiece of a Gothic mausoleum, stood an avocado bidet.

"There's your pride and joy," said Ally. "What's all this cost if you don't mind mah asking?" he added with that wrinkled forehead expression of his.

"Nigh on a grand."

Ally whistled. "Feck," he said, "you only paid ten grand for the place."

"Yeah," said Simmo, "but removing supporting walls and fitting steel lintels costs."

The two men walked around the side of the house and Simmo tried the back door. Unusually, it seemed to be locked. Now his missus would never let him in through the front door due to his filthy boots and overalls so he scratched his head as he fumbled in his pocket for the key. In the meantime Ally had walked round to the back of the house. He pressed his face, shielded by his large hands, to the wet glass. Staring into the lounge through the French windows, his view was initially blurred by the rain and condensation and he struggled to make out a shape, only to see a face he didn't recognise metamorphose into the form of a big arse going up and down on Simmo's wife. And as the penny dropped he could hear the sound of Simmo mumbling, "Got you the bastard!" as he found the right key for the lock and was shouldering the swollen back door open.

Ally came charging round but Simmo had already disappeared into the house. He could just hear the words "What the fuck?!" followed by "I'll kill you, you bastard!" in a high pitched screech from his friend, who was now brandishing a large Stillson wrench that he'd grabbed from one of the plumbers' tool bags. He'd raised it above his head and great dribbles of saliva were accompanying the banshee's wail escaping his lips. Moving with a speed and stealth not normally seen in the big man, Ally grabbed Simmo by the shirt collar with one hand and the wrench with the other and dragged him backwards kicking his heels until he fell on his arse on the soggy doormat outside the kitchen door. He flung the wrench over the hedge

Gigolos

into the garden next door, with an accompanying crash of glass as it found the greenhouse where prize-winning tomatoes probably wouldn't appear this summer. Dragging a stunned Simmo to his feet, he stood between him and the door and began shoving him back towards the Cortina.

"They're nae fecking worth it!" screamed Ally into his stunned friend's face as he turned him around and pushed him out into the front garden. "Who the feck is he?"

"The fucking bathroom salesman, Bob the Bidet," said Simmo bitterly, glaring at the font of all evil standing on the lawn.

"Is that his car?" said Ally.

"What?" Said Simmo, still stunned. "Dunno, looks like the type of thing a cunt like him might drive."

Ally's eyes lit up – "Get hold!" he said, and the two men picked up the bidet from the pallet and stepped over the low garden wall. The door opened a bit on the van and one of the men shouted, "Oi, that's going in!" to which Ally replied "Too fecking right it is pal!" as with a mighty heave the two men hurled the bidet through the front windscreen of the Mercedes.

The other man in the van said to the one leaning out, through fits of giggles, "Oh fucking leave it!" "What's the boss gonnae say?" the other replied.

"I don't know," said the laughing man, regaining his composure, "but I expect he'll be glad he didn't park his Granada there."

Despite the trauma of these events Ally and Simmo scrambled giggling into the old Cortina and Ally pulled away, wheels spinning like something out of Starsky and Hutch.

Steve Poultney

"God I could do with that drink now," said Simmo, slapping himself on the forehead.

"Just as well I managed tae lift this then, innit?" said Ally, who somehow during the melée had acquired Simmo's well-aged scotch.

"How the fuck did you do that?" said Simmo, momentarily impressed.

"Aye; we were poor but we were good shoplifters," replied Ally, tapping his nose.

Simmo turned his head away and looked out of the window, tears running down his cheeks. He hoped the deaf old sod next to him couldn't hear him snivelling. Ally plonked the bottle of scotch in Simmo's lap and he held it like a baby, letting out a gut-wrenching sob as he squeezed the bottle tight. They drove on in silence with just the squeak of the windscreen wipers and the occasional flick of a match as Ally chain smoked yet another rollie.

Ally's flat was on the second floor of the tenement. It was drab and had all the attributes of the single male: sink crammed with soiled dishes and an ashtray pilled so high that it resembled a model of the Taj Mahal. Simmo shifted a pile of clothes from the chair and slumped into the faded fabric. His eyes wandered round the few photos and the faded Celtic poster hanging on the walls. His gaze settled on an old fashioned black and white print in a battered frame, of a man in a flat cap and wearing what looked like plus fours with a rifle slung over his shoulder, and then another of a pretty red-headed girl with a grinning Ally, his arm hanging around her shoulder.

Ally emerged from the kitchenette, two dusty glasses clutched in his big fist.

"You gonnae open it then?"

Gigolos

Simmo realised he was still clutching his talisman. Ally plonked the glasses on the small coffee table and Simmo reluctantly poured two healthy drams. He absently rubbed his face and to break the silence, he asked "Who is the man in the picture?"

"Huh?" grunted Ally.

"Was he a big game hunter?"

"You heathen!" Ally retorted, wrinkling his forehead, "that's mah Uncle Sean, and he only shot things for noble causes."

"Don't get you."

"He was in Dublin.... 1916...a fecking patriot."

"Oh," said Simmo whose own parents came from Ireland.

"Aye, the bastards shot him defending the GPO...he survived, but there were arguments after the civil war, so the family moved over here."

Simmo shuffled again. "So who's the girl then?"

Now it was Ally's turn to shuffle. "Lorna was her name...we were in love," he sighed, wrinkling his forehead again, "but she was a prod and the troubles were raging and well... it just wasn't possible, too many oars poked into our lives...old scars... all that bollocks..."

Simmo thought he saw the beginnings of a tear in Ally's eye but his friend rapidly changed the subject by asking "so what were you saving the whiskey for?" He poured another pair of very large drams before sticking another rollie in his mouth, lighting it from an ancient gas fire long missing its protective grill and where a black-brown stain betrayed its secondary purpose as a cigarette lighter. Ally's face lit up like an imp in the reflection from the sickly yellow flame.

Steve Poultney

Simmo, too, stared into the flame, and as he spoke he became detached, as though as on some hippy astral projection, pouring out his heart in a long, surprised torrent as his mind took him back to Liverpool, where he and his Mrs C were born and bred. It had been good back then. Laird's was in full swing and they were both happy in that little terraced house in Anfield. And he had been thrilled at the prospect of the baby and, although unplanned, Mrs C, too, was over the moon.

Ally silently topped up the glasses but Simmo barely noticed, drinking mechanically as the whiskey slipped down his throat.

All the anti-natal stuff had gone fine and she had had a relatively easy time of it, with little morning sickness - in fact she didn't really show until right near the end. Simmo had bought the scotch to wet the baby's head. It was a cold January dawn when he took her to Mertil Street maternity hospital, and although the windscreen was clear he had to crank up the heater as it was slowly icing up...He took her in and returned for the bags; there was no panic at all...

He remembered the kafuffle as he was shoved out of the way and lost his grip on her hand. The screams and the silence, that was the worst - and their expressions, the downturned mouths, the sorries, and then the beautiful baby girl that lay dead in his arms...Later the priest, that fucking bastard priest.

"It's God's will," he said.

Simmo had grabbed him, arse and collar, by the cassock and propelled him out of the little room and down the ward screaming "Fuck off, fuck you, fuck your God, and fuck our lady of perpetual bingo! Get out! Go on! Get out!"

Gigolos

Simmo looked at his friend through red rimmed eyes. Ally looked at the three quarter gone bottle ashamedly.

"I did nae know," he whispered, shell shocked. "I would never have… "

Simmo interrupted, "well today is as good a day as any for drinking it". It was he who now topped up the glasses.

When they had regained their composure Ally asked, "Is that why you moved up here?"

"Yeah…Sort of a new beginning and of course the money was better."

Simmo began to feel tired and a little chilled. In fact it was after this tragedy that their lives had gone cold, a slow freezing the way a frost creeps up a windscreen in the early hours of a January morning. And it was at about this point when Mrs C had sort healing by retail therapy.

Ally lit another fag from the gas fire, staring into the yellow flame. He would have to ring the council; the bloody thing wasn't burning right…

A snore distracted him. Simmo, who wasn't a big drinker, had fallen asleep in the chair with his glass, still half full, dangling precariously from his hand. Ally eased it from his loosening grip and finished it in one easy gulp. Leaving the sleeping man where he was, he went to clear the bed in the spare room, making it up with his two spare sheets and some moth-eaten army blankets which had probably last seen service in the Crimean war.

"I've nae got a case," Ally muttered, wrapping a pillow up in an old bath towel. Seeing him still asleep in the chair, he put Simmo's coat over him, put his own coat on and went out to get a few bits – and of course a few pints - whilst he was at it.

"Poor sod," he said quietly as he gently closed the front door.

The weekend passed in an alcoholic haze. The telephone rang on three separate occasions, the two men glaring at it like a suspect device. As it rang for a fourth time Ally said "well it's nae for me, nobody ever bloody rings me," and Simmo, knowing that it could only be Mrs C calling, screamed down the phone "Fuck off! It's over!"

After slamming the receiver down, the pair of them nodded at each other and carried on drinking in silence. Ally was still using his tumbler but Simmo now clutched a cracked Typhoo mug, his glass having finally succumbed to one of his drunken slumberings.

Their main mission for that Monday morning was to get their names on the redundancy list. The mood in the yard was muted, with hardly any of the craic and usual shenanigans amongst men now facing an uncertain future. There were talks of strikes and endless ballots but, like the great ship on the slipway, once this thing had started to slide there could only be one outcome: the yard was going down.

The days passed slowly with Johnny Walker accompanying the men of an evening, mellowing their thoughts in his own special way. Unusually for the two of them they finished early on the Friday, no overtime being available. Getting back to the flat there was a pile of junk mail and the local free newspaper. As Ally stooped to pick it up the device in the corner rang menacingly. In two strides Simmo

Gigolos

angrily crossed the lounge, further enraged by hitting his leg on the coffee table in his urge to reach the phone. Snatching up the receiver he screeched down the line "I don't ever want to fucking see you, so just fuck off and stay away!" before slamming the thing back down without giving the caller the chance to respond.

The perplexed man on the other end of the line scratched his head and said to one in particular "If you don't want your gas fire fixing fair enough, but there's no need to be so rude about it. "

"That's fecking telling her!" said Ally from the kitchenette, where he was stuffing the junk mail into the overfilled bin bag and cursing the *Reader's Digest*.

He came back in with two steaming mugs of tea and the local rag tucked under his arm. The tea was black and sweet with a curious odour in the vapour.

"Oh God," said Simmo, staring at the cups as the distinct smell of poitín temporarily stifled the stale stench of cigarette smoke.

After passing Simmo the poisonous brew, Ally plonked himself down at the table and opened the broadsheet. It was a collection of all the usual bollocks – jumble sales, public notices and local headlines. The front page led with the yard closure, but Ally had had enough of that so turned his attention to the second page where there was a picture of a middle-aged woman in a large hat and a gold chain of office around her neck. The caption above it read 'Vandals Trash Provost's Mercedes'. Simmo could hear Ally muttering.

"What's up?" he asked.

Steve Poultney

"Some knob's just smashed up the Provost's car; I'll read it to you."

"The Provost's car was parked in Kings Road last Friday morning. As part of her Civic duties, she was visiting one of the elderly residents who had just received a telegram from the Queen."

Simmo's jaw and the penny both began to drop as Ally read on.

"The yobs had apparently hurled a b –Oh Christ!" Ally stalled and spluttered.

Simmo choked on his poitín as Ally struggled to finish the sentence.

"A-a-a- bidet through the windscreen in an unprovoked and pointless attack. Police are asking for witnesses to come forward, "but at the moment," the spokesman for the Strathclyde force commented, "we have nothing to go on"." After a short pause Ally looked over at Simmo.

"Are you sure last Friday was nae the thirteenth?"

Simmo looked up from the mug he had been staring into, his eyes watering from the caustic vapour. "Every day is bloody Friday the thirteenth for me mate".

The weeks went by, the redundancy paperwork was submitted and the knock on the door from the Strathclyde police never came. Their evening, however, was disturbed some days later by an unexpected caller. A taxi driver introduced himself, saying that there were some bags in the cab to be delivered to Simmo. Most of Simmo's clothes and possessions had been stuffed into carriers and his one and only suitcase, half filling the cab. Not much for a lifetime, Ally mused as he gave a hand to carry it in. Simmo just stared blankly at the mess. A small

Gigolos

note was tucked into one of the bags informing him that his wife would leave the garage unlocked on Sunday if that "lanky mate" of his wanted to pick up his tools; after that they were going to the car boot sale.

The note also asked Simmo to post Mrs C his solicitor's details and informed him that she was keeping possession of his only suit seeing as she had bought it for him to wear when they had got married.

Ally scratched his head in the usual manner and asked "is there going tae be a custody battle for it then?"

There was a brief pause before the two men fell about laughing.

"What are we going to do Ally?" said Simmo, absently fingering the letter.

"Well," said Ally, "I'm thinking we could kidnap the suit, cut off one of the lapels and send it tae her with a ransom note. "

"No, you idiot," Simmo laughed, "really, what are we going to do?"

"Well," said Ally, wrinkling his forehead, "I think we could do with a bit of a wee holiday when the money comes through, a take stock type of thing, and come up with a plan."

Mmmm...thought Simmo, a plan... sounds good...."Where were you thinking of going then?"

"Amsterdam."

"Never had you down as a windmill and tulip man."

"Nae you daft bastard, more them funny coffee houses and the naked women in the shop windows," said Ally with a wink.

"Oh!" gulped Simmo.

"Aye we could do with a blow."

"Blow job more like," retorted Simmo with a smile. He thought about the last holiday with Mrs C, a coach trip to Rimini. She didn't like flying...thirty six hours on a sodding coach...he shivered.

"Take it you've got a passport?" asked Ally, waking Simmo from his thoughts.

"Yes, it's probably in the carrier bag with all the other crap."

"I'll check out the travel agents," smirked Ally, "Amsterdam it is then."

"I thought you liked Benidorm?"

"Aye, I did, but that's where I met Carole, on one of them 18 tae 30 things."

Simmo started to smile.

"I thought you met her through the allotment? "

"Nae, we met on holiday, but it was only afterwards when we got back I realised that," Ally's voice dropped to a whisper, "that we shared a passion; a passion," he continued earnestly, "for..." and he looked around as though someone else might be listening, "... beetroot."

Simmo started to laugh hysterically. "BEETROOT?!" he spluttered.

"If you're gonnae be like that then I'm nae gonnae tell you."

"No, go on." Simmo wiped a tear from his eye. "This is fascinating."

"Well we grew the beet on her allotment but," he said in a conspiratorial whisper, "in her shed she had a still, and it was there she made it. Oh, ambrosia...!"

"Rice pudding?" Simmo asked, somewhat confused.

"Nae, you philistine! Ambrosia, nectar of the gods. D'you nae know your classics?"

Gigolos

Simmo was seeing a different side to Ally, whose eyes now shone with an almost religious fervour.

"She made the world's finest beetroot poitín."

There was a short pause while Ally refilled their glasses. Simmo leaned forward in his chair.

"Aye it was like a dream until that fateful night... we'd had a wee dram from the first batch and were making hot, passionate love behind the beetroot boiler when there was a terrible explosion; aye, it blew all the windows out for half a mile. The boiler saved us... it took all the blast. But I had a terrible stinging sensation on mah face..."

"God," Simmo gasped, "were you burnt?"

"Nae, far worse... it was the raw beetroot juice from the press... It splashed down mah face in a purple zigzag... Ah...Ah..."Ally too leaned forward in his chair. "... I looked like fecking Ziggy Stardust!"

Simmo was now crying with laughter.

"Six months of Omo and Scotch-Brite it took to get that purple shite off mah face...Then the coppers came with their bloody guns and sniffer dogs... took a while to convince them it wasn't a bomb-making factory...They let me go in the end, aye, but they kept her in and charged her. Three months she got, and they confiscated what was left of the still....She was never the same after being inside...her passion changed...she started growing cucumbers, about the same time she moved in with that lady tennis player."

"Straight sets?"

"I nae think so," replied Ally, shaking his head and trundling off into the kitchen.

True to his word Ally began drafting plans with the travel agent. Simmo, lost in his own hurting world and a semi-permanent state of intoxication, was quite relieved to leave it all to the big man. Ally had also found him a solicitor, and although he didn't really care the legal process had probably begun.

Simmo had been at Ally's flat for weeks now and, when he actually thought about it, Christ! Nearly three months. God, he thought, he had become some sort of automaton, fuelled on the black oil of Ally's poitín... he was going to have to get a grip on himself... His mind wandered to a Stranglers' song before returning to the present.

It suddenly dawned on him that their notice period was drawing to a close and that soon they would be joining the ranks of the unemployed in a place where work had become scarce. In the relative silence the cogs of his mind whirred relentlessly, and he found himself considering Ally's idiosyncrasies: the way he wrinkled his forehead, the way he pissed without lifting the toilet seat and, most peculiarly, his strange habit of wiping the kitchen work top in circular motions with a filthy tea towel, fag in mouth, transfixed on the one spot.

"Fuck," he thought, "what we are going to do?"

His train of thought was totally derailed by a screaming Ally who had almost severed his ear with an old fashioned none-too-safe 'safety' razor.

"What's up?" asked Simmo?

"Mah feckin' ear!" screeched Ally," I nearly did a fecking Picasso!"

"I think you mean Van Gogh," laughed Simmo, as Ally mumbled something incomprehensible and blundered off into the bedroom, a dirty vest pressed to his ear.

"He was an impressionist!" Simmo shouted after him.

Gigolos

"I dinnae care if he was fecking Dick Emery!" Ally retorted. "Oh, mah bleedin' ear!"

He came back in with a bottle of Johnny Walker, the ultimate cure for melancholy, a bleeding ear and all other ills. He had stuck two pieces of sticking plaster in an 'x' over his ear, the vest still clutched in his other hand. He went to pour Simmo one but was stunned when his friend refused and disappeared off to bed, saying he needed an early night.

"You're nae sickening for something?" asked Ally behind him.

"No mate I just need some sleep and to get my head together."

And with that he left Ally alone, scratching his head.

That night Simmo dreamed. All kinds of images passed through his mind... One of Mrs C's headmaster father lecturing him about how "frankly, Simon" he had expected greater things for his daughter... And another of how, after the death of his own father at an early age, his uncle was telling him fabulous tales of his adventures in the merchant navy, which too had fallen into disarray with the coming of containerisation and Philipino crews. His uncle's advice had been to "become an engineer. Then if some woman gets her mitts into you and you come ashore you will always have a trade."

Having started in the ship yard he had discovered a talent to weld as much as Mrs C, with her art degree, had a talent for still life. There had been so much animosity between the families over religion that they had taken off to a registry office to get married. He dreamed of the strange after-party thrown some weeks later to celebrate their wedding;

his mother calling Mrs C's father a "pompous twat"...
Luckily enough the only casualty of the evening was a
glass ashtray thrown by a drunken reveller...It all
went round and round in a vortex until his mind,
overloaded, finally shut down and took him into the
oblivion where dark thought lapsed into dark
feeling...

Ally had the devil's own job waking him up.
Simmo had slept for nearly two days solid, the drink
and the stress haven taken its toll. The bed looked
like he had been playing rugby in it.
"How d'you feel, wee man? You should nae come
off the drink like that."
Simmo groaned. "What time is it?"
"You should be asking what day it is, you missed
Monday completely... they have gone and brought the
leaving date forward tae Friday."
Simmo sat up and rubbed his eyes. "What? This
Friday?"
"Aye."
"Fuck," was all Simmo could say as he slowly
hoisted himself out of bed.

On the Thursday the men selected for the first
wave of redundancies were called to the office and
given their wages and final cheques. Having cleared
their lockers and collected their tools they were duly
escorted off the premises, the additional security
making sure that anything belonging to the yard
remained on the yard and that there was no
vandalism. Some shook hands, others laughed
clutching their fat cheques and others just wandered
off in silence.

Gigolos

"Aye," said Ally, scrutinising his final wage slip, "at least they paid us for the Friday." And putting his arm around Simmo he continued "Let's put this in the bank; be just our luck tae lose the bloody things."

The high street was busy with Thursday afternoon shoppers. Ally drove like a man possessed to make it to the bank before it closed, snatching the only parking space from an irate van driver and shutting him up instantly with a wave of his big fist, the continual honking of car horns from behind the van forcing it to move on. Simmo struggled as usual with the bloody door, compounded by the front wheel of the Cortina being on the pavement and the boot being full of tools. They made a dash through the throng and caught the bank with minutes to spare.

"Next on the agenda," said Ally, "we catch the travel agents."

It was about a ten minute walk and Ally strode ahead with Simmo almost having to jog to keep up.

"Hello again," said the pretty girl sat behind the desk.

"Aye," said Ally, "me and mah wee friend here are ready tae book that trip tae Amsterdam."

Simmo hated the way Ally always referred to him as his wee friend, but supposed that at five foot five stood next to Ally's six foot two he did appear a little short.

The girl disappeared off into the back of the shop and reappeared with a couple of different glossy brochures. Simmo was staring out of the window into the late afternoon traffic and only caught brief snatches of the conversation between the girl and Ally.

Steve Poultney

"Aye, and nothing tae fancy now... aye mid-week fine, package or schedule whatever the cheapest..." etc., etc...

A brochure for New Zealand caught Simmo's eye; he and Mrs C had once considered moving to...

"Oi!"

Simmo jumped.

"Cheque book!" demanded Ally.

Simmo slapped his forehead. Ally groaned and tore up the cheque he had just written, quickly writing another and handing it to the girl as he whispered "it's a good job his head is bolted on."

Both men signed where the girl had put an X in blue biro on the forms.

The business concluded, Ally announced it was time for a pint. Simmo declined with a shake of his head, saying he needed to get some new clothes for their forthcoming trip and agreeing to meet in the pub opposite in about half an hour...The diet of drink, bacon butties and chips had somewhat enhanced Simmo's once skinny waistline. Ally just grunted and headed for the bar.

Simmo wandered around the big department store aimlessly. Mrs C usually picked his clothes... He eventually arrived at the counter with a couple of pairs of jeans, a decent if not a little bland blue shirt and a fleece-lined denim jacket. Then, on his way back up the road, in a snazzy shoe shop window, he spotted them. His eyes were drawn to a pair of cowboy boots, black and pointy with a red flame pattern. But what really attracted him was the two and a half inch heel and, despite already having used a

Gigolos

large lump of his final wage packet, he had to have them.

Leaving his old work boots behind, he left the store sporting his latest acquisition. In his haste to get to the travel agent he had left his old coat on the back seat of the Cortina and was starting to shiver in the cold Glaswegian evening air. He hooked the new jacket out of its bag and hastily ripped off the labels. Looking in the grimy window he was quite pleased with what he saw.

Ally's eyes widened as Simmo crossed the bar.

"See you've gone up in the world then," he smirked.

"Do you like them?"

"Err... I did nae say that!"

Simmo teetered up to the bar and ordered a pint. Ally wrinkled his forehead and gently rubbed his hand in that peculiar circular motion he utilised when in deep thought or about to say something profound.

"Well I nae thought I would be going away with the midnight cowboy, but seeing you teetering across here it looks like I'll be goin' with bloody Dolly Parton!"

"Fuck you!" said Simmo, locking eyes with Ally for a few seconds before the two men burst out laughing.

Finishing their beer, they headed back to the Cortina. Ally had to steady Simmo, grabbing his arm as the smooth leather soles of his new boots lost traction on the wet diesel-smeared tarmac. "For Christ's sake don't go breakin' your leg before we even get there," Ally spluttered, climbing into the car.

Simmo's attention was drawn to something stuck to the windscreen: a parking ticket. He snatched it off the windshield and went through the palaver of opening and closing the door.

"They cannae give me a ticket, there's nae bloody parking meters around here!"

Simmo peered at the ticket and then, looking at Ally, pointed to the tax disc.

"That's the fecking Reader's Digest's fault!"

"Huh?" said Simmo, bewildered as usual.

"Aye, I probably threw the road tax thing out with all their bloody shite."

Simmo couldn't help but smile as Ally forced his way out into the rush-hour traffic, the Cortina groaning under the weight of their tools.

The taxi driver raised his eyebrows when he saw the shorter man in the cowboy boots struggling with a humongous suitcase. Somehow they managed to get it in, with Simmo squashed into the gap left between the door and the case on the back seat. Ally had ensured that Simmo had his passport but kept hold of the tickets, travellers' cheques and the guilders he had drawn for both of them from the post office on Friday, not trusting his companion not to lose the cash. He chatted away with the cabby in the front whilst strains of The Clash emanated from the stereo - *'Should I stay or should I go?'*

"Very appropriate," Simmo thought, his mind wandering back to Liverpool, to Eric's where they had punk rock matinées... The Clash, Ramones, X-Ray Specs... the bloody Beatles long forgotten by the new wave crowd...

He had hardly noticed the drive to the airport in his reminiscence and he almost fell out as Ally yanked the door open, the suitcase acting like a giant spring

Gigolos

propelling him sideways. The taxi driver rolled his eyes again.

"If you don't mind mah saying so, they will nae let you on the plane with that." He pointed to Simmo's suitcase. "There's restrictions on luggage unless it goes in the hold but it will cost you a small fortune, that's if they'll take it at all."

Ally and Simmo pondered over what to do with the offending luggage, Ally in the end exclaiming "what have you got in that bloody thing?!"

"Just jeans, underwear, socks, a spare sweater, toiletries and my travelling alarm clock."

"Christ! Why did you nae buy a new one?"

"Dunno". Simmo sighed.

Time was getting short and they had called the check-in.

"You'll have tae get some carrier bags from the shop!" Ally yelled, "And we'll have tae dump the bloody case, its nae use tae man nor beast. Off you go or we'll miss the bloody flight."

Simmo went to the nearest shop and asked for some bags, to which a po-faced battle-axe told him he would have to purchase something... He started to panic and picked up the first thing he saw - a large expensive teddy bear wearing a kilt - and asked for half a dozen carrier bags which the woman grudgingly gave him.

Ally, unusually for him, was starting to panic too.

"Quick," he said, "take your passport and your ticket over there - I've already done mine - and leave me the bloody case! I'll pack your gear while you check in."

Simmo went through the rigmarole and Ally caught up with him clutching four stuffed carrier bags along with his own holdall. He thrust the bags onto

Simmo who still had the giant teddy stuffed under his arm.

"Quick man!" he shouted, shoving Simmo along and in their urgency leaving a trail of socks and underpants like a latter-day Hansel and Gretel as the handles and sides of the bags burst. They were just closing the gate as Ally propelled Simmo through. They had to dash across the tarmac and charge up the stairs of the Dan Air plane to the accompaniment of "why are we waiting?!" sung by their fellow passengers. There was a rapturous cheer as a grown man clutching his teddy bear burst through the door followed by a tall sweating madman with murder in his eyes. Simmo blundered blindly past the two vacant seats before Ally's big hand dragged him back. They barely had time to sling their excuse for luggage on the rack before the seat belt sign was lit, and as they sat down and fastened their belts the aircraft door closed with a clunk somewhat reminiscent to a Cortina.

Within minutes they were taxiing down the runway, with Ally still gasping both for breath and a fag. Simmo too was out of breath and still clutching the bear tightly, there being no room on the luggage rack for such a large beast.

It wasn't long before the seat belt and no smoking signs flickered out. It was then that a head appeared from over the seat in front of them, and a camp voice let out "I only usually throw knickers at Tom Jones, big boy!" as he twanged a pair of underpants into Ally's face before disappearing back behind the seat. Ally looked at Simmo, the teddy bear and the underpants, raised his eyes to heaven and in a very reverent voice asked God what he had done to

Gigolos

deserve this, to which the camp voice swiftly replied "amen".

The hostess was kept busy proffering Ally a seemingly endless supply of drinks. Simmo stared out of the window at the clouds whilst Ally, chain smoking, produced one of his own. The flight was relatively smooth and for the first time in months Simmo was actually becoming interested in something again. He had a fondness for art, something he had shared with Mrs C, so was looking forward to visiting some of the museums and galleries. He and Ally had swapped seats shortly after take-off, it being easier for Ally to holler at the hostess from the aisle. The bear occupied the seat between them but said very little.

Ally would occasionally cock his ear at a noise from the aircraft, or the engine.
"I dinnae like the sound of that," he muttered, looking nervously across the bear at Simmo.
"What's up?"
"Did you nae see those two geezers at the side of the plane before? Them in the overalls with their tool bags."
"No," said Simmo, who had had the bear and the bags to contend with.
"Aye a, tall one and a short one, could've been aviation's version of us."
"Christ... well at least ships don't fall out of the air...."
Ally took little comfort from this last remark and was quite relieved when the seat belt and no smoking signs came back on again and the aircraft began its descent.

Steve Poultney

They were among the last people to leave the plane. The camp voice and his companion strolled along arm in arm just ahead of them, with a few odd stragglers in their wake. The customs men seemed particularly interested in Simmo and Ally and wanted to know whether either of them had a case. Ally flashed a warning look at Simmo, who quickly denied having any luggage. After a brief conversation amongst themselves the officers waved them on, with Simmo's bags now depositing their own version of a paper trail on a foreign shore.

"What do you think that was all about?" asked Simmo, trying to keep the last of his sundries from escaping, the bear still tucked firmly under his arm.

"I dinnae know but I've always found it best with authority tae deny everything...even if you haven't a clue what they're going on about."

Sound advice, thought Simmo.

They flagged a cab at the airport and asked for the hotel. Now Amsterdam is a pretty liberal place and if either of them had had a smattering of German, never mind Dutch, they would have realised that the translation of the hotel name was the Pink Palace, a gay hotel. The penny didn't drop with Simmo at all but after a few minutes it certainly had with his friend.

"Simmo", Ally whispered, "there's nae women here."

"Oh! Is this place something akin to the Y.M.C.A. then?"

"Aye, I think you could say that...or maybe something far worse..."

Gigolos

The camp couple from the plane were at the reception in front of them. The taller of the two looked at Ally and winked.

"Didn't expect to see you boys here."

The other man looked at Simmo and gesticulated.

"Sure he is, look at his kinky boots!"

Simmo went bright red as the shorter one said to them cryptically "remember boys, when in Rome do as the Vulcans do," and winked.

Simmo and Ally looked at each other; the quip was lost on them.

"What's Mr. Spock got tae do with this?" asked a confused Ally scratching his head.

"Tut tut," went the tall one. "Rubber up lads, condoms... remember it's not just the boys that can get it."

This was the mid-eighties and an Aids pandemic was sweeping a largely indignant world. Ignorance and indifference was seeing this deadly killer creeping into the heterosexual world and Ally and Simmo were in the vice capital of Europe; such advice could well save someone's life.

Ally had booked a twin room but was mortified to find it had only one double bed.

"What the feck?!" he yelled, "Do they think we're fecking Laurel and Hardy? This will nae do..."

Simmo, being a little more diplomatic than Ally, returned to reception and managed to book another room, explaining that his friend's snoring would keep him awake all night otherwise - a statement which wasn't far from the truth, as Ally snored like a bull rhinoceros letting off steam during the mating season. It cost a little extra but Simmo really didn't fancy sharing a bed and shuddered at the thought.

They spent their first evening wandering around the red light district, Simmo's eyes agog and Ally giving the bum's rush to the pimps, pushers and working girls. Simmo's feet were aching from the tight new boots and high heels so they found a quiet bar away from the main drag and settled down for an evening of drinking. Simmo had managed to pick up a few tourist leaflets and a street map whilst they were waiting for a taxi from the airport, and was musingly looking through the museums and galleries.

They arrived back at the hotel a little worse for wear; they had consumed copious amounts of walnut schnapps and on the second landing Simmo wobbled and slowly slid down the wall like a sinking yacht, arms spread like sails. Ally picked him up and, having rescued the key from his incoherent companion, deposited him unceremoniously prostrate on the bed. He did try to remove the cowboy boots, but really couldn't have done a better job of welding them to his feet himself. He switched out the light and shuffled off to turn in.

Simmo awoke with a blinding headache, compounded by a hammering noise, which transpired to be Ally at the door.
"Are you up wee man? Tis only half an hour till breakfast."
"Erm... yes...I think..." He was looking around in vain for his travel alarm clock, concluding that it must have been lost along with most of his underwear.

Gigolos

"Give me a knock when you're ready tae go down."

"I will," replied Simmo, crawling groggily out of his pit. During the night he had somehow removed the cowboy boots but was still wearing one sock and a T shirt. The shower was strong and hot, rinsing some of the fuzziness out of his head. His wash bag was one of the few items to have survived the journey and in it were all the essentials: tooth brush, razor, soap, shaving foam, aspirin and the welder's essential, Preparation H - you couldn't sit on cold steel welding in the Glaswegian climate without developing a case of the farmer Giles... On completing his ablutions he gulped down a handful of aspirin and dressed quickly. He had intended on wearing his old trainers but they too had apparently gone AWOL. He also surmised that not a complete pair of socks had survived, but no one would see the odd ones under the cowboy boots, and after a quick lick with the comb he set off to find Ally.

They were the last to enter the dining room and the only seats available were with the couple from the plane. Simmo grabbed two coffees from the urn on the counter as Ally muttered something about bacon and eggs. One of the men opposite shook his head.

"Its continental breakfast here boys," he said, pointing to the array of cheese, yoghurt and croissants laid out on the counter, "go help yourselves."

Ally had the look of a man facing famine.

"Christ, I know how mah ancestors must have felt," he said to no one in particular.

Simmo produced one of the leaflets from his pocket. On the front of it was the Rijksmuseum.

Steve Poultney

"Look Jeremy," the shorter of the two men opposite said, "an art lover!"

"Paul here is an artist," the other man explained, nodding toward his companion.

"Really?" said Simmo, "I am so looking forward to seeing the Rembrandts although -" he leaned forward slightly - "I prefer Durer."

"Am partial to a little Jura mahself," Aly chipped in.

"Not whiskey," sighed Simmo," the artist, you buffoon!"

"Err that's what I meant."

Ally was floundering in the conversation so was grateful when it was interrupted by the young waiter clearing the table who Paul began speaking to in perfect Dutch. Simmo caught snatches of the conversation - Glasgow, airport, bomb, and hoax. Paul looked perturbed.

"What's up babe?" asked Jeremy.

"We were so lucky to get away yesterday! They closed the airport; ours was the last flight out. Apparently there was a bomb scare; the army had to blow up a suitcase after a passenger reported it ticking."

Ally spurted out a long stream of coffee and gasped for breath as Simmo too realised what had happened to the alarm clock and his trainers, and gulped. Paul glanced at him briefly before resuming the conversation. Ally was getting a little irritated now and, pushing his chair back with a screech, announced that if the ladies would excuse him he would leave them to their 'Grand Masters'; he was off to find a drink and a bacon butty.

Gigolos

Simmo wouldn't see him for the rest of the day so he took himself off sightseeing, savouring the architecture and canals. He hadn't meant to upset Ally; he didn't know how he would have coped without him.

He found the Rijksmuseum without incident and had a pleasant afternoon there with the old masters; although his mind did wander to Mrs C... it was she, after all, who had awoken his interest in art. He could appreciate how much she would have enjoyed the gallery and could almost feel her looking over his shoulder. Other than the odd solicitor's letter he had heard nothing from her... He started wondering what she was up to, but then the face of Bob the Bidet crept into his mind and put a damper on his mood.

"Fuck 'em!", he muttered, as Ally would say... and thinking of Ally he thought would head back to the hotel where the evening meal was already paid for.

Simmo found Ally in the hotel bar with a big smirk on his face. There were no prizes for guessing what the Scotsman had been up to all day.

"Take it you've had a good afternoon then," he giggled.

"Aye..." Ally had a faraway look on his face.

"I was thinking..." said Simmo.

"Go on then."

"Maybe we could check out one of those coffee houses?"

"I dinnae see why not."

Simmo's feet were killing him.

"Do you mind if we get a cab?"

"Aye," replied Ally, maintaining a whimsical air.

Steve Poultney

The evening meal was surprisingly good and the pair of them found themselves quite sated. Simmo had ordered a bottle of wine with the meal but after the first glass Ally had ordered a beer, complaining that it tasted like vinegar - this coming from the man who thought beetroot poitín the be all and end all... in the end he was feeling quite mellow, having consumed three quarters of a bottle, and they agreed to meet in the bar after a shower and a change of clothes. Simmo came down first and asked the man at the counter if he could recommend a coffee house and order them a taxi to take them there. The receptionist shrugged when Simmo mentioned a cab but ordered them one anyway. Ally appeared and managed to squeeze in a hasty beer, finishing it just as the taxi arrived.

"You'll have tae find yourself some new trainers," he commented, Simmo nodding in agreement, "you're going tae give yourself bunions or a broken ankle otherwise."

He would try and find a shoe shop tomorrow, Simmo thought to himself.

The coffee houses dotted around seemed vaguely familiar to Ally as they got out. The taxi driver winced as Simmo, used to closing the Cortina's door, gave the cab's an almighty slam. Ally soon realised that the ten minute ride had dropped them in a side road about 400 hundred yards from their hotel. He groaned but Simmo had paid by now and the taxi was already pulling away. Shaking his head, he turned to follow his friend, who was now hobbling determinedly towards the closest establishment. On entering, the odour hit them straight away.

Gigolos

"I think they may be on the wacky backy," said Ally ironically, wrinkling his nose as his eyes took in the scene and his lungs inhaled the drug-fuelled miasma. Cannabis of all varieties was clearly for sale over the counter, with elaborate menus describing their wares and effects. Simmo ordered two large coffees whilst Ally quizzed the young man behind the counter as to what he recommended, quickly arriving at a decision and ordering some red Lebanese.

There was a surprisingly good atmosphere in the packed café, with people of all ages and decent music playing in the background; to their relief they even managed to find a table. Simmo eyed Ally as he expertly rolled a five skin spliff and lit it, taking a long, deep draw and holding in the smoke. A young man at the next table smiled at Ally.

"Good shit man!"

Ally smiled and gave him a thumb's up, passing the joint to Simmo after another heavy toke. Although he had occasionally tried it in his youth his hand wavered, Mrs C being very anti-drugs. Ally questioningly raised an eyebrow and Simmo thought, "Oh fuck it!" and took the spliff. The young man opposite nodded his head in approval and Simmo took a long, deep drag. He held it down for a few seconds before starting to cough a little. He went to hand it back to Ally but Ally shook his head.

"Go on, have a few more wee drags," he said encouragingly, "you did want tae try all Amsterdam can offer."

Simmo nodded, struggling to keep the hot smoke down, and let it out this time not with a cough but with a grin. The young man opposite nodded again and said "Welcome to Amsterdam," to which Ally replied "great tae be here." The youngster was seated with two other men of a similar age to themselves. They spoke very good English but Simmo found himself floundering in the conversation as it turned to football, a subject he cared not in the least for. Ally and one of the men were revelling in past glories, agreeing the merits of Johan Cruyff and comparisons of Celtic and Ajax, pondering the fact that the game was far better in the 70s...Simmo was lost in his own thoughts when the younger man asked him what he did for a living.

"Erm," said Simmo with a start, his mind rushing as he returned from the void.

"We're welders...fitters...erm, that is we were..."

He trailed off as the young man looked at him quizzically and nodded as if to go on.

"We have been finished up....made redundant..."

"Redundant?" the young man asked, unsure of its meaning.

"The shipyard is closing so we have been paid off, finished."

"Ah yes, I understand now."

The man sat in the middle had said very little so far, but having flashed the younger man a quick glance now questioned Simmo.

"So what do you intend to do? I gather there is little work in the UK."

Simmo pondered "I...erm, we... are not sure..."

"Have you considered investments or property development?" the man asked.

"I'll nae gamble mah hard won cash on the stock market, "Ally chipped in.

"No, that's not what I meant. Would you consider running your own business, something like, say, a bar?"

Gigolos

Simmo, suddenly famished, derailed Ally's thoughts.

"I'm starving!"

He pushed his chair back as though to get up but the man who had been talking to Ally gestured to him with his hand to sit down as he spoke rapidly to the young man in Dutch who, smiling, disappeared off only to return a few minutes later with a tray of cakes, plonking them down between Ally and Simmo.

"Enjoy."

Now Ally, who had been chain-smoking joints all evening, could surmise what was in the cakes but Simmo, in his naivety, had no idea. The so-called "munchies" were another new experience, and of course he hungrily devoured them with relish. He soon found himself staring at the table where the crumbs and bits of tobacco appeared to be performing in a kind of flea circus. He began to feel quite numb, and was sure he could catch things moving on the periphery of his vision. Drifting in and out of this reality he could hear the conversation but his mind was detached and floating... For the first time in his life and in an almost biblical revelation he suddenly understood the concept of "spaced out"...

The conversation had turned to bars and tropical climes... Simmo was trying to listen to Raoul...was that his name? ... Things grew fuzzier as Simmo started to laugh hysterically to himeself, muttering "Raoul... growl...fowl... bowel!!!" His face was aching as the tears rolled down his cheeks - to coin a phrase he was, in fact, off his face...

Ally, on the other hand, was deep in conversation and they were invited into a small room at the back. As with all things intoxicating Ally did not seem in the least inebriated, but to Simmo crossing the room was like walking on a giant mattress watched by an audience of over-extenuated clowns. He flopped into a chair in a performance Andy Pandy would have been proud of, large rivulets of sweat running down his forehead and into his already well moistened eyes, blurring his vision as the salt in the sweat reddened them further. Looking a little concerned, the young man brought him a glass of iced water.

Over the course of the next half an hour or so his head began to clear a little. There was a folder in front of them which Ally had apparently been studying for some time. Raoul was showing them pictures of a beautiful island - sandy beaches, blue skies, smiling tourists and a panoramic picture of a long curving beach on a lagoon, with a shining white bar on the shore and a couple of odd buildings at the other end of the sands...Simmo's mind drifted again as there was talk of exchange rates, guilders and legal gobbledygook. Ally appeared to be driving a hard bargain, although Simmo had no idea what he was bargaining for; every now and then he would briefly get a grip, only for his mind to send him out to the twilight zone again.

Ally was shaking hands with Raoul now and the other three men all looked very pleased. For an instant Mrs C's face flashed in front of him mouthing the word "NO!!" but Simmo dismissed her with a wave of his hand. In front of him was a document a couple of pages long and Ally was nodding at him. Raoul placed a biro in Simmo's hand and after a little difficulty he signed his name beneath Ally's scrawl. Raoul turned it over two or three times and Simmo signed again in the place Raoul guided his hand to. The two other men added their signatures as Raoul

Gigolos

patted Simmo on the back, congratulating them on becoming the proud new owners of an up-and-coming bar enterprise.

Ally and Simmo left the bar, Ally tucking the envelope containing the paperwork into the inside pocket of his jacket. The cold night air was sobering Simmo up somewhat, though he still felt a little out of sorts. Shortly behind them another man left the bar. He was of medium height but very skinny and sallow looking, with obvious needle tracks up his arms. He had overheard the conversation as they were sat in the front of the coffee shop and he was convinced that they would have large amounts of cash on them.

"This way," Ally said to Simmo, "I think I know a short cut." Simmo followed his friend down a long dark alleyway; Ally was talking away all the while.

"Aye it's a grand opportunity; we'll be our own bosses," he prattled on.

Simmo wasn't so sure. His mind was still too addled to think straight, but Ally was convinced he had got the place at a knock down price - and what else had they to do...?

The usually quiet Ally was still chattering away when a figure jumped out in front of them. It was the skinny man from the bar and he was brandishing a knife. "Money," was all he said. Simmo started fumbling in his pocket but Ally just stood considering their would-be assailant as the man waved the knife impatiently at him. With the speed of a cat Ally suddenly grabbed the man's right wrist and put in a header that Johan Cruyff would have been proud of. As he spiralled to the floor Ally quickly wrestled the knife from his semiconscious hand. He was in no mood for this kind of tosser and advancing on the body drew the knife back to slash him.

"Nooo!!!..." screamed Simmo.

Ally turned to look at his friend and there really was murder in his eyes.

"No," said Simmo again softly, shaking his head.

Ally let out a blood curdling scream making Simmo's hair stand on end and smashed the knife into the wall, instantly snapping the blade at the hilt. He bent down over the prostrate junkie. Simmo at first though Ally was going to try and give him first aid or something, but realised to his shock that he was helping himself to the man's money, also removing a small plastic bag from his pocket and tipping its contents onto the wet pavement. The powder in it may have been brown but Simmo couldn't really tell in the half light. Simmo stared at Ally, hands on hips; he was looking at the notes in his hands. Ally just shrugged and spluttered.

"Aye well the bastard was gonnae take mine!"

Simmo just shook his head. The junkie whimpered something in Dutch and Ally retorted with "Aye I'll help you alright," and gave him an almighty kick. Simmo dragged him away.

"Come on Ally, he's had enough."

"Aye, but he'll nae be getting up and following us."

He put his arm around Simmo's neck. "Come on wee man, we've got a bar tae celebrate."

"So much for a quiet night," thought Simmo, leaving Ally still drinking in the bar. The beer had been tasteless and all that he wanted to do now was go to bed. The following morning he felt shaky and quite down. He was rather hoping that he had dreamt

Gigolos

the previous night's events but felt sick to the pit of his stomach, sure that they had enlisted themselves on a road trip to disaster. There was a knock on the door. Not Ally's usual hammerings.

"Simmo, Simmo, open up; its me."

Simmo, fearing the worst, opened the door a crack. There stood Ally holding the envelope, looking at it like it was a parcel bomb.

"I think," said Ally...

"Come in," said Simmo interrupting him.

"I think we may have spent half our money on a bar in God knows where."

Ally came in and flopped down on the bed. Simmo snatched the envelope from him and started scrutinising a very legal looking contract, witnessed and dated by two signatories. The address appeared to be that of a lawyer... a certain Mr. Raoul Van Horen.

"Shit," murmured Simmo scratching his chin, "I'm no expert but this all looks very legal to me."

They took a cab across town to Van Horen's office. A middle aged woman who either didn't, or pretended she didn't, speak much English let them sit there for over an hour until eventually Raoul turned up. The secretary flashed her eyes at him and he turned to Ally and Simmo, who were sat slightly obscured from view behind the door. He greeted them before they had time to speak.

"Good morning gentlemen, what a pleasure it was doing business with you last night. I am so pleased to have started you on your entrepreneurial career."

He invited them into his office and gestured for them to sit down.

"Well you see," Ally began, "now that we've had a wee chance tae think about it, we were thinking we may have been a wee bit hasty."

Raoul eyed them coldly. "You gentlemen have signed a legally binding contract in front of two independent witnesses, not to mention Karl the bar owner."

Simmo gulped "But we were stoned..."

"Mmmm..." Raoul leaned back in his leather chair, hands behind his head, and then he leaned forward across the desk, resting one hand upon his chin. "Gentlemen, cannabis is legal here, and if you are foolish enough to smoke it before attending a business meeting... "

He let the inference hang in the air.

"Now just wait a minute here pal," Ally protested, but Raoul silenced him by raising the palm of his hand.

"I had a phone call from Karl this morning. The police have been in the coffee shop asking questions. Two men half killed a drug addict last night, mugged him and took his money and effects; two men fitting your description."

Simmo looked at his feet and Ally glared.

"Now Karl suffers from selective amnesia, it comes and it goes. I suggest you go gentlemen, before Karl's memory returns. I will expect your cheques within the agreed period. And don't try to renege; remember I have the law on my side and there are substantial penalty clauses should you fail to pay. Now good day, gentlemen."

Simmo and Ally shuffled out of the office. They had a look of beaten dogs about them. There seemed few options open now, other than to return to the hotel and pack.

Bars and Scars

Ally and Simmo stepped out of the solicitor's office into the cold Glaswegian drizzle, Simmo clutching a brown manila folder.

"Aye," said Ally, "looks like we've been stitched up."

Simmo was lost in thought. The solicitor had looked into the matter, concluding that in the eyes of the law it was a legal sale and that they should not have signed anything without taking proper legal advice. On the plus side all the paperwork was in order. Van Horen had forwarded the deeds, such as they were, along with a copy of the bill of sale and accounts. Investigations on their behalf had also concluded that the address checked out and the bar did indeed exist - and there was some land with it. But as to its true value, the solicitor had found few real estate companies on the island and the only one to respond to their correspondence had valued it at several times under the figure they had paid for it.

"Well then." Simmo sighed. "At least the bloody thing is real; I suppose we ought to go and check it out... Maybe it will be ok, or if not then we could always sell it on."

Ally rubbed his chin but said nothing.

The flat seemed bare without the furniture, the patches on the yellowed walls a reminder of where the pictures had once hung. The two men had meagre possessions and what little they had was crated up and in the hold of a ship somewhere, probably crossing the Indian Ocean. Ally had sold the Cortina - Simmo pitied the poor sod who had bought it - and so the two of them were just hanging around waiting for the cab to arrive. Ally had put all the important stuff in his suitcase other than the tickets, passports and visas.

"You've nae got a bloody alarm clock in that new holdall of yours?" asked Ally, cocking an eyebrow.

"Not this time," replied a sheepish Simmo, "just some new clothes and a couple of pairs of trainers."

"Well thank Christ for that!" said Ally, breaking into a smile.

Three loud toots on a car horn announced the arrival of the cab.

"Off you go," said Ally, "I'll lock up and follow you down."

Simmo set off down the stairs. Ally lit a final fag off the gas fire before turning the knob, which was loose on the spindle, tightly enough to extinguish the flame but not fully tight enough to lock the ignition valve closed. Taking one last look around, he blew out a long puff of cigarette smoke then closed the door, posting the keys through the letterbox as the council had instructed him to do.

The cab ride was uneventful; they had allowed plenty of time for the journey. Both men were lost in their own thoughts and said very little. The taxi driver tried to strike up a conversation but could only get one word answers from Ally, who as usual was sat in the front, and so he eventually gave up. The check-in went ok, other than the fact that Simmo's new holdall was still considered too large for hand luggage and had to go into the hold. Simmo had thought it prudent to wear dark glasses in case anyone

Gigolos

recognised them after their last escapade. Ally just shook his head.

"Do you think they will recognise us?" whispered Simmo.

"Nae, they'll be lookin' for some daft shite with a feckin' great teddy bear."

Their flight was called and they boarded the large Boeing. Simmo had the window seat. Ally leaned over and tried to look out of the window, saying to Simmo "can you see any geezers in overalls?" Simmo looked around but there was no sign of Ally's fearful apparition. "Nope," he replied. Ally just sighed and relaxed into his seat.

The plane was quite plush compared to the last Dan Air jet they had taken to Amsterdam, the interior of which had been of the same ilk as an old school bus; this much wider plane seemed almost palatial, but Simmo supposed it would have to be considering the length of the flight. The first part of their journey would take them to Los Angeles; there they would change flights to take them out to Tahiti. From Tahiti a local flight would carry them over to the islands, after which there would be a short boat ride out to theirs. They were to meet the current bar owner, a Mr. Chin Lee, at their new premises.

Simmo decided he quite liked flying. Ally, on the other hand, was a nervous wreck, and when some hours into the flight the seatbelt sign went on and the captain announced that there may be a little turbulence ahead, he looked panic-stricken. The buffeting lasted about twenty minutes or so and most of the time Ally had his eyes shut, his hands tightly gripping the seat. Simmo could hear him mumbling and promising a tenner to Saint Anthony if he made it stop. Simmo was frightened to say anything to him in case he spooked him even more - he just had visions of Ally making a bolt for the door, which would not be a good move at forty thousand feet.

After the turbulence had stopped, Ally, having consumed half a dozen large whiskeys, was now as calm as he was likely to be, so Simmo quizzed him.

"I thought St. Christopher was the patron saint of travellers?"

"Aye so he was; he got struck off though."

"Huh?"

"Aye just after the titanic sank."

"Fuck off!" cried Simmo, exasperated to have fallen for it hook, line and sinker.

He went back to reading his book, 'Great Aviation Disasters'. Ally groaned on seeing the cover and shut his eyes; he was tired and was going to try and sleep the rest of the flight out. Simmo, too, must have nodded off as they were woken by a gentle voice announcing that they were on the final approach and needed to fasten their seatbelts.

The heat hit them immediately, especially as they were still dressed for Glasgow. Ally was grumbling and peeling off layers like an onion. Simmo removed his coat but left it at that – his holdall was being transferred to the next flight so he had nothing to put the rest of his clothes in. Reluctantly he went into an airport shop. To be on the safe side he thought he would buy a can of coke, only to find the bemused sales girl shaking her head at the pound note he held out to her.

"Payment in dollars please, sir," she said, pointing towards the bureau de change opposite.

Gigolos

"They only take dollars in this neck of the woods," said Simmo to Ally.

"Might be something to do with being in America," Ally surmised, scratching his head and adding "Christ, I had nae thought of that..."

"Thought of what?"

"What are we going tae use for money when we get there?"

Ally made enquires at the bureau de change. The girl behind the counter made a quick phone call. "Dollars or Polynesian francs," she confirmed. Simmo and Ally looked at each other and shrugged. "Dollars," said Ally, making a snap decision, so the pair of them hastily swapped their pounds at an extortionate exchange rate. Simmo returned to the shop and asked for a can of coke and a carrier bag, into which he stuffed his thick sweater. They wandered around the airport for a little while before Ally finally said "come on wee man, let's find a drink. " They had two hours to kill before the flight to Tahiti.

Simmo suggested getting something to eat.

"I cannae eat anything, mah stomach is turning somersaults."

"Don't worry, you'll be alright."

Ally didn't look so sure. Simmo tried to draw him into conversation but his friend wasn't relishing the thought of another flight and was quite mute.

"Come on mate," said Simmo soothingly as the flight was called, "we're halfway there; we'll be on the other side of the world tomorrow."

Ally just grunted. It was dark boarding the plane and he was not in the mood for reassurance.

"Relax... I know you, a couple of drinks and you'll soon crash," said Simmo. Ally glared at him and

Steve Poultney

Simmo spluttered "... I mean...you'll soon nod off... Be there in no time...." Ally just grunted again.

They filed along the aisle and the pair of them found their seats, Simmo taking the window one as usual and Ally looking around for the emergency exit signs. He gripped the seat even though the plane took off smoothly, climbing quickly with the seatbelt and no smoking signs soon going out. Ally was pleased that there was little to see in the darkness and, from the occasional glances he took at the window, was much relieved that he hadn't seen his spectres as they took off. He managed a rollie and a large scotch as the cabin settled down, the lights soon to be dimmed. With the cabin lights out Ally shut his eyes, just to rest them mind, and it wasn't long before he drifted off into an uneasy sleep.

Both men slept long into the flight. Ally had relaxed a tiny bit, but once he was properly awake his ears quickly attuned to the slightest noise or bump, making him twitchy again.
"Did you nae hear that?" he would say to Simmo now and again. Simmo was immune to Ally's imaginary sounds, but on the odd occasion when he did hear something, he would shake his head anyway.

It was morning now and they were going to put a movie on for the last hour or so of the flight. Simmo suggested Ally put the headphones on to take his mind off it. Ally did as he was told but was still convinced he could hear imaginary knocks and bumps...Simmo settled down to the movie - it was *The Towering Inferno* and he felt Ally wince when the helicopter crashed, but it seemed at least to be

Gigolos

keeping him occupied. Simmo didn't know who was the more relieved when the seatbelt sign came on and the captain announced their imminent arrival - Ally to get off the plane or Simmo to get away from Ally's constant jumping and twitching every five minutes. The plane made a textbook touchdown.

"You can open your eyes now mate, we're down," said Simmo, giving Ally a shake and adding "Tahiti; wow."

"Aye." said Ally, "didn't they eat Captain Hook here?"

"Huh?" replied Simmo. History wasn't really his strong point, but he added "I think you mean Cook and I don't think they ate him, but I think he did come to a sticky end..."

"Simmo, I cannae see any information about our next plane," said Ally, scrutinising the departure board. Simmo walked up to the nearest desk, an Air France one as it happened.

"Excuse me, do you know where the check in is for this airline?" he asked, showing their tickets to the woman behind the desk. She looked at it for a moment then shook her head. Simmo thanked her then wandered over to another desk. There was a queue of people in front of them and he waited patiently for it to go down, only to get the same reaction. This pattern was repeated twice more until a smart young lady with an American accent and a dazzling smile saw Simmo's crestfallen look and told him to hang on while she made a phone call. She directed them towards the freight terminal from where their particular airline apparently operated.

It was a fair old walk to the terminal. There had been air conditioning in the main building but once they left it the heat and humidity hit them and Simmo could feel his feet squelching in his cowboy boots. They wandered around aimlessly looking for a desk, a security man who spoke little English eventually ushering them to a drab office. They showed a young man their tickets, who directed another man to take them to their gate.

"Hurry, hurry, hurry," he beseeched them in broken English, "plane go soon!"

After a cursory glance at their tickets they were pointed at a plane standing on the hot tarmac. Ally shielded his eyes against the glare and Simmo thought wistfully about the sunglasses stuffed in his coat pocket, which in turn was stuffed into a carrier bag.

"Hurry!!" shouted the young man.

"What the fuck?!" squawked Ally, goggling the plane.

Simmo couldn't believe his eyes. There in front of them stood an aircraft that would not have been out of place in the Korean War. Ally started to splutter and Simmo, unsure as to whether his friend was going to voluntarily ascend the steps to board the plane, gave him a hasty shove in the back.

"I dinnae think -" gasped Ally, but Simmo pushed him up the stairs one step at a time. Ally had to duck to get through the door, holdall held out in front of him like a talisman. The flight attendant wrestled the bag from him, putting it on a rack next to the door similar to that found on a double-decker bus. She pointed at two seats, and before Ally could protest she clapped her hands saying "sit, sit, sit!" Ally flopped down as Simmo watched the other passengers simultaneously turn their heads silently in their direction. He also observed that they were the

Gigolos

only Europeans on the plane. He sat down, the carrier bag balanced on his knee. The flight attended shouted something and the passengers all started to buckle up their seat belts. Simmo fumbled for a while and managed to fasten his. Ally was sat there frozen and Simmo had to nudge him out of his daze.

"Eh?" he mouthed, stupefied.

"Come on mate," said Simmo gesturing to the seat belt, "clunk click."

Ally's hands were shaking so much that Simmo had to fasten the belt for him. It took the flight attendant two goes to shut the door, sparking a *deja vu* in Simmo's head. The engines sputtered into life with a throbbing vibration and a noise like a swarm of bees. The aircraft began to move and taxi out onto the runway. Ally was trying not to look out of the window but caught sight of two geezers, one short and the other tall, both dressed in company overalls. The taller one appeared to be looking straight at him and Ally couldn't tell if he was waving or making the sign of the cross.

"Did you nae see them?!" Ally screeched into Simmo's face, but when Simmo leaned over all he could see was runway speeding past.

Ally was still gripping the seat with his eyes shut when the flight attendant said "you may belt off and smoke now." Ally's hands were trembling so badly that Simmo, who had never rolled a fag in his life, had to make one for his friend and light it for him. Three large whiskeys and five fags later, Ally was starting to calm down. The vibration from the engines had lessened and the bee noise had been left behind. Simmo's book was in his coat pocket, which was maybe just as well, but he could feel a lump under his foot and reached down to see what it was.

Steve Poultney

"It's a feckin' parachute!" Ally started screaming as Simmo pulled the object out, and it took both him and the flight attendant all their powers of persuasion to convince Ally it was a life jacket.

"Well at least we won't bloody drown when we fall out of the sky," he retorted, closing his eyes and pretending to be asleep. He continued mumbling to himself and Simmo reckoned Saint Anthony would be able to build himself a bloody basilica with a helipad by the time they got down.

How long had they been travelling for - eighteen, twenty hours now? Simmo pondered, his eyelids beginning to droop. He had never worn a watch - he had seen one of his fellow apprentices nearly lose a hand getting one caught in a lathe chuck back at Laird's. He drifted into a sleep where something akin to Cousin Itt from the Adams Family was trying to open a travelling alarm clock, whilst parachuting out of a Cortina. Mrs C was shaking him, saying "wake up, wake up." He came to with a start. The flight attendant was gently shaking him, "seat belt," she said. Ally was snoring. He was still wearing his seatbelt; he hadn't taken it off. The plane banked at a crazy angle and Simmo could make out a mountain before it swooped down. He gripped his seat, the engines roaring and Ally's snoring resonating with their groan; then they were on the ground. Simmo could feel the strain of the breaks gently pulling forward and then easing off as the plane came to a halt.

Most of the other passengers had shuffled off by the time Simmo woke Ally.

"Wake up Ally, we're here!"

Gigolos

Ally opened one eye.

"We've landed Ally, we've made it!"

"Oh thank Christ," said Ally, "no wonder the Pope always kisses the bloody floor."

Simmo headed out of the door, the glare - now even stronger - reflecting off the sea. Ally grabbed his holdall. The flight attendant asked him: had he been scared?

"Nae," replied Ally, "just a little indigestion, that's all. "

Simmo was much relieved to see a more modern aircraft at the airport, being boarded by what looked like tourists. He had a sneaky suspicion that their last flight had been one of Ally's penny-pinching exercises but still, he thought to himself, you get what you pay for. He chuckled at this notion and Ally asked him what he was so bloody happy about, but Simmo just smiled and replied "oh, nothing...." so Ally said "you'd better get over there with that lot off the plane and get your holdall then." They stood there whilst all manner of luggage and other items, including animals in cages, were unloaded. In the end Simmo asked the man who seemed to be in charge where his holdall was. They were getting nowhere until an English-speaking passenger interjected. He spoke to the airport official in his own language then asked Simmo whether he had checked his bag in at Tahiti?

"Erm no," replied Simmo.

"When was the last time you had it?" asked Ally

"When we checked it in at Glasgow."

"Christ! It could be fecking anywhere by now!"

"I thought it would be sent on automatically," said Simmo, forlornly.

Steve Poultney

The passenger shook his head and explained that Simmo would have to call the airline and explain what had happened, and then see if they could find it and maybe forward it on.

"Bollocks," said Simmo, taking a sharp intake of breath. And then he thanked the passenger for his help. Ally just stood there shaking his head.

"You've nae lost your passport as well have you?"

"No..." It was in his coat in the carrier bag.

"Wonder you've nae lost your head by now," groaned Ally. "Come on, let's get out of here."

They breezed through customs, what there was of it, with passports stamped and visas checked, and then out into a slightly cooler - now darkening - landscape. Simmo spotted the passenger who had helped him earlier.

"Excuse me, where do we get the ferry to this place?"

The passenger regarded the crumpled piece of paper Simmo was holding and pointed them to a coach.

"It takes about fifteen minutes by road, then a further twenty or so on the boat," he said, looking at his watch. "You have missed the morning one, but there is one in the afternoon. It leaves at four-thirty."

It seemed prudent to board the coach rather than hang around in town. The journey was pleasant enough, although the coach was rather hot and stuffy. The friendly passenger's name turned out to be Jamaal and they asked him about their island. He explained that there was only really one town and a couple of small villages. Ally showed him a picture of the bar and Jamaal said that he knew the place and that it was very nice. He was surprised that he hadn't

Gigolos

heard it was up for sale, but he had been away in India on business... in recent years the tourist trade had picked up on the island due to the development of a number of new hotels and a relaxation in the gambling laws.

They spent a pleasant afternoon with Jamaal, and over a light lunch he explained to them the history of the islands - culture, customs, currency - in fact all the things that Ally and Simmo hadn't even considered. He also explained that if they wanted to get anywhere with the local authorities then bribery was the usual way. Jamaal looked at the sky, which was now quite black.
"It is unfortunate for you my friends that you have come at the rainy season."
"Rainy season?" quizzed Ally.
"Yes my friends, not quite a monsoon but certainly very wet."
At which point the heavens literally opened, sending everyone scarpering under cover.

Totally soaked and dripping, Ally and Simmo disembarked from the small ferry boat. The crossing had been a little choppy, but the men were both quite used to this. Simmo had spent his last year of school at a nautical academy in North Wales, and although he hadn't done it for many years he was quite a proficient dingy sailor. Only a small handful of other people got off with them and most of them were local. A short fat American was heading for the only vehicle resembling a cab they could see.
"Excuse me," hailed Ally, "would you be knowin' where this place is?" he asked, handing the Yank the photo of the bar.

"Why yes, it's lucky for you guys I'm going there myself - care to share a cab?"

The American only had a brief case, so he and Ally placed their meagre luggage in the boot. Simmo kept hold of the carrier bag - he had lost enough for one day - and all three of them quickly climbed in out of the torrential rain, accompanied by Simmo's usual slamming of the door. The taxi driver said something in his own language, and he and the Yank both laughed. Their new companion garbled on about this and that, finally asking Ally what their plans were for their holiday, given that it was the rainy season. Ally explained that they had a new business venture - that they had bought a bar.

"Oh," said the Yank, a little perplexed, "which one?"

"The one in the picture," Ally replied.

"You're sure it's this one?" he queried, staring hard at the picture and then at Ally.

"Yes that one."

He passed him the bill of sale and the Yank asked the taxi driver to pull over for a minute and to turn the interior light on. He poured over the paper, digesting it a couple of times before breaking into a grin.

"What's wrong?" asked Ally. The Yank was now laughing.

"What's up? That's the right address now? We're nae on the wrong bloody island are we?"

Simmo gulped. He had a flashback to Mrs C's drug-fuelled warning.

"No," said the Yank, it's the right address all right but you're looking at the wrong bar."

Ally didn't understand.

"Look carefully at the photograph."

Gigolos

"Aye?" said Ally, screwing up his eyes to focus in.

"Can you see the white building at the right hand side?"

"Aye..."

"Follow the beach back to the left...now there, just in the corner, can you see it?"

"What?!" said Ally, widening his eyes in disbelief. "It's nae that rusting tin shack is it?"

"Oh God," groaned Simmo

"That feckin' Raoul!" Ally's eyes were ablaze now. "Are you sure?"

"Oh quite sure guys, 'cause I own the bar on the right. I'm Frankie by the way."

He spoke to the driver, who extinguished the light and drove on. He and the Yank chattered away in French, and the only word Simmo could make out sounded like 'patsy'.

The taxi took a sharp turn down a bumpy muddy track and pulled up outside Ally and Simmo's new home.

"Well good luck fellas!" shouted Frankie over the wind and rain as they got out. "Call up to my place for a drink sometime."

The taxi driver started to turn the cab around.

"Hold on there!" shouted Ally, waving his arms.

The taxi stopped and Frankie slid the window open a little.

"Mah bag," said Ally, pointing at the boot.

"Sorry," laughed Frankie as the driver popped the boot, adding "We gotta get goin', this road will be a goddam river shortly."

Ally and Simmo crossed the muddy yard and walked up the three steps onto the veranda. The rain drummed incessantly on the roof and the pair of them were soaked to the skin. There were a couple of dim lights to be seen inside. Above the door hung a faded sign that once may have said 'cocktails'. Simmo and Ally looked up at it, like moths looking at a flame... BURRRRR!!!... It suddenly buzzed as water from the dripping roof seeped into one of the terminals. The neon flashed brilliantly for a moment, spelling out a word from the broken letters ... 'C..O..C..K..S'.

There were three or four old men inside the bar. They all stared at the dripping muddy foreigners in front of them. A short pretty skinny girl with long black hair stood behind the bar polishing a glass.

"You ever seen *American Werewolf in London*?" said Ally to Simmo.

"Errm... Mr Chin Lee?" said Simmo to no one in particular.

The girl looked at one of the men at the bar, who gave the slightest of nods.

"He Chin Lee," she said, nodding at the man.

"We're the new owners," Ally said to the girl.

There was a conversation between Chin Lee and the girl.

"When you take over?" she said.

"Now I suppose," said Ally.

"All here, all ready for you."

"That's good," said Ally," I suppose we ought to have a wee drink then." He ordered two large whiskeys, adding "and what does your former boss want to drink?"

The girl seemed to have a little difficulty with the word 'former', but got the whiskey down off the top shelf. She had to stand on tip toe to reach it and, stumbling backwards, she dropped the bottle,

Gigolos

shattering it on the floor. She drew a sharp intake of breath as, with a roar, Chin Lee charged around the bar and began slapping her around the head and face.

"Now wait just a minute there pal!" Ally was furious.

Chin Lee shouted something back at him, but Ally's long arm reached over the counter and seemingly in slow motion lifted the man over, his hand firmly gripping him around his throat. Chin Lee's feet were kicking a good six inches off the ground. His eyes rolled into the back of his head and a stream of stinking urine ran down his leg. Ally was suddenly distracted by the girl punching and kicking his back and legs. He let go and Chin Lee crumpled to the ground.

"You no can do!" she screeched, "I his!"

"I don't care if you're his girlfriend, I will nae stand back and watch a grown man beat a woman." In his mind's eye he could see his own poor mother...

"You no understand. I not his girlfriend I ... his..." the girl faltered.

Ally looked at Simmo who just shrugged. The other men in the bar looked on in surprise - Ally must have looked a giant - and an angry giant at that. Chin Lee dragged himself to his feet and snarled something at Ally, who simply replied "and the same tae you with knobs on pal."

Chin Lee headed for the door and screamed "Rikitea!" sharply at the girl. She looked at Ally and then at Chin Lee, but didn't move. Chin Lee advanced on the girl but Ally stepped in between them and he backed off.

"Best you stay with us tonight sweetheart," Ally said to Rikitea, "let that bastard go and cool off."

Chin Lee had one final outburst, pointing his finger at Ally before storming off. Two minutes later they heard the sound of an engine as a large jeep came from the back around the side of the building and Chin Lee sped off into the night. Ally said to Rikitea to offer the gentlemen in the bar a drink. The men kept mum at first, but soon there were nods and smiles all around as the beer began to flow...

God knows what time they threw the last drunk out.
"Where do we sleep?" Ally asked the girl. Rikitea lowered her eyes and took Ally's hand. He cocked an eyebrow at Simmo, who coughed loudly and looked at Rick... Richt? Oh fuck, he couldn't say her name.
.…."No Rhik, he attempted, "where do Ally and I sleep?" Rikitea looked relieved, then a little puzzled. "You queer boys?" She asked.
"It's you and them feckin' cowboy boots!" screeched Ally, pointing at Simmo's feet, "no wonder we keep coming up on the gay radar."
Simmo just laughed. "No, erm, Rikk, we're not gay.
Again Rikitea looked puzzled.
"Not queer ... we like girls."
She didn't look convinced, but shrugged her shoulders and took them to the living quarters. There were three rooms, a large one with a big double bed and two smaller ones, both a little like cells. One had an ancient set of bunks on which Ally's Crimean War army blankets would have looked right at home. Rikitea dumped Ally's holdall down onto the bottom bunk and showed Simmo to the larger room, leaving Ally scratching his head. For her own part she crept off to the other small room with the single bunk.

Gigolos

There was a dressing table sparsely populated by a hairbrush, a cracked mirror, a faded photograph in a wooden frame and a few odd bits of makeup scattered around. Simmo kicked off the boots with some effort and crawled into bed. He wasn't sure if he could hear the girl crying or if it was the creaking and groaning of the tin roof under the relentless drumming of the rain.

Simmo was awoken from his dream by Ally screaming. Still half asleep and totally disorientated he flung open the door and ran straight into a deep wardrobe, getting himself tangled in what was presumably Chin Lee's finery. "Christ I must be in fucking Narnia!" he giggled to himself. He heard Ally scream again, and having burst free of the wardrobe picked up the only weapon he could find, an ancient wooden coat hanger that had escaped with him out of the wardrobe. He charged into the main bar where Rikitea stood brandishing a baseball bat. Another ear-splitting scream came from the toilet. God, shuddered Simmo, fearing the worst. He and Rikk - Christ he couldn't say her name - burst in, weapons raised above their heads. There were three traps in the gents, and the door to the end one was ominously closed. Simmo pushed it slowly open with the coat hanger with Rikitea beside him, bat raised like a samurai sword. The hinges creaked slowly, reminiscent of something out of a Hammer film or more likely a *Carry On* spoof... and there was Ally, all six feet two of him, crouched on top of the lavatory beneath which a large, garish snake was curled. Simmo honestly didn't know what to do and looked to the girl for help. After slowly lowering the bat she looked first at Simmo, and then at Ally, a dumbfounded expression crossing her face.

"What wrong?" she asked.

"Can you nae see the feckin' snake?!" screeched Ally clutching his knees to his chest.

Rikitea cocked her head slightly and pointed to the creature. "This good snake, eat all rats." Ally could only whisper "Get it away." Tossing the bat aside Rikitea pulled the snake out from around the pan by its tail, and then stooping to pick it up she carried it out into the bar. She motioned to Simmo, who had followed behind her, to open the door. Ally was still on his perch, so to speak. Rhik (or however you said it) carefully stepped out into the rain and placed the snake gently on the floor. It promptly slithered away under the veranda. Rhik smiled and said "he like us... no like rain." Simmo, still holding the coat hanger, hastily put it behind his back and smiled in return.

They went back into the bar and Simmo shouted "it's safe to come out now Ally! Rikki Tikki Tavi Mongoose has got rid of it for you!"

Ally returned, looking a little shaken, and poured himself a large one.

"Thanks Rikki Tikki," he said, raising his glass.

'Rikki Tikki' giggled, and then she eyed the two men coldly before bursting out laughing, and shaking her head wandered off back to her room. Simmo could have sworn he heard her mutter "pair of plicks" as she disappeared inside.

Despite the rain it was still hot and humid. The torrential showers would briefly stop as soon as they began, only to resume with a further intensity. Rikki Tikki, meanwhile, had been busy unpacking Ally's gear. She had folded the smaller items and put them

Gigolos

in the drawers, then hung up the rest in the small closet. Simmo's only two items of clothing - the coat and pullover - were now on the hanger he had found and sat resplendent at the front of the Narnia wardrobe. Rikki Tikki stocked the bar, brushed the floor and produced a small stepladder for changing a defunct light bulb.

"Err, Rikki Tikki..." asked Ally "...what do we pay you?" A shadow crossed her eyes and she said quietly, "you no pay me." Ally and Simmo exchanged glances but said nothing. Rikki Tikki carried on, disappearing off into the kitchen where a fabulous aroma of cooking escaped. Suddenly Ally and Simmo were salivating; neither of them could remember when they had last had sat down for a proper meal.

Later in the afternoon a couple of locals arrived, slowly followed by a few more who were probably curious about the new owners. Rikki Tikki had them enthralled with a story, and by her gesticulations Simmo gathered she was relating the tale of the snake.

The evening passed pleasantly enough and money was going into the till. Ally had presented himself behind the bar, but as he couldn't communicate with all but one of the customers he stood to one side, towel in hand, gently polishing a spot on the counter doing that circular motion thing, rollie in the other hand and a faraway look on his face that was so reminiscent of his stance in the kitchen back in Glasgow. He had kitted himself out in an old pair of sports shorts, green flash pumps and a vest, it being much too humid for anything else. Simmo, however, had a dilemma: he only had the clothes he stood up in. He knew, somewhat ashamedly, that Rikki Tikki would wash them after he went to bed, but the tight heavy corduroy jeans clung to him and he could feel the onset of sweat rash... Despite Rikki Tikki's best efforts his only t-shirt, a white Sandinista Clash one, had become heavily sweat-stained. He wasn't sure what to do...

They hadn't seen sight nor sound of Chin Lee and eventually Simmo started rifling through the wardrobe. They were of a similar height, although Simmo's waistline was a dam sight smaller. Most of the clothes were white, so he settled on some baggy peg trousers, a wide black leather belt, a silk shirt that had a collar with a wingspan similar to Concorde and a pair of Bay City Rollers style platforms. There was a black silk handkerchief stitched into the pocket of the shirt that Simmo, to his consternation, found that he could not remove; but then to top it off he found a white wide- brimmed hat with a black ribbon around it. He suddenly decided he looked pretty cool - sort of Jackson Browne meets Hinge and Bracket. He laughed to himself, and was going to take off the hat but (just as Mrs C might say) it set off his outfit...

Ally's jaw dropped as Simmo sauntered into the bar.

"Jesus Christ!" he exclaimed after a short pause, "You look like the Naked Civil Servant!"

Simmo, looking affronted, walked over and stood next to Ally.

"Well at least I don't look like a wooden horse reject in a stalag luft PE kit!"

They both turned to look at Rikki Tikki and Ally prompted her, saying, "What d'you think?" She regarded the pair of them, shaking her head slowly

Gigolos

before announcing, through fits of giggles, "I think you look like pair of fluckin' gigolos!" The three of them burst out laughing. Eventually Ally managed to splutter out "great name for a bar, d'you nae think?, at the same time wiping a tear from his eye.

"Why not?" said Simmo, regaining his composure.

"Especially if you're gonnae dress the part wee man," said Ally, giving Simmo a dig in the arm and setting them all off laughing again.

Rikki Tikki returned to her station at the bar, leaving Ally and Simmo play-fighting and calling each other names in the middle of the room.

The dray, for want of a better name, came out to the bar once a week, bringing the essentials from beer to beans, from tampons to toilet paper and from condiments to condoms. Rikki Tikki explained to Simmo that she usually hitched a ride back into what passed for the town with the dray; she took the takings - what little they were - to the bank and picked up other bits and pieces. She suggested he came with her.

"You need open bank account."

Simmo slapped his forehead - of course! At least then they could move the rest of the money from the UK. Rikki added they could also find him some shorts and t shirts – oh, and some flip-flops and of course a pair of sneakers...

"Sneakers?" quizzed Simmo.

Rikki pointed down at her feet.

"Oh!" said Simmo, cottoning on, "*trainers!*" He drew the word out slowly. "But how will we get back?"

"Bus to top road then walk."

Steve Poultney

Simmo didn't fancy a couple of miles squelching through the mud, but he had after all said he would go. The dray looked like something left over from M.A.S.H. but the big truck was more than capable on the muddy, rutted road. The track opened onto the beach road that took people to the top bar. It was relatively smooth and asphalted.

"Wish this was our road," Simmo sighed.

"It is!"

"What do you mean?"

"You own road, from top road to bar. When Frankie do his place it only way through, through here; he have pay use road."

"Really?!" said Simmo, the fact slowly dawning on him, "Ah...I see..."

"Frankie want buy bar but Chin Lee no sell to Frankie. No trust him."

"Have you ever heard of Raoul van Horen?"

"Yes I think. He from Holland, had big plan but no get it going."

"What was it Rikki Tikki?"

"Him and Chin Lee want build hotel but couldn't. Bar not make much money... road pay bills."

"Is there anything else we own?" Simmo was more than curious now.

"Land behind bar too."

Simmo nodded; he knew about that.

"And fishing rights to lagoon," she added, nodding

"Fishing rights?" Simmo looked a little unsure.

"Yes, good fishing here once, then they dredge lagoon... All gone..."

"Dredge?" Simmo shrugged, not quite understanding.

Van Horen want build boat harbour."

Gigolos

"What, like a dock?"

"No..." Rikki paused for a moment, trying to think of the right words, "for big yachts."

"Oh..., more like a marina then?"

"Yeah," said Rikki, nodding her head, "marina! That the word, all do with hotel, but hotel never happen. Van Horen no have permission to dredge lagoon, big stink over it, no give him permission build hotel after that."

"Oh," was all Simmo could muster.

Rikki and Simmo had a great time in town, despite the frequent torrential rain. Rikki picked him out some fabulous clothes which she haggled for expertly. Simmo even managed to open a new bank account, with Rikki's help of course. (Ally wouldn't trust Simmo with the important paperwork, insisting that he gave the passports and the bill of sale etc. to Rikki.) The bank, overjoyed at the prospect of a large deposit, was unusually efficient in telexing through accounts and money transfers.

"Should all go through in week or so," Rikki related to Simmo. She and the teller were huddled in deep conversation.

Simmo stared at the two of them as the teller shook his head and Rikki pressed her point home. In the end the teller held up his hand, palm out, five fingers showing. Rikki turned to Simmo and whispered "Fifty dollars." Simmo eyed her suspiciously and she looked hurt.

"You no trust me?"

"Erm no I - erm- I mean yes" Simmo hadn't meant to offend her.

"Trust me?" She eyed him again. Simmo looked petulant but nodded and handed her fifty dollars. He watched her slide it over the counter and it vanished into the teller's jacket like a pickpocket act in reverse.

Rikki took Simmo by the hand and led him out of the bank towards the market square where the buses stopped.

"What was all that about?" whispered Simmo.

Again she eyed him coldly: "You no trust me?"

"No it's not that," he replied, exasperated, "I'm just trying to understand what's going on."

Rikki looked at him hard again, and then her face relaxed and softened with just the faintest hint of a smile.

"Money for road was still going Chin Lee."

"Oh fuck," said Simmo, slapping his head again.

"Money now go you and Ally bank."

Simmo gave her a great big hug. "Sorry Rikki," he beamed, "I am new to all this."

Rikki smiled and shook her head. "Saw theatre once when small..."her eyes had a faraway look before she added, focusing on Simmo's face, "was much funny. Babes in Wood."

As suddenly as the rain had started it stopped, like turning off a tap. The sun broke through and this time it stayed out. Rikki had Ally help her remove the shutters and glass panels to the shed at the rear, whilst Simmo moved the tables and umbrellas from inside. Rikki produced a ladder and inspected the roof. She shouted instructions to bring various tools and she quickly drew up a maintenance schedule that any shipyard would be proud of. She knew that within a week or two the tourists would begin to flock in, and after speaking to Simmo and Ally she enlisted the help of a couple of the old boy regulars and the bar began a stunning metamorphosis. The dray had the

Gigolos

appearance of a carnival float, with palms and all manner of exotic shrubbery arriving with it. The boys, too, had smartened up their appearances. Rikki had ordered them t-shirts with 'Gigolos' emblazoned across the front. And then there was the *pièce de resistance*, which the boys knew nothing about, a brand new sign with *Gigolos* standing out in bold letters and a subtle light incorporated into the frame. Rikki supervised the final positioning of the sign and the three of them stood back admiring their achievement.

The final job was the road, the rainy season having taken its toll. Rikki ordered a couple of lorry-loads of stone and Simmo spent a week from dawn to dusk barrowing stone and filling in potholes. Not only did he have to fill them in, he then had to tamp it all down. It was a laborious business but slowly a transformation was happening - not just to the road, but also to Simmo as his once flabby body began to ripple with muscle. The final task was to erect a smaller version of the *Gigolos* sign at the end of the road, this in turn being adorned with exotic shrubbery.

The customers slowly began to trickle in. Rikki was doing her best to teach Ally how to make all the various cocktails, a task at which he was failing miserably. He could, however, pour a reasonable pint and was doing a fantastic job of polishing one particular area of the bar. Try as she may Rikki couldn't break Ally's habit of smoking on counter duty. "It's nae good," he protested, "I need something in mah mouth." Simmo suggested that if he felt the need to smoke, why not try chewing on a pencil instead? It wasn't long before Ally was on forty HBs a day.

Unusually, a smart black Mercedes jeep turned up early one afternoon. Simmo was at the bottom of the drive strimming around the entrance. He couldn't see in through the blacked-out windows but something about it made him feel uneasy. He was about three-quarters of a mile from the entrance to Gigolos, so he dumped the strimmer and set off at a jog. The jeep crunched on the gravel of the car park and slid to a halt. Chin Lee climbed out of the front passenger side and a huge geezer got out of the back, holding the door open for a short Polynesian-looking bloke impeccably dressed in a smart silk suit. Out of the driver's door climbed an equally large and muscly man who could have made a bookend with the other one. Chin Lee led the men up the veranda steps and burst inside. Ally was stood behind the bar chewing on a pencil. Rikki was startled when she saw Chin Lee, but gasped at the sight of the smartly dressed dude. Ally didn't register what was happening at first, until Chin Lee started shouting and pointing at Rikki. Most of the foreign customers in the bar realised something was going down and started shuffling out of the rear entrance down toward the beach. The dapper man spoke in a quiet husky voice and the few locals who had stayed to view the spectacle also disappeared. In the meantime Ally had picked up a long-necked bottle of red wine and positioned himself slightly in front of Rikki. Chin Lee stood in front of Ally and began shouting in his face. Now Ally, in spite of his size, could move with the speed of a cat if need be.

Gigolos

"Big man with your mates are you?" he drawled in the gruff Glaswegian accent he resorted to when riled. And before he had finished speaking, lightning fast, Chin Lee had gone down in a shattering of broken glass and red wine. The dapper bloke just shrugged while the two big geezers looked on unimpressed. The dapper bloke removed a cigar from his inside pocket and one of his minders moved with a speed equal to Ally's, producing a Zippo and a flame just as he put it to his lips, and the cigar was alight. He took a large drag, gently blowing out the smoke as he surveyed the scene. Then he spoke, catching Ally by surprise: his voice was a perfect imitation of Marlon Brando's portrayal of the Godfather.

"Well now Scotsman, it seems like we have a little situation here... It seems that Mr. Chin Lee may have been a little hasty... It seems that you have something here belonging to him."

"Come again pal?" replied Ally.

"The girl... she is a bond woman." He took another long pull on his cigar.

"I nae understand," said Ally, who in reality wasn't as green as he was cabbage looking.

"Let me spell it out: he owns the girl. At least he does for another three years and seven months. Is that not so Rikitea?"

He looked at her hard and Rikki bowed her head. Ally took a step forward but the dapper bloke held up his hand, not in the least bit perturbed.

"Listen to me, Scotsman, there may be a simple way out of this situation."

"Go on." said Ally softly, judging the distance between him and the dapper man. "Who is he Rikki?" he asked, his eyes not leaving sight of his adversary.

Steve Poultney

"He the Don... The Pedalo Don," She replied, her head still bowed. "He run the beaches," she added.

Ally raised an eyebrow, perplexed.

"A simple solution," the Don continued, "would be for you to buy her, pay what is owed on the contract and of course a little compensation for..." He looked down at the prostrate Mr. Chin Lee.

"And how much that will cost me pal?"

"Three thousand dollars."

Ally whistled. "How about two thousand five and I'll compensate Mr. Chin Lee mahself."

The Don blew smoke and started to laugh. "You drive a hard bargain, Scotsman. I like you." He nodded and one of the boys produced a document from his pocket. "This is her contract."

Ally in turn nodded at Rikki. "Go get the cash - you know where I keep mah money."

Rikki soon returned with the payment and Ally gestured her to put it on the bar. The Don sent the boy with the contract over to the bar, picking up the cash and leaving it on the shiny spot that Ally loved to polish. The Don nodded and Ally nodded back, neither of them breaking eye contact.

"What about him?" asked Ally.

"Ah, Mr. Chin Lee; we are retiring him," the Don replied, gesturing offhandedly at the prostrate man.

"What - permanently?" Ally had a grave look on his face now.

The Don leaned forward and whispered conspiratorially "yes; he's moving... to Eastbourne."

One of the boys picked up Chin Lee and slung him over his shoulder. The Don looked about the bar. "Nice job, Scotsman," was all he said. He whispered something to Rikki, who replied and bowed her head, then the Don turned on his heel and left. Simmo was

Gigolos

just in time to see one of the minders slinging the unconscious Chin Lee into the back of the jeep, watching it pull away the instant the passenger door shut. He leaped up the steps, bursting through the door and skidding across the wooden floor.

"Is everything all right?" he panted, worried.

"Ally just buy me," said Rikki, with head bowed, and tears in her eyes.

Simmo's head swam from the charge up the drive. He watched Ally walk over to the bar and appear to study the contract, but it was in a language that he didn't understand and besides which he didn't care any way. He took a cigarette lighter out of his pocket and ceremoniously set light to it over the ashtray.

Their first taste of officialdom came the following week. Ally, as usual, was stood polishing the bar whilst Rikki and Simmo were busy ferrying drinks in and out. But then a smartly dressed man approached Ally with a prohibition notice in his hand. The gist of it was that their bar had a raw sewage outlet going out into the sea and that they were to cease trading forthwith until they did something about it. Ally waved Rikki over and she spoke sharply to the man in their own language – indeed, she appeared to be haggling with him. After a while the man nodded. Rikki leaned over to Ally.

"Two fifty," she whispered. The man eyed Ally, po- faced.

"Jesus wept!" muttered Ally, winking at Rikki, who disappeared into the back and came back with an envelope which she placed on the bar. The official casually picked up the envelope and stuffed it into his pocket, then turned on his heel and left.

Steve Poultney

"Shit!" said Simmo to Ally.

"Aye, quite literally," Ally responded tersely.

It was a common practice according to Rikki: "They all on take." She explained that the man would keep coming back for his money; that it happened to all the bars unless they did actually put a septic tank or some such other arrangement in. Most bars didn't bother as it was cheaper and less hassle to pay him.

Simmo and Ally stood in the water a few yards off the beach. A brown stream of sewage seeped from the pipe, reminding Simmo of the pier head when he was a child.

"Jesus, what are we going to do?" he asked Ally.

"Well it's nae wonder the bloody tourists don't swim in the sea here is it? I bet Frankie doesn't pump his bloody shite into the sea... aye, and he probably bloody tells 'em to stay away, that the sea is foul up here."

Rikki, practical as ever, told them that Chin Lee had had plans drawn up to deal with the sewage, but when he and Raoul couldn't get the hotel off the ground he never bothered.

"He still have drawings in back."

Ally pawed over the drawings: scratching his head, chewing on his pencil, scribbling on them, crossing things out, and muttering and mumbling, leaving Rikki and Simmo to run the bar. He eventually explained to Simmo that he reckoned they could do it at a knock-down price. Raoul's plans were for a fifty bed hotel complex...

"Aye," said Ally, we only need something a fraction of the size that Raoul was planning."

Gigolos

He proposed that they put a chamber and soak-away further inland on some of the land they owned, then disperse the waste with a macerator pump. Rikki suggested building a concrete chamber shuttering the sides rather than a tank; she also knew that one of the old boys who drank there had a brother with a digger. Simmo was gobsmacked.

"How the fuck do you know about bogs and drains?"

"Aye well, we put one in at mah Gran's when I was a kid; she lived in the wilds high up above Inverness." Ally looked smug. Simmo turned and looked at Rikki.

"Uncle builder," she replied, equally smug.

"I'll go get my spade then," Simmo chortled, and the three of them laughed.

They enlisted the help of a couple of the old boys; Rikki sourced the materials, although there was some debate over the pipes, and at times she was at loggerheads with Ally... Simmo saw a different side to Rikki: she would bang the flat of her palm on the table, and Ally in turn would pull tongues and silly faces at her. He noticed something else too: the way they looked at each other. Could it be the first sparks of attraction...? But then the reality of running the bar would kick in and he dismissed his thoughts. Their work load was relentless. To get on with the construction meant getting up at six o'clock, with Simmo and Rikki cramming in a few hours' building work before opening the bar. They hardly saw Ally in his role of architect, site manager and labourer.

It was the quiet part of the morning. Rikki was busy outside arranging the tables when a tall, slim, good-looking girl with a boyish haircut walked into the bar. She didn't have the look of a tourist about her. She sauntered up to the counter and ordered a coke.

"You don't seem very busy," she spoke, making small talk.

What was her accent? Her English was word perfect.

"Parlez vous Francais?" Simmo tried.

"Oui," she replied, followed by a stream of French.

"Sorry," Simmo stumbled, "erm...my French isn't very good."

She cocked an eyebrow, and slowly smiled. "Well at least you tried." Simmo looked down, blushing, and for some strange reason started polishing the bar, Ally style.

"Is it only you and the girl working here?" She motioned toward Rikki, who was busy sweeping the veranda.

"No there's my partner as well, he's outside somewhere working on the tank."

She gave him a confused smile. "Tank?"

"Erm yeah, it's to process the sewage."

"Oh, that type of tank!" she chuckled. "That's good; we've been on at the authorities to do something about it for ages." She was beaming now. "There are some quite rare species in these waters."

"We?" replied Simmo, suddenly suspicious.

"Yes, I am a marine biologist. There is one in particular, a left-spiralling sea snail; I won't bore you with its Latin name, but it is so unusual and almost unheard of in this part of the Pacific."

"Oh," said Simmo.

Gigolos

Rikki came over with some empty glasses and looked at the pair of them, and Simmo found himself stumbling over his words again.

"This is...erm... sorry, I didn't catch your name?"

"Pascale," the girl replied, and without thinking Simmo blurted out "She's from France!" Rikki eyed Pascale and then, much to Simmo's surprise, the two girls started up a conversation in French. They laughed at some private joke which Simmo surmised was probably at his expense. Pascale raised her glass at Simmo and said "cheers!" before walking outside to find a seat on the veranda out of the sun. Both Simmo's and Rikki's eyes followed her out.

"She nice girl," said Rikki. "Bar polished plenty enough," she added, giggling.

Simmo realised to his consternation that he was still imitating Ally's usual stance. He fumbled with the cloth before slinging it under the bar, doing his best to act casual. Rikki just eyed him sideways, laughed again and went about her tidying.

From then on Pascale was often in the bar, usually of an evening, although she was never alone and almost always with the same man. It was now peak season and there were a lot of unaccompanied women who, tired of watching their husbands gambling at Frankie's, would wander down the beach to the quieter *Gigolos*. To his surprise Simmo found himself becoming quite popular with the forty-somethings. He had never been very good with women and wasn't sure how to react to this new found attention. Occasionally he would catch Pascale looking at him, but there was never time to strike up a meaningful conversation.

Steve Poultney

Simmo was surprised when Pascale appeared very early one morning leading a horse, just as he and Rikki were about to join Ally up at the tank.

"Could you help me please? She asked Simmo.

"What's the matter?"

"She's thrown a back shoe and its half hanging off. I need a pair of pliers or something …

Simmo strode over and whilst Pascale held the bridle he stood to one side and ran his hand down the horse's leg, picking up her hoof.

"Mmm," he said gently, setting the hoof back down, "wait there a minute."

He disappeared off to the shed. In with the stuff he had had shipped over from Scotland was a tool roll. He had meant to throw it out years ago but for some sentimental reason he had kept it. His mind wandered back to his youth....It had started off as a summer job working in riding stables on the outskirts of Liverpool. At first the job was all mucking out, which mainly consisted of shovelling shit. But over the weeks, he learnt how to groom and tack up the horses, a task that he had taken to readily, and Simmo learned quickly. The woman who ran the place saw some potential in him and offered him riding lessons instead of cash. So gradually over that summer, the thirteen year old Simmo had learned to ride and to look after horses. He was there for three summers - and most weekends - before going off to the nautical school in Wales. In the peak season he would take riders out pony trekking, and learned how to take off shoes if one twisted or became really loose on a ride. He mused that was where he first met Mrs C… Her dad paid for her to have lessons there…then he went away, and they lost touch before meeting again at college… Simmo came to, shaking his head

Gigolos

wistfully before returning to the task in hand. He reappeared with pincers, buffer and a small hammer. Pascale and Rikki both looked at each other as expertly, with the hoof clamped between his legs, he removed the twisted shoe. The other rear shoe was also coming loose, so Simmo raised the clenches with the buffer and hammer. It took a little longer to remove this one but the whole process lasted a little under ten minutes. Pascale and Rikki seemed impressed.

"Where you learn use them tool?" asked Rikki.

Simmo tapped his nose. "Front ones are ok for now but she will need them all doing soon," he said, stroking the mare whilst blowing gently on her face. He asked Pascale to trot her up and down a couple of times, observing her gait.

"She looks fine," he said. "It will be ok to ride her back on just the front ones."

Ally had been stood there for some time; in all honesty he was quite impressed.

"Oi, cowboy, seeing as you're so good with your hands do you nae mind lending me one?"

Simmo nodded but his eyes never left Pascale's.

"What are you doing?" Pascale asked Ally.

"Just finished wiring the pump," he replied proudly, "it's all ready tae try. I just need someone tae check the pump's pumping the right way whilst I switch it on."

"Oh! Well, I must be there for the grand inauguration."

She giggled and Ally gave a very formal bow before the four of them, horse in tow, walked the couple of hundred yards to the tank. Ally pointed to the hatch.

"Aye, the inlet pipe is down there, just behind the ladder... Simmo, shout when you're ready and I'll switch on."

Ally walked back down to the little shed which housed the pump and the control panel. Simmo poked his head down the hole. He could just make out a bung in the pipe that they had put in there to stop the render blocking it. Pascale and Rikki were deep in conversation in French, presumably about horses...Simmo stretched down but couldn't reach the bung. "Bollocks," he said as he started to climb down the ladder, shouting back to Rikki "for Christ sake tell him not to switch on!"

As his head disappeared down the hatch Rikki only caught "switch on" and immediately shouted at Ally to do so. As Simmo removed the bung there was an almighty gurgling noise and a tremendous "whoosh!" Simmo was blown clean off the bloody ladder as Rikki screamed "sitch off sitch off!!" Ally hit the stop button, worried the pump was going the wrong way, and started walking back up the hill just in time to see what appeared to be a turban emerging from the hole. As he advanced further he realised it was a none- too- pleased Simmo, his head and shoulders adorned in used toilet paper and covered from head to toe in shit. The girls were rolling around laughing; the horse wrinkled its nose and pawed the ground. Ally looked at the sight and started to laugh.

"Take it it's going the right way then," he gaffed.

"Give us a fuckin' hand!" said Simmo. He stretched out his arm but Ally just laughed, shook his head and stepped back. Simmo scooped a handful of filth off his shoulder and went to throw it at Ally but lost his grip and literally fell back in the shit. The two girls were in near hysterics now and the tears were

Gigolos

running down Ally's face. Eventually Simmo scaled the ladder and heaved himself out of the hatch. He nodded politely to Pascale, snubbed his nose at Rikki, gave Ally the finger and without further ado took himself off to get cleaned up.

Pascale returned to the bar to see Simmo one evening a week or so later; in her hand she had a rather fine bottle of Chivas Regal.
"This is for you."
"Really?"
"It's from Jean Paul." Simmo frowned, cocking his head.
"It's his family who have the horses."
"Oh... erm... Thank you...Is Jean Paul the guy I usually see you with in here?"
"That's him."
"Is he your boyfriend?"
Pascale shuffled a little, and after a moment she replied "it's complicated."
"Oh."
"And you?" asked Pascale.
"He isn't my boyfriend," quipped Simmo.
Pascale looked at him, perplexed, before the pair of them started laughing.
"No!" she giggled.
"If you mean do I have a girlfriend, then the answer is no. I seem to be married to this bar." When he thought about it he - in fact the three of them - hadn't had a night off since their arrival, which must have been a good four months ago now.
"Do you ever get an evening off?" Pascale asked him.

Simmo shook his head. "I suppose in a couple of weeks' time, once the season proper ends, then maybe."

Pascale mused for a moment, and then she inquired, "Have you mornings free?"

"Why?" Simmo was busy stocking bottles.

"How about we get up early tomorrow? I can borrow a couple of horses... I know some beautiful little coves and there will be no tourists about that early; we could have a long gallop in the surf..."She stared at him intently.

Simmo looked a little unsure. "What about ... erm ...Jean Paul?"

"He won't bother; he isn't much interested in horses."

Simmo looked at her hard. What was her expression? Was it beseeching, pleading....or bewitching....? He paused before nodding. "Why not? All work and all that..."

"Settled then," said Pascale, smiling.

The only suitable footwear Simmo had for riding in was his cowboy boots, although he considered the heels a little high - but then it had never stopped John Wayne... Ally was still in his pit but Rikki was up and about, although it was barely light when Pascale rolled up in an open-top jeep. Simmo waved to Rikki on his way out, pulling the door closed behind him. In three strides he was across the gravel and launched himself into the jeep, Pascale wincing as he slammed the door. It was about a fifteen minute drive to the Ranch - Jean Paul's parents' place. Pascale handled the jeep expertly on the twisty island roads, although Simmo found himself gripping the seat. His only experience of driving on the island had been as a

Gigolos

passenger on the dray, the local bus and of course in the shared cab ride with Frankie.

The Ranch, as it was called, would not have looked out of place on *Dynasty*. Simmo whistled as they drove through the automatic gates. The main house was a large white colonial-looking affair, with a couple of expensive motors parked outside. Pascale eased the jeep round to the rear of the building where a substantial stable block stood, bordered by a sizeable manège. Pascale pulled up. They had said very little on the drive there, as conversation had been drowned out by the noise from the convertible.

Simmo looked impressed. "It's quite a set up," he said.

"It is. Jean Paul's mother was a very keen equestrian before her accident; maybe not quite Olympic standard but certainly in the higher echelons."

"Oh…" Simmo rubbed his face. "Was it a riding accident?"

"No, a motorcycle."

"I'm Sorry."

At a loss for anything else to say, Simmo followed Pascale through the yard. There appeared to be a couple of Lusitanos and some smart-looking sports horses. A groom met them near the end of the building. "Bonjour," said Pascale, striking up a conversation in French as he led them to where two horses were already tacked. The groom nodded in Simmo's direction and Pascale smiled as she asked him "he wants to know whether you would prefer to ride western."

Simmo looked down at his boots and shook his head. "Had a nasty experience of that once; had a horse throw a bucking fit with a roping saddle on and I got thrown up high and came down right on my ..."

"Horn?" enquired Pascale, smiling again.

"Suppose you could call it that," smirked Simmo, inadvertently rubbing his goolies.

The groom, ever attentive, asked Simmo if he required a hat, and seeing that Pascale was slipping her own on he nodded and said "six and three quarters" to the groom. It was the groom's turn to look surprised now, but moments later he returned with a jockey skull-type riding helmet, a perfect fit. Pascale had popped herself onto the mare she had been riding when the shoe came off. Simmo's horse was a large bay gelding of at least sixteen hands. The groom asked "would sir like the assistance of a mounting block?" but Simmo just smiled and shook his head. Whilst the groom held the horse Simmo set his stirrups to hole number ten, (God, he hoped his legs hadn't shrunk over time!) and taking the reins popped himself up onto the gelding's back, quickly adjusting the girth and raising himself a couple of times in the stirrups just to check. They were, perhaps, a little short on number ten, but better to be a little short if they did indeed gallop down the beach. The groom looked a little more relaxed and Simmo winked at him as he and Pascale set off towards the sea.

They rode single file along the narrow track down to the beach. Once there Simmo drew abreast of Pascale, and the pair laughed and chattered for a while before breaking into a trot. It was early and they were the only people on the sands. Pascale guided them over to the edge of the sea. "Come on!" she giggled, breaking into a canter. Simmo shortened his

Gigolos

reigns and followed, his thoughts returning to his youth when they would take the horses in the lorry up Southport way for an early morning gallop on the beach... Pascale took her horse into a gallop and Simmo, who had been miles away, had to raise himself in his stirrups and push himself backwards as his horse took off after her. They galloped for about half a mile or so, Pascale easing back down gently to a trot and then a walk. Simmo bounced round a little, easing up, and at one point he thought he may lose a stirrup, but quickly regained his seat. They walked their horses slowly along the surf, riding on in relative silence for a while.

In a couple of hundred yards or so the beach narrowed. There was a small wooden fence, reminding Simmo of the breakwaters you saw back in the UK, protruding out into the sea.

"Race you!" Pascale yelled. Simmo's horse stuck its tail high into the air and broke into a gallop, aiming at the weathered planks of the breakwater. Pascale yielded her horse over to skirt the breakwater, but Simmo's, try as he may with rein and leg, ploughed straight on towards the looming fence. Simmo was aware that although it only looked three foot from this side, it could be four, five or even six foot on the other. He tried to pull up but was only shortening his stride, and realised that he, either with or without the horse, was going over that fence. At the last minute he forced his heels down, and in a scene reminiscent of Thelwell the horse threw in a big one and they both flew over the breakwater. Simmo, a good eight inches out of the saddle, let out an almighty shout of "WAAYYY!" as the horse took off. They cleared the fence by a good foot, and luckily it was only about ten inches lower on the other side.

Steve Poultney

The landing was a little bumpy, but Simmo soon regained control, bringing the gelding down to a canter and then to a trot. Pascale had more or less avoided the breakwater with just a little skip over the part closest to the water.

"Wow!" she said, "he loves to jump."

"Now you tell me! Ride him in a bloody Pelham next time!" Simmo panted, "I couldn't stop him!" But he was grinning like a Cheshire cat as the pair of them brought their horses back to a slow walk. Pascale giggled, "Oops! I forgot how strong he could be." Simmo pulled tongues at her.

After a little while the beach curved into a small cove where a shallow stream gurgled out into the sea. There was a small grassy paddock, fenced with a little gate. Pascale dismounted, opened the gate and went through, beckoning Simmo to follow, and he too dismounted. She suggested they un-tack the horses and rest them for a while.

"Once they have cooled off we can water them a little further up the river."

"Sounds good to me," Simmo nodded.

So after un-tacking the horses and closing the gate, they placed the tack on the fence and strolled towards the sea. Pascale took Simmo's hand and rested her head on his shoulder. They stood next to the surf gazing out across the blue ocean.

"Let's swim!" Pascale cried suddenly, peeling off her top. She wore no bra and her breasts were small but pert... Simmo felt an immediate movement... They stripped quickly save for the barest pair of briefs that Pascale wore and Simmo's shorts. Pascale plunged into the warm sea and Simmo quickly followed suit. They swam for a while in the shallow

Gigolos

water, splashing each other and generally fooling around. Pascale threw her arms around Simmo's neck and, thinking she was going to duck him, he shut his eyes. But instead she pressed her lips to his and kissed him passionately. Fifty thousand volts passed through Simmo's body and he kissed her back, more passionately than he had ever kissed anyone in his life. They made love there and then in the surf, briefs lost to the sea. The first time was frantic, the adrenalin still flowing through Simmo from the excitement of the ride. The second was slow, each exploring the other, needing, wanting, the pair of them lost in the moment... Eventually sated they collapsed into each other's arms in the warm surf, neither of them saying anything; just being.

It was Pascale who eventually broke the spell. "I think the horses will need a drink before we return." Simmo nodded, a faraway look on his face. They found their clothes - minus underwear - and returned hand in hand to their mounts, tacking them loosely and leading them further up to the river.

Neither of them said much on the way back. Simmo was a little uncomfortable in his jeans without any underpants. Both were smiling and would look at each other now and then and giggle.

"Last canter? Pascale suggested.

"Just a little... am getting a bit rubbed...and don't forget I'm out of practice!"

The short canter took them almost back to the ranch.

"Thank you for a perfect day. You ride very well," said Simmo, panting a little

"You are not so bad yourself," said Pascale, not quite sure if this was innuendo. "How long is it since you last rode?"

"Mmmm... let me think... must be five or six years ago, easy... We would usually try to take in a ride on holiday.

"We?"

"Erm... me and my wife..."

Pascale drew her horse to an abrupt halt, Simmo following suit. She eyed him quizzically.

"We...erm... split up." Pascale was staring at him hard now. "She..erm...she...she...she wanted a bidet!" he blurted out. Pascale's jaw dropped open. "It's a long story..."

"Are you still married?" Pascale asked, frowning slightly.

"I...erm, I don't know." Simmo replied honestly. He hadn't heard from the solicitor in ages. He was sure in his mind he had told them of his change of address... at least...he suddenly sensed, rather than felt, the horse lurch under him as Pascale kicked her mare into a canter and the gelding took off after her. She slowed the horse down at the last minute, going from canter to walk as she entered the yard. Simmo had dropped to a trot as he followed her in, but Pascale was already off the mare and handing the reins over to the groom. As Simmo approached she shouted to him "Maurice will take you back to Gigolos!" Maurice the groom nodded politely.

"Good bye Simmo," she said, putting her hands to her face. He thought he could hear a quiver in her voice and her eyes were moist. Simmo dismounted, but Pascale had rounded the corner and quickly disappeared. Maurice coughed loudly and motioned to Simmo for his reins, leaving him scratching his head.

Gigolos

Ally and Rikki stood back admiring their handywork. They had been refurbishing the vintage cocktail sign, restoring the faded background, renewing the wiring and cleaning up the terminals along with the reserve battery. They had hung it on a framed board with the *Gigolos* logo overhead, mounting it above the door inside the veranda. They were all ready to switch it on when Pascale's jeep rolled into the yard. Simmo jumped out, giving the door an unceremonious slam. Maurice winced then shrugged as he drove off. Ally and Rikki exchanged glances.

"What d'you think wee man?" Ally asked, nodding at the sign.

"Huh?" replied Simmo, somewhat distracted.

"The sign!" said Ally, beaming, "go on Rikki, switch it on." The sign flashed brilliantly, but as Simmo watched a couple of the letters started to dim before going out completely, spelling out the word 'C-O-C-K.'

"Very apt," said Simmo, rubbing his chafed legs before disappearing through the door.

"I nae understand it," said Ally wrinkling his forehead and taking a deep drag on a cigarette.

Rikki mumbled something in her own language and then said, shaking her head, "he not good," before she too went in through the door.

Rain and Pain

The season gradually petered out, the tourists becoming fewer and fewer. Ally and Rikki were busy discussing plans to improve the bar. Rikki suggested extending the veranda area and putting in a dance floor. Ally was raving on about having scantily clad dancers but every time he mentioned it Rikki would beat him with a rolled up tea towel. "Aye but it would bring the tourists in," Ally beamed. "They close us down for indecency!" Rikki would retort.

As the weeks went by Simmo was unusually quiet and becoming more and more introverted. Pascale had only been into the bar a couple of times. She was usually with Jean Paul but never alone. Simmo caught her glancing at him from time to time. He had tried to make idle chat with her but the last time she had cut him short with "how is your wife?"

They had owned the bar for a good six months now. Ally had tried to cheer Simmo up but he was morose and lost in his thoughts, so in an effort to distract him he suggested to Simmo that they go and check out the opposition.
"What do you say wee man? Rikki and one of the old boys can mind the bar...Well?" asked Ally. "Come on, we'll go see how that Frankie does it."
Simmo was quite blasé, but Rikki joined in with "go, go, go! We manage here ok." So under duress Simmo buckled and agreed to go with Ally the following night.

Gigolos

Simmo walked into the bar wearing a Hawaiian shirt and the smart pants Rikki had picked for him. "Thank Christ for that," said Ally, "you're nae going dressed as a member of the Stylistics tonight." Simmo flipped Ally the finger.

It was about a mile walk to Frankie's, and try as he may Ally struggled to get a word out of Simmo. In the end he stopped walking.

"For Christ's sake what's up with you man?" he bawled in exasperation.

Simmo looked down at his shoes and shuffled his feet, hands in pockets.

"*Well?*" questioned Ally.

"I erm, well, erm...I think I'm in love," Simmo blurted.

"Well a blind man could see that," replied Ally, "so what's the problem then?

"I think I blew it."

"Go on."

"I...erm... told her I was married," he said glumly.

Ally scratched his head. "But it's over with you and Mrs C, isn't it?"

Simmo paused. "Erm... I suppose it is."

Ally raised an eyebrow. "Are you nae having regrets then?" he pushed.

"Erm no... Erm... it's just that I never expected to meet someone like Pascale. And we've been so busy...and... erm...I don't know what to say to her... I want to tell her how I feel and to tell her the truth about what happened, but the only thing I could say to her was that she wanted a bidet."

Ally shook his head, trying to stifle a laugh. "Well I'm nae expert but I think you really need tae get her on her own and tell her how you feel, without mentioning any items of sanitary ware. Now come on you soppy bastard, I need a beer."

There were steps up from the beach to Frankie's, leading onto a terraced area with tables and grass umbrellas, subtly lit with coloured lights. Music could be heard playing gently from hidden speakers in the trees. Inside was the main bar with a dance floor, numerous tables and a small stage, with another room off this where the gaming tables were, and a passage leading to another small bar extending out to an open dining area. Ally whistled and said to Simmo "and tae think we thought we'd bought this." Simmo nodded, quite impressed.

Frankie's appeared to be quite busy, despite the lateness of the season. Near the bar, sat at a table, were Frankie and three other men, one beside him and two others with their backs to Simmo and Ally. The taller of the two backs appeared familiar to Simmo, and as he and Ally drew alongside them on their way to the bar they were hailed by Frankie.

"Hey boys how's it going?"

Simmo and Ally turned to face them.

"Aye not tae bad," replied Ally.

Frankie turned to the men who were looking curiously at them. "These are the gigolos," he explained and the men started to laugh. Simmo recognised the taller of the two men at the rear of the table as Jean Paul and shuffled a little uneasily. Ally just winked at them and carried on to the bar.

"Aha, so you're the cowboy," said Jean Paul nodding at Simmo. He said something in French to his companions and the men burst out laughing again. Simmo stared hard.

"Tell me Simon, are you comfortable amongst thoroughbreds?"

"Well," said Simmo, pausing and registering the inference. "I find them too interbred and stupid as fuck to be honest."

Gigolos

He shrugged and followed Ally over to the bar. They took their beers and went outside onto the terrace.

"What was that all about?" asked Ally.

"Oh, Jean Paul was trying to take the piss out of me, so I shut the cunt up."

Ally nodded, impressed. "Aye wee man, I get the impression we're considered the poor relations." He wrinkled his forehead.

"Worst of it is, I suppose, we actually are," said Simmo.

Over the course of the evening Frankie's began to fill up. A number of cars arrived and a couple of minibuses. The music gradually became louder and the boys had to push their way across the now crowded dance floor in order to get to the bar. At a table near the bar sat the Don. He waved Ally and Simmo over. Ally eyed him steelily.

"Gentlemen, good to see you here."

He beckoned them to sit down. Ally slumped down at the table and Simmo stumbled, having been jolted by a slightly tipsy woman and spilling some beer on the table in the process. The Don beckoned a waiter over, who quickly dabbed it up with a cloth. The Don offered Ally a cigar but he declined, produced his own battered Golden Virginia tin and fished out a rollie. Simmo pulled up his chair. They huddled together to talk over the music which was by now very loud. The Don then offered Simmo a cigar too; Simmo refused with a shake of his head. The Don made a little chit chat, gently blowing smoke, before leaning forward to ask Ally a question.

"Tell me, how would you like to see your place busy like this?" he asked, gesturing to the packed dance floor.

"Mmmm...," Ally mused, all ears but giving nothing away, "and how would you propose tae go about that?"

"Did you see the minibuses outside?"

"Aye... go on."

"Suppose those minibuses were to stop at Gigolos as well as here?"

"And what would this cost us?" Ally was wary of a catch.

"Very little really," replied the Don, puffing deeply on his cigar. "As I see it, you have cleaned up the beach and smartened up your bar... the locals and the tourists seem to like you...I see some potential here..."

"So what's in it for you pal?" asked Ally.

"I want to put some pedalos on the beach there, sell a little ice cream, cigarettes and coca cola." Simmo started to smile, but Ally cut him short with a glance. "Maybe a floating platform..." The Don looked at Ally intently. "I think that maybe we could do with a little more competition around here," he continued, glancing over in Frankie's direction. Ally pulled a face.

"Listen to me, Scotsman," said the Don, looking Ally straight in the eye. He waved his hand in the general direction of Frankie and Jean Paul's party. "They have... let me think of the right words... No respect, they still think that they are our colonial masters..."

"There's the same attitude in Whitehall," nodded Ally, "they cannae understand why the Scots don't want to be bloody English."

"The Don lifted his glass: "to nationalism!"

"To nationalism!" agreed Ally, also raising his.

Simmo nodded, his face flushed red from the beer.

Ally cast his eye over to Jean Paul's table "They do think they're a cut above the rest of us." He looked back at the Don. "And I suppose at some time you will call upon us for a favour in return."

The Don laughed, posturing, his hands palms upward. "Well?" he said, after a pause.

Ally leaned further forward and Simmo was not sure what he was going to do. Ally's hand shot out quickly and shook the Don's "How about we give it a wee trial and see how we all get on... "

The Don nodded and Ally went off to the bar to get the three of them a drink.

The Don asked Simmo how he was enjoying the islands. Simmo considered this then shrugged, explaining the bar took up most of his time.

"Little acorns," said the Don. "I started out with nothing...these things take time and conviction."

Ally returned and the beer started to flow. Ally and the Don were deep in conversation and laughing and joking... apparently the Don had spent some time in Scotland many years ago. At one point the conversation looked like it was getting a little heated. Simmo's head was now starting to swim. The gist of the conversation between Ally and the Don was about Rikki and this bond woman thing. The Don assured Ally that he didn't condone that sort of thing, and was actually against it, but Chin Lee had asked him, in here in front of Frankie and his cronies, to mediate, so to speak... putting him on the spot... and the Don's solution had meant nobody lost face and that, in fact, he respected Ally for what he had done. Ally shuffled a little uneasily before offering his hand again, which the Don squeezed firmly.

Simmo suddenly got up, feeling a little queasy from the heat coming off the dance floor and the flashing lights. He headed outside thinking the slightly cooler air might clear his head. In retrospect this wasn't a wise move. The night air hit him and he went from pleasantly tipsy to full-blown drunk.

An equally tipsy forty something woman threw her arms around his neck and they started to dance. It was very late in the evening by now and smooch music was bellowing from the speakers in the trees. Simmo hadn't seen Pascale come into the bar earlier in the evening. She had been purposely avoiding Jean Paul, who had taken up residence at the gaming tables. She was waiting for an opportunity to speak to Simmo on his own but she didn't want to interrupt their business with the Don. Pascale had spent the early the part of the evening at Gigolo's, mainly stood at the bar, talking to Rikki. Rikki had explained Simmo's circumstances to her, filling her in on what had happened between him and his wife as Ally had explained it to her. Seizing her chance she followed Simmo outside, but her expression soured as she saw a plump middle-aged woman trying to snog Simmo. With that she turned on her heel and went back inside. Simmo caught a glimpse of her just as she turned. "Shit," he said, sobering somewhat, pushing the woman away and then having to fend her off. He shouted after Pascale but she had disappeared into the noise and throng of the bar.

Simmo was a little disoriented and lurched across the dance floor stumbling and bumping into people. He couldn't see Pascale but saw a tall, red-haired man leaning across a table, with his back to him. Thinking it was Ally, he tried to call to him but the geezer was deep in conversation with the people at the table. In a bid to get his attention Simmo approached and pinched him on the arse. The man straightened himself to his full height and instantly turned an unfamiliar face to Simmo. In an attempt to defuse the situation he blurted out "sorry...I thought..." only to make it worse by saying, "I thought you were one of us." Whack! A fist came out of nowhere and he was sent reeling across the dance floor. As the geezer advanced on Simmo, who had been pushed back by the dancers, Ally put down the drinks he had been carrying on a nearby table and shoved through the crowd. He tapped the big man on the shoulder.

"Leave it alone pal, he's pissed."

As the other man squared up to Ally, Simmo shouted and distracted him, pointing at his friend and shouting "he's one of us!" The geezer looked from one to the other accompanied by fits of giggles from other revellers, before shaking his head and walking away muttering "goddam fags".

Simmo, now sporting what would be a fine shiner in the morning, was trying to tell Ally about Pascale, but the beer and the blow to the head had taken affect and his ramblings were gibberish. Ally shouted over to the Don, nodding in Simmo's direction. "It's past Prince Charming's bed time." The Don nodded and beckoned a waiter over, giving instructions. The waiter helped Ally load the punch-drunk Simmo into the Don's car, and few moments later his driver came out and took them home.

It was nearly afternoon when Simmo appeared from his pit. Rikki and one of the old boys were at the bar. The old boy pointed at Simmo and he and Rikki started to laugh.

"He say you look like panda!" giggled Rikki.

Simmo peered into the mirrors behind the bar and groaned. "Ugh," was all he could muster, looking at his black eye and further compounding his raging hangover. Ally looked up from the table where he was sat, his reading specs perched on the end of his nose. Simmo grimaced, catching the sunlight reflecting from the spot Ally liked to polish on the bar, beaming like a Martian death ray.

"Aye," Ally spoke, "and I thought we were gonnae have a quiet night out."

Simmo suddenly felt ill as he had a flashback of Pascale turning on her heel. He vaguely recalled getting punched but couldn't remember for the life of him why. He could remember dancing...

"What happened?"

"Careful whose arse you grab!" laughed Ally.

Simmo scratched his head. "I grabbed some woman's arse?" he asked, shocked.

"Nae, much worse than that wee man," said Ally, still laughing, "the arse in question belonged tae a bloke, and a big fecking geezer at that."

"Christ," said Simmo.

"Nae harm done said Ally, "it livened the place up a bit it, so it did."

"Where did you get those?" said Simmo trying to change the conversation, at the same time looking at the newspapers in front of Ally.

"Ah," said Ally, the Don's driver dropped them off this morning. Mainly English, but with a couple of Glasgow Heralds thrown in for good measure. Most of them are ancient but some are only a couple of weeks old."

One in particular had drawn Ally's attention. He held the front page up to Simmo, who stepped forward to focus his eyes, the effort causing more pain. "Massive explosion rocks Glasgow tenement," said the headline. Simmo shook his head, recognising the picture of the block.

"They suspect a faulty gas fire," said Ally with an all too familiar look. Simmo just shook his head again and sloped off for a shower, hoping the hot water would ease his aching face and wash away the banging in his head.

The Don appeared early a few mornings later in a truck with half a dozen pedalos loaded onto the back. His two boys helped with the unloading. Oddly, part

Gigolos

of this included a box with lifejackets of all sizes. Ally held one up.

"Health and safety," grunted the Don, "cheaper than paying the officials."

They also unloaded a chest freezer and some old-fashioned trays, the type cinema usherettes used years ago. The Don also produced a drawing for the bathing platform he was planning on building.

Ally looked at the drawing. "This will nae do," he said, shaking his head, and so he, Rikki and the Don sat down at one of the tables to scrutinise the drawing. Ally explained that it would sit too high in the water.

"How do you know this?" asked the Don.

"Well I used to build ships for a living."

Ally promptly started making notes on the drawing. The Don asked him to come with him and inspect the premises where he made pedalos and oversee the building of the platform over the rainy season. Ally readily agreed. True to his word the minibuses started to arrive at Gigolos and the bar became busy once more. Ally was complaining that they would need more staff. Even with the old boys helping out collecting glasses and tidying up the three of them were hard pressed to cope.

One bloke had become a regular over the last couple of weeks, a man called Byron. He was an English academic who had fallen on hard times; he didn't want to pay the over-inflated prices at Frankie's - or so he said - and had taken to propping up the bar at Gigolos.

"Sad tale really," he told Ally early one evening, "I was a doctor of chemistry teaching at Oxford. Some of the students in my charge put me up to making a kind of amphetamine, just as an experiment mind, though I must say we revolutionised the process...ah! to challenge those enquiring young minds... still, I digress, and how was anyone to know that they would go on to produce it on a commercial scale...? The dean took a very dim view, very dim indeed. I was suspended on full pay pending an investigation... I was cleared by the police of course, but the board thought it best that I should further my career at another educational establishment." Byron took a large gulp from his gin and tonic. And do you know what the ultimate irony was?" Ally shook his head. "The board sold the rights to my discovery to an American pharmaceutical company... bloody cheek... that was my intellectual property. Still, I suppose after the lab burning down incident I was on a sticky wicket somewhat."

"What happened tae the lab?" asked Ally, now intrigued.

"Silly me ... always forgetting things... I omitted to turn the gas off."

Ally just shook his head, absently polishing the spot on the bar. "Aye," he agreed with a sense of *deja vu*, "easily done."

Byron prattled on, relaying one tale of woe after another.

"So how do you come tae be out here then?" enquired Ally? "Are you on holiday?"

Byron took a long sip from his drink. "Well I was, well sort of..." Ally gestured with his hand for him to go on. "Well, I inherited a yacht."

"A *yacht*?" gasped Ally, curiosity now fully raised.

"Yes," replied Byron, "nothing too fancy, just a 40 footer."

Ally whistled, and then said "Shit!" as he overfilled the beer he was pouring.

"An uncle of mine retired out here, and after his demise I was his only living relative."

Gigolos

Ally began pouring another beer. "So what happened tae your yacht then?"

"The thing is I know nothing about sailing, so I hired a rather attractive female skipper."

"You never did," said Ally, smirking.

"It's all true... The idea was to sail to New Zealand where I hoped to find a teaching position, or if not then sell her and go home – the yacht, I mean, not the skipper. But as so often happens, fate got in the way. We were supposed to moor in a lagoon on one of the remote islands." Byron paused whilst Ally served a customer before continuing. "I mean, we arrived safely enough." Ally's brow began to wrinkle. "But she was going to slip into something cooler and go below. She saw me let go the anchor and the yacht did indeed come to a halt, but in my haste to follow her below, I never checked; well, I didn't damn well know the actual anchor chain wasn't fastened to the windlass thingy." Ally groaned. "Next morning we were high and dry on the reef. Two days of Robinson Crusoe before any help came, and the only way to release her was to cut the bloody keel off." Here Byron paused and shook his head sadly, before concluding, "Oh bugger, I loved that yacht."

The bar was becoming busier and busier, with Ally serving drinks like prohibition was about to be announced. Simmo was outside sorting the pedalos for the night and Rikki was running about like a headless chicken.

"And so, Alastair," Byron droned on, "that brings me to my present predicament...I am on my uppers... have been since they barred me from the tables...not a pot to piss in."

"I nae understand," said Ally, "and by the way pal, the name's *Ally*."

"Oh, awfully sorry," said Byron, "Frankie's - that was the last place, you see."

Ally didn't see.

"I got a little carried away," Byron continued.

"You did nae try to burn down the casino then?" quizzed Ally, wondering what the hell Byron had done to get barred.

"Well it was simple arithmetic really, only I got a little greedy... did it once too often."

Ally, in the midst of pouring beer and trying to mix cocktails, still didn't get the gist.

"They accused me of cheating... which of course I wasn't... I just counted the cards."

"Aye, I think I get you now," said Ally, cottoning on.

"There was a charming young French girl... Sorry her name escapes me...well... she told me to scarper... she had overheard them talking and I think there may have been a lot of unpleasantness coming my way."

Rikki barged in with a big order. "So what are you going tae do now?" asked Ally, trying to pour beer and serve shots all at the same time.

"Well that's the thing... my ticket home has expired and I haven't the money for the flight back... none of the other gambling establishments will let me across the threshold."

The bar was by now three deep with customers on all sides.

"Can you count then?" asked Ally.

"Naturally." Byron replied.

"And pour beer?"

"I imagine so."

"Then give us a hand behind this fecking bar!"

And so Byron joined the crew of Gigolos. Rikki made him up a bed in the loft of the shed, and with the addition of a few bits of furniture and a lamp it was really quite cosy and Byron's few meagre possessions fitted in quite easily. Over the next few days, Rikki taught him how to mix all the cocktails on the menu, but was irritated by the chemist's attention to detail that Byron paid to his concoctions. "Just pour bloody thing!" she would rebuke him. As a pedalo ride salesman he was useless, just sitting there on the beach, his mind miles away.

The Don had become a regular visitor, probably to check on his investment. He and Simmo stood observing Byron, chuckling good-humouredly.

"Hasn't got a clue has he?" said Simmo.

The Don just shook his head. "So how would you do it, Simmo?"

"Erm," said Simmo, rubbing his chin, "I think you would need a bit of banter, a bit of the old patter with the customers."

"Go on."

"Flash a smile, push the cold drinks, and crack a joke or two."

"You've got it! Let me show you." The Don instantly broke into a Spanish style accent: "hey pretty lady, you want cokey coley, cigarettes, nice ice cream cool you down? You like my pedalo? Lovely ride...(he emphasised *lovely ride*)... I peddle if you like...show you how... "at which point he winked (and this had a definite air of innuendo to it).

Simmo stood open mouthed.

"You try," said the Don. Simmo raised one eyebrow. "Don't think you can pull it off?" The Don smirked, blowing out cigar smoke at the same time.

"No problem," said Simmo, straightening his shoulders and staring the Don straight in the eye, "watch this."

Simmo strutted over to where Byron was sitting, his eyes vacantly staring out into the sea and his mind lost in numbers bordering on infinity, calculating the number of grains of sand that it would take to fill the empty coke can he held in his hand, and then pondering how many atoms that would be.

Simmo gave Byron a light dig with his toe. "Oi!" Byron was startled from his thoughts. "You go and give Ally and Rikki a hand in the bar; I'll look after the beach."

Byron shook away his thoughts, reeled off a six figure number and shuffled off, leaving Simmo shaking his head. Simmo took the tray out of the fridge, hooked it around the back of his neck and arranged his wares. He looked over to the Don, who stood on the veranda, one hand in his suit jacket pocket and looking on impassively. Simmo approached the nearest two girls lying on the beach. He looked over to the Don, who gesticulated the way an opera singer may demonstrate throwing his voice and then shouted over to Simmo in that weird Spanish accident.

"Hey Pedro! How's it going?"

Simmo, in his new guise as Pedro, went straight into his patter, accent and all. Much to his surprise he soon had the girls laughing and giggling, even throwing in some corny old jokes. He returned to the Don having sold two cokes, two ice creams, a packet of cigarettes and a pedalo ride.

"Not bad," said the Don.

"Here, hold this!" said Simmo/Pedro, thrusting the tray on to the Don. "I got two beautiful ladies to take on a cruise," he cackled in that phoney accent of his.

As the weeks went by, Simmo gradually slid more and more into his alter ego, to the point where he got

Gigolos

Rikki to streak his hair. She cut the arms out of his T-shirts and made cut-offs out of his last two remaining pairs of jeans. The pedalo business was now bringing in a healthy profit, with the Don taking in a sizable chunk. Simmo was also notably missing after the bar closed and sometimes well before it finished, presumably entertaining his new-found lady friends. Also - and much to the disdain of Ally and Rikki - Simmo wasn't rising from his pit until much, much, later in the mornings, quite often accompanied by whichever of his conquests had spent the night with him.

After a couple of weeks of this Ally was starting to get really annoyed. He wasn't particularly bothered by Simmo's nocturnal antics but it was the fact that Simmo was disappearing earlier and earlier each evening, leaving him, Rikki and the hapless Byron to cope on their own, that irritated him. It was after an exceptionally busy night, when the Don had arrived with an additional two minibuses full of business men and local officials, that it came to a head the following morning when Simmo appeared from his room with not one but two of his lady friends, wanting Rikki to make all three breakfast.

"You can feck right off pal!" yelled Ally, "this isn't a fecking hotel. We've all been up since stupid o'clock, while you've been... "Ally didn't finish, he just let the words hang in the air. "And them pedalos ain't gonnae bloody well launch themselves!"

The two women looked at each other and shrugged before kissing Simmo and shuffling out through the door.

Simmo responded, in his Pedro voice, "oh but they nice ladies."

"Couple of old tarts more like!" yelled Ally in response.

The two men glared at each other, but Rikki stepped in between them, speaking softly to Simmo.

"You use be a nice boy. Go sort boats... I bring you something later."

Simmo turned on his heel, only to walk straight into Pascale, who had silently come in through the side door and had witnessed the whole affair.

"Fuck," said Simmo.

Pascale just looked him up and down, shaking her head at the same time.

"Well?" said Simmo, rather abruptly, hands on hips.

"I came to tell, no it doesn't matter... "

"Go on... tell me what you were going to say."

"I came to tell you that Jean Paul and I have split up...but... do you know what Simon? I think Rikitea is right... you're not a nice boy."

Simmo's mouth hung open but no words would come out. Pascale shoved past him and went over to the bar, speaking to Rikki in French. Rikki opened a cold bottle of coke for her; Pascale tossed a few coins on the bar and went out through the door towards her jeep. All eyes were on Simmo; even Byron had roused himself from his endless calculations to observe the debacle. Simmo shuffled a little uncomfortably under their stares, before shaking himself and going out after her. Pascale was finishing putting the canvas hood up on the jeep.

As he came out of the door the sky and the sea looked as though they were one, and a defiantly reddish purple. Simmo shouted over to Pascale but his voice was drowned out by an almighty crack of thunder from overhead, lightning streaking across the sky. The jeep pulled away, tyres screeching and scattering stones. Simmo sprinted over the yard towards the gate but the jeep sped past him as the first big drops of rain began to fall. Simmo stood there in the deluge staring after her, soaked almost instantly. Ally moved to follow him out but Rikki stopped him. "I go," she said. Rikki watched the bedraggled Simmo slowly return, accompanied by another loud crash of thunder. The lights in the bar flickered a couple of times and then went out. Only the sign above the door remained lit and that was arcing and flashing in the torrent seeping through the veranda roof. Simmo didn't bother looking at it; he knew what word it would be spelling out.

"Come inside, I cook for you," said Rikki.

Simmo just shook his head as he squelched up the steps. Somehow he didn't feel very hungry anymore.

Double Beds and Broken Heads

Although they knew the rainy season was coming they weren't prepared for its sudden onset. Tables, loungers and all the other associated equipment needed bringing in. It was hectic rearranging the junk in the shed so that they could get the shutters out. The loungers and tables had to be stored and it was difficult to find space for the soggy mattresses to dry. Ally had problems with the backup generator, which refused to start despite his ritual swearing incantation, leaving Simmo and Byron to hump the shutters over and hang them up by themselves. Byron was too finicky, trying to line them up square and uniform.

"Just let's get the bloody things up!" yelled Simmo over the rain and wind, "we can sort them out later."

The force of the rain and spray stinging their faces made it difficult to see. The darkness came early and Rikki found a some oil lamps and lit them, placing them strategically around the bar, and then of course the lights came back on. Ally appeared ten minutes later muttering about how lucky he was to have got the generator going and that it would need a new set of piston rings judging by the smoke and lack of compression. Byron was shagged, not being used to physical labour, and collapsed dripping into one of the chairs. Simmo asked Ally whether he would mind giving him a hand to drag the pedalos into the yard, as this was turning into quite a storm.

Gigolos

"Aye," said Ally, "and for good measure we'd better lash them to the uprights on the fence."

Simmo nodded; there was a coil of rope in the shed. Fair dues to Byron, he insisted on coming outside along with Rikki and one of the old boys, and between them they half dragged, half carried the boats into the yard, leaving Simmo to lash them down.

The wind rose to a full tropical storm that raged for three days. Rikki was worried there might be a storm surge, but had a little difficulty in conveying this to Simmo.

"Might be big flood, big flood!"

Simmo was a little puzzled, but Byron picked up on this and explained that it was not a tidal wave as such, but that wind and air pressure would raise the sea level. Luckily enough the sea stopped short of the bar, although with the wind, rain and driving spume and sands, it was difficult to gauge exactly where the sea ended and the land began.

"We've always got the pedalos!" Simmo quipped, trying to lighten the mood; but no one laughed.

Byron had taken up residence in a corner of the bar to save risking the elements going to and fro to the shed. There were a few scary moments when the building shook violently and the four of them thought it might be ripped off its foundations by the force of the wind. Later, on the second night, the gale tore one of the shutters loose, clattering and banging against the side of the building hard enough to crack the glass pane.

"Christ!" said Ally. "Come on wee man, better do something before it comes off."

They hastily donned cagoules and went outside into the full onslaught of the wind as they struggled to lock the slippery wet shutter back in place. Ally let out an almighty scream as the shutter, driven by the full force of the wind, caught him on the side of the head and cut deep into his eyebrow. It had knocked him down, and he lay there out cold, his body occasionally twitching slightly.

"Ally, Ally!" yelled Simmo, but there was no response and he could see what appeared to be more than a trickle of blood pouring down the side of his friend's head. He wrestled the door open and shouted into the bar.

"Give me a hand, quick! Now! Ally's hurt!"

Byron and Rikki rushed over, the door now flapping wildly in the wind. Ally was too heavy for Simmo and Byron to pick up, so the two of them dragged him unceremoniously by the feet whilst Rikki struggled with the door, and with dogged determination they managed to heave him inside. Simmo, who had history with troublesome doors, finally managed to get the bar door closed with a resounding slam.

Rikki was shouting at Byron: "Get first aid kit! Quick, quick, need it now!" she screeched.

In the meantime Simmo had pressed a clean bar towel to Ally's gushing head. Byron returned with the first aid stuff. Ally groaned a little - water was dripping on him from Simmo's head.

"Ally, Ally, you ok?" Simmo asked anxiously. Rikki cut him short.

"He out of it, look like concussion, hope head not broken. Help me!" she added. Between the three of them they managed to move Ally onto the big double bed in Simmo's room. Rikki felt around Ally's head. She disappeared then came back with scissors, and a needle and thread.

"What are you going to do?" gulped Byron.

"Me stitch, you hold head."

Gigolos

Byron looked a little faint; he thought he could see bone where Rikki had wiped the wound.

"I'll hold his head," nodded Simmo, and turning to Byron soothingly added "why you don't put the kettle on whist Rikki knits and pearls?"

Byron nodded and headed back into the bar, and Rikki trimmed the hair away from the wound. Ally groaned a little whilst Rikki, with an intent look of concentration, neatly stitched the gaping wound on the side of his head. Stitching the eyebrow proved the most difficult, with the stitches pulling through the skin and forcing her to re-stitch further out from the wound and raising his eyebrow. It didn't take her too long, easing the skin together and stitching it as best she could.

"Is he going to be all right?" asked Simmo, who had seen a fair number of accidents in the shipyards.

"Think so." said Rikki.

"There's no chance of us getting a doctor?" Simmo asked, already knowing the answer.

Rikki just shook her head. "I look after him. You go, he be fine with me," she whispered, nodding.

Simmo crept out and closed the door behind him.

"Is he ok?" asked Byron.

Simmo shrugged. "I fucking hope so," he sighed, taking a large gulp of the tea that Byron passed him. "We may as well sod off to bed; see how he is in the morning."

But thoughts of bed were soon abandoned as the loose shutter started clanging in earnest again.

"Come on," said Simmo to Byron, and with a great deal of effort and swearing on Simmo's part they managed to get it back in place without further injury, the catches holding firmly this time.

The wind howled and the bar shook. Simmo drifted in and out of vivid dreams, awakening in a sweat with the thread of the dream just out of his grasp. Byron and Rikki were up and about when he finally gave up on trying to get back to sleep.

"How is he?" asked Simmo anxiously.

"He awake now," replied Rikki. "Me think he gonna be ok. He mend."

"You sure?"

"Me sure," Rikki replied, her hand waving as if she were holding a glass, "he asking for whiskey!"

Simmo laughed... his favourite medicine.

"I promise him one if he good and rest," Rikki continued.

Simmo laughed again. "Don't forget to put it on his slate!"

Rikki just pulled tongues and went back in to Ally.

Eventually the wind died down, but the rain persisted. The bar was more or less intact, but the shed hadn't fared well at all. Half the roof was missing and most of the equipment in there had been crushed by falling debris. There was no mains electric, but surprisingly enough the generator had remained going, largely thanks to Byron and Simmo battling the elements to top the fuel and oil up and keep it running. Sand had piled up high along one side of the bar and the shed, and had half- buried the pedalos. Byron and Simmo managed to clear some of the debris from the shed and fashion a temporary roof over the generator, using a couple of roofing sheets that weren't too badly crumpled. Most of the other sheets had gone.

"Must have been blown to kingdom come," said Byron.

"Probably in Kansas by now!" said Simmo, rubbing his chin absently and holding a large metal funnel over his head in an impression of the Tin Man.

Gigolos

"Just as well you weren't in here," he commented, looking at a joist that had fallen where Byron's bed had once been.

"Mmmm," Byron replied, the implications of where the joist had fallen dawning upon him, "it's a shear fluke nothing damaged the generator."

There was a slight smell of fuel, and the water on the floor had a greasy film floating on it, but Simmo couldn't see any obvious leaks. He checked the level of the oil tank - ok for now, he thought - he would ask the dray man to bring him a barrel of diesel and a couple of gallons of engine oil.

The two of them were exhausted by nightfall; they had secured most of the shutters and brushed and shovelled most of the sand from the veranda in the brief lull between rain squalls.

Rikki had come out to see what they were up to and called them in for sandwiches and a brew. The rain had returned with a vengeance, and whilst she was shouting to them over the noise of the rain she had absently picked up a sea shell off a pile of sand they had shovelled up. She showed it excitedly to Simmo, but he couldn't quite make out what she was saying over the sound of the deluge on the veranda roof; so Simmo being Simmo just nodded and said "that's nice." Rikki said something else which he didn't catch, before shrugging and heading back in.

Simmo was quite surprised the following morning: unusually Rikki was nowhere to be seen. He assumed she must be in with Ally, so without thinking he went in to see how he was, only to find Ally and Rikki making love. Rikki was on top, Ally moaning gently. Caught off guard and blushing deeply, Simmo spluttered out a "sorry" before beating a hasty retreat back out of the door, for once not rattling the frame.

"Is he up and about?" asked Byron who had heard bumping and banging from the room.

"Oh yes, he's definitely on the up!" Simmo giggled.

Later on Rikki came into the bar. Byron, as usual, was reading a book; Simmo wondered where he kept getting them from but shrugged it away as Rikki shuffled over to talk to him.

"Me ask you something." She looked at him earnestly.

"What's up Rikki?

"I want look after Ally..." Simmo observed her, she was biting down on her lip, "I look after him all time."

She spoke softly, and again she shuffled on her dainty feet, absently twirling a strand of that long black hair. Simmo nodded for her to go on, slightly raising his eyebrows.

"Want to move in big room with him."

"My room?" asked Simmo. She straightened herself up and cocked her head to one side. "Mmmm, well..." said Simmo pausing. Rikki fixed him with a hard stare and Byron glanced over his book at the two of them. "You will have to..." he drew this out slowly, "give me a hand to move my gear out and of course help me get rid of all Chin Lee's ole shite."

Rikki broke into a beaming smile, threw her arms around his neck and gave him a kiss. The moment was further enhanced with the lights flickering a couple of times as the mains power came back on. Rikki was almost skipping as she went back to the bedroom. Simmo nodded to Byron who had heard everything but was trying to look like he hadn't.

"No bloody rest for the wicked, I'd better go and shut down old Smokey," muttered Simmo, snatching up a cagoule before disappearing out into the rain.

Gigolos

"Oh to be young and in love," sighed Byron, humming a tune he had heard covered by a band curiously called the Flying Pickets.

Early that evening a couple of the old boys returned to the bar. The storm appeared to be the main topic of conversation. Apparently Frankie's had fared far worse than they had, having completely lost the roof. Simmo tried to look concerned but secretly thought it served the smug bastard right. Ally was well enough to make a guest appearance, with Rikki fussing over him. Byron had dragged the big comfy chair from the bedroom in for him, but Rikki was carefully rationing his drinks. Simmo stood at Ally's spot at the bar observing that the shiny spot was losing its hue.

A large jeep pulled up and half a dozen people piled into the bar, soggy from their dash across the yard. These were some of Frankie's regulars in search of an alternative watering hole. The atmosphere was quite jolly and the beer flowed into the night, Ally and Rikki disappearing early, leaving Simmo and Byron to their own devices.

The arrival of the dray the following day was a great relief. Although they had power, the phone lines were still down. Rikki went off to town with the driver; Simmo remembered to order the diesel for the generator, and thought it prudent to order more beer and mixers. Rikki had organised help from the old boys in the tidy-up operation and the digger man was coming over too.

Ally was now quite steady on his feet, although he had quite a scar, and Rikki's stitching of his eyebrow gave the impression that one eye was slightly bigger than the other. Ally was busy drawing up lists of materials for repairs; he was also working on plans to extend the bar by removing the veranda and building outwards, then incorporating a new veranda. The Don brought Rikki back from town and both he and Ally were genuinely pleased to see each other. The Don would source the materials for him and Ally had promised to come over and inspect his workshop. The two discussed prefabricating sections for the extension in the workshop. They also discussed the planning aspect: for the right consideration, the Don would ensure that all would go through smoothly with no interference from the authorities.

"Aye," said Ally, "but you'll have tae come and fetch me, I've no way of getting over tae your place."

The Don rubbed his chin for a minute, and in his best Marlon Brando voice offered him the use of a jeep. "After all," he replied, "you would be doing me a favour."

They were very busy over the next few weeks, shifting sand and effecting repairs, especially to the shed. Rikki insisted on driving Ally over to the Don's place. She too was embroiled with the planning and design but she was no shirker, up before everyone else and getting the bar ship-shape before they left.

The evenings, too, were surprisingly busy, the yard filling up with jeeps and all manner of 4x4s. Ally brought back an ancient juke box in the back of the series 2 Land Rover, an offering from the Don.

"Aye, we've a wee bit of entertainment for the evening."

"Fucking great if you like Vera Lynn," replied Simmo sarcastically.

"Well we could always punch the middle out of some of those old punk singles of yours," Ally replied,

Gigolos

breaking into *Alternative Ulster* and po-going up and down, "aye that's your favourite ain't it wee man?"

"I'll pogo on you in a minute!" Simmo retorted.

"More of a Ramones man myself," chipped in Byron, singing *Beat on the Brat* in an Eton choral style and leaving both Ally and Simmo open mouthed, "saw them New Year's Eve '79 at the Rainbow. Quite a concert that was," he reminisced.

"Gig," corrected Simmo, "Not a bloody concert, a *gig*!" He shook his head. Byron gave him a thumbs up, but Rikki looked perplexed "I find nice music, people dance not bounce like that tiger in Winn Poh!" They all laughed

"Aye," said Ally wiping a tear, "I don't think we're quite ready for punk rock yet."

Rikki was explaining something to one of the old boys when he amazed them all by shouting out "Johnny Rotten! Save Queen, yes?"

Simmo shook his head and said to Ally "you've started something now... they will all have bloody Mohicans and pink hair by next week."

Rikki helped Simmo move his belongings from the big room. They binned most of Chin Lee's stuff; it seemed he had a passion for particularly pongy aftershaves. Rikki wrinkled her nose and pulled a face.

"Make me cringe," she said.

"Best tip it down the bog," Simmo suggested.

"Better than beach," she replied as she scuttled off to tip the potions and lotions down the toilet, not flushing it as they appeared to be removing the limescale.

Ally had been out in the shed checking the pipework for the generator, which had suffered a little damage from the falling debris during the storm. He nodded to Byron before disappearing off to the toilet for a constitutional. The pungent odour of cheap aftershave was overpowering, but he needed to go. As usual he had a rollie hanging off his bottom lip. On finishing his business he chucked the fag end down between his knees, but instead of the usual hiss there was a flash and a jet of blue flame, rattling all the doors in their frames and closely followed by an almighty scream. Rikki and Simmo looked at each other.

"Don't tell me he's found another bloody snake," laughed Simmo.

"We go see," Rikki replied.

As they went into the toilet they discovered Ally, pants round ankles, sitting in the sink.

"What the fuck?" asked Simmo.

"The fecking bog!" screeched Ally, "the fecking bog's just exploded!"

Simmo looked at Rikki, the realisation dawning on him.

"Chin Lee's aftershave," he whispered to Rikki with a conspiratorial nod; she nodded too.

"Mah feckin' arse!" moaned Ally.

Simmo, seeing his friend wasn't seriously hurt, began to giggle; Rikki too started to chuckle.

"it's nae funny," retorted Ally "it's singed all the hair off mah balls!"

Simmo and Rikki were now in fits. Ally was franticly splashing water over his nether regions. Simmo could barely talk but managed to gasp out "it's a pity we chucked that bidet away!" and even Ally couldn't help laughing. But his roaring laughter and associated jiggling caused the ancient sink to loosen even further from the wall and Ally, perched on top of it, fell gracefully like a giant redwood to the floor, the pipes ripping out and squirting the three of them with a high pressure jet of water. Ally grappled for the stopcock whilst Simmo slid down the wall unable to stand with hysterical laughter. It took the three of them what seemed like an eternity to recover their senses.

Eventually, when Rikki regained her composure, she said to Simmo, "You go; I got some lotion cool him down."

"I'll get a mop," replied Simmo, still giggling, and he retreated leaving Rikki to apply her balm. He went back into the bar as Byron and one of the old boys appeared from outside.

"I am starving," said Byron, "I could eat a horse. Don't suppose you know what's for dinner?"

"Boil in the bag," replied Simmo as he wandered off into the back to find a mop and bucket, the joke being lost on Byron.

Ally was in a bit of a quandary and was rubbing his head where Rikki had stitched it. It still felt a bit raised and lumpy where she had removed the stitches. As soon as the rains stopped he wanted to get on with the building work, and as no repairs could be started at Frankie's either he wanted to get on with it and steal a march on the tourist trade. He reckoned that it would be slow for the first couple of weeks but he was gambling on the lack of competition to capture and retain new customers. His plan was not only to prefabricate everything for the extension but also to attach flooring, pipe work, cables, windows etc. to as much of it as possible so that it would bolt together like a giant jigsaw. He surveyed and marked out the foundation pilings, allowing an extra depth on top of his calculations, bearing in mind the devastation of the recent storm.

The digger man dug the holes and Ally, with the help of the old boys, constructed elaborate structures over them and shuttering on the inside, enabling them to fit the reinforcement and pour the concrete.

This was quite arduous, particularly in the squally rain, but under Ally's supervision the foundations went in. Simmo was worn out from mixing concrete in the giant mixer that was attached to the digger man's other tractor. Byron and Rikki concentrated on running the bar.

Another problem was that most of their outside equipment - tables and loungers - had been trashed, but again the Don said he could probably help.

The fabrications were going well now, with most of them completed. Removing the veranda would be relatively simple; it was a wooden structure so a bit of a chainsaw massacre after removing a few sheets from the roof would suffice; the digger man could then just drag it all away. All they had to do now was to wait for the rain to stop.

"Aye," said Ally to Simmo, "I reckon we can do this. The Don's got a couple of good blokes over there, says he'll send them over tae give us a hand. Most of the panels are loaded on his lorry ready tae go."

"You sure?" asked Simmo, trying not to sound sceptical.

"Aye, the bloody Yanks could knock out a whole liberty ship in a week during the war, don't see why we couldn't have a prefab up in a couple of days. Relax wee man, what could possibly go wrong?"

Ally slapped his big arm around Simmo's shoulder, who just shuddered at the thought.

Simmo was up early; he sat out on the veranda sipping a coke, staring out at the lightening sky and sea. It was probably the sudden stopping of the rain that had awoken him. Although he had witnessed the end of the rains last year he was still amazed at the abruptness of their ceasing. Just like turning off a tap or a sink's stopcock, he mused.

He hadn't slept much the previous night. Ally had the building work planned to the same detail as operation bloody overlord, everything ready just waiting for a break in the weather. As he sat there staring, he wondered where the time had gone. A maelstrom of thoughts passed through his mind; their arrival, their disappointment, Rikki and of course Pascale... he sighed... He had really blown it there, he sensed. He hadn't seen her around at all - she seemed to have disappeared from the face of the earth.

He could hear Ally crashing and banging inside, and caught the first whiffs of frying bacon floating through the air, making him salivate slightly. Ally poked his head out through the door.

"Come on in wee man," he croaked, spluttering through the early morning coughing fit, the first rollie of the day hanging from his lip. "You're gonnae be needin' a good breakfast inside you I'm thinking, we're gonnae be busy for a while."

Simmo looked up, his thoughts dissipating like the drifting tobacco smoke. "You know them things will kill you?" he remarked. Ally removed the cigarette from his mouth, looked at it, frowned, and then stuck it back in, gazing intently at Simmo.

"Aye," he said, his face forlorn. "Had an uncle once, cigarettes killed him."

"Oh, I'm sorry," said Simmo.

"Aye, it was a terrible, terrible thing to behold." He looked Simmo square in the eye. "Aye, the poor sod was run over by a lorry." Ally shook his head.

Simmo looked puzzled. "Erm, I thought you said cigarettes killed him?"

"Aye," said Ally, looking at his feet, "and so they did ... the lorry was carrying twenty pallets of Benson and Hedges."

"Fuck off!" giggled Simmo, drawn in by Ally's mock sincerity.

"Nae it's the truth, they paid for the funeral. He was a big man so they got him a king size coffin... and insisted on a cremation...presented her with his ashes in a limited edition John Player special formula one ashtray... aye, and on top of that, mah auntie got five hundred Embassy vouchers in lieu of compensation... she's still got the bloody fondue set she bought with them."

Simmo laughed, shaking his head at the same time, as the two of them went back inside. Ally had the bit between his teeth now. He was back on top form.

Tom Cruise and Uplifting Booze

Ally's version of Operation Overlord rolled out after breakfast. The phone lines were back in commission and he had primed the Don, the digger man and the old boys that as soon as the rain stopped: "don't wait tae be called, get your arses over here!" Simmo stood on the veranda surveying the scene as trucks, diggers, men and equipment arrived, with Ally and Rikki explaining to each group who, what, where, when and why. Simmo could hear a Winston Churchill voice in his head accompanied by the Battle of Britain march in his ears... *and this was their finest hour.*

Ally was everywhere. He had disconnected the electricity to the veranda and had Byron and Simmo take down the signs. The cocktail sign buzzed menacingly but didn't spell out anything rude for once. Simmo couldn't believe the pace of the operation. Whilst the sheets were coming off the roof, chainsaws could be heard cutting through walls and floors, the digger was shackled and the whole of the veranda area removed. At the same time the floor section was being assembled and, with only one or two minor alterations, was lowered in large sections, with the help of the digger, into place.

The pace didn't slacken for a moment. Rikki followed in Ally's wake relaying instructions and answering queries, occasionally pouring over the drawings and debating some of the finer points with him. The Don's lorry was busy back and forth bringing supplies. Ally was also examining roof sheets and timber to see if any could be salvaged to repair the shed, with Rikki marking the keepers and binners, although unfortunately most had seen better days.

They did well that first day getting the floor, walls and a couple of roof trusses in place. And despite the fact there wasn't a great deal of free space in the yard they opened up for the evening with most of the workforce taking advantage of the couple of free drinks Ally offered them. The major construction took another three days to finish, with a further three of final fixing and decorating. The Don's lorry took away the scrap and all the useless timber was taken up near the tank, and in celebration there was going to be a grand bonfire and barbeque.

The Don was congratulating Ally. "You did it, Scotsman!"

Ally looked a little coy. "Aye well," he said, "we had tae work tae some tight schedules back in the yard."

Simmo was impressed: Ally's attention to detail had been superb. Everything that had to marry up had done so perfectly. The only real snag was a broken upright on the old part of the bar that had snapped when they were pulling the veranda away with the digger, but Ally had one of the Don's men fashion two angle iron sections which they bolted through it, making it stronger than it was before.

As he staggered away from the bonfire, Simmo couldn't understand why his legs were pissed but the rest of him wasn't. He put it down to the cocktails Byron had been mixing for them whilst Ally manned the barbeque. A 'Harvey Wall Holder', Byron had called it, and Simmo could well understand why. Ally had his arm around Rikki and was singing away, *Danny boy, Athenry* - in fact working through his full repartee. Simmo joined in with the chorus.

Gigolos

"Come on now wee man, I know you know this one!"

Simmo held up his hand and shouted "going to give Byron a hand!" over the crackle of the wood.

Ally nodded and turned to throw more meat on the barbecue, before bursting into *Scotland the Brave*. Simmo shuffled back up to the bar, on legs he was convinced belonged to someone else. The bar was quite busy and Byron was rushing round like a scalded cat. He had one of the old boys behind the bar helping him, the one who spoke a little English. They had taken to calling him Sid Vicious, or Sid for short, in recognition of his knowledge of a certain John Lydon. Byron handed Simmo another one of his concoctions.

"I call this one Comfortably Numb," he chirped.

"After Pink Floyd?" quizzed Simmo.

"No... it's because I've lost all sensation in my hands."

Simmo giggled. "Go on then, let's give it a try."

After his second one, Simmo too had that floaty feeling. Through slightly bleary eyes he could observe a number of vehicles arriving in the car park. One was the Don's jeep; he was with his two boys. He recognised Jean Paul and his cronies instantly in the other, larger jeep, but no Pascale. Simmo asked Sid to go and get Rikki as more headlights were appearing outside. Jean Paul's crowd had found a table in the old part of the bar. One of the things Ally had overlooked was furniture for the new extension, so there were just a few odd chairs and the juke box out there. It was quietly playing Doris Day, making the atmosphere somewhat surreal. There were a number of women in the bar, and even more surprisingly one or two couples were dancing. Simmo had only the briefest of chats with the Don as he was struggling with the beer pump. He slapped himself on the forehead and excused himself as he realised the gas was running out. He had remembered to order everything but the bloody gas. He explained to Rikki what had happened, slurring a little from the last two cocktails. More headlights appeared outside.

"Christ," said Simmo, "I don't know how much longer the gas will last."

"It's a pity about Frankie's," Byron shouted to him over the noise, "we could have borrowed a bottle of gas from him."

This remark set a quite tiddly Simmo thinking. "Come on!" he yelled suddenly to Byron, hastily adding to Rikki "we won't be long!" Rikki shouted something back at them but Simmo didn't catch it.

"Where are we going?" asked Byron. He too was a little the worse for wear.

"On a little boat ride," giggled Simmo, unlashing one of the pedalos from the fence, "give us a hand."

Between the two of them they managed to drag the pedalo to the sea, but Byron was a little perplexed.

"Err if you don't mind me asking, Simmo, why do we need the pedalo?"

Simmo replied in a dreadful pirate accent. "well you see me hearties, we're off to do a little raiding - Captain Simmo and his motley crew are going to plunder a bottle of gas from Frankie's."

"Why don't you just ask the Don to run us up in his jeep?"

"What sort of a pirate be you?" Simmo retorted as Byron started to laugh. "And besides," he continued with perfect drunken logic, "no one will suspect us launching a raid from the sea!"

Anyone watching their painful progress might have considered them to be zigzagging to avoid u-boats or something, but eventually they landed on the beach by the steps up to Frankie's.

"Shush!" said Simmo rather too loudly, but Frankie's was quite deserted. They crept inside and searched around the back of the bar until they found a small wire-meshed compound containing gas bottles. Now in their haste neither of them had thought to bring a torch or tools of any sort.

"Shit!" said Simmo, looking at the padlock and chain in the moonlight and sinking despondently to the floor. "Well that's us fucked," he added to no one in particular.

Byron scratched his head Ally style, then ran his hands over the hinge pins. "Might I make a suggestion, Captain?" He too was in buccaneer mode by now.

"What?"

"I think there is enough slack on the chain to lift the gate off its hinges..." Simmo dragged himself up to look, the combination of Harvey Wall Grabber and Comfortably Numb greatly affecting his coordination.

He looked at Byron. "You sure you haven't got any Scouser in you?" Byron shook his head.

"Then sir," he hiccoughed, I bestow upon you the title of honorary Liverpudlian - now give us a hand to lift this fuckin gate!"

They successfully managed to lift the gate off its hinges, leaving it hanging at a funny angle on the chain. Simmo was poking around with the gas bottles.

"What are you doing?" slurred Byron

"Looking for a full one," Simmo slurred back. Pleased that he had found a full one he called "lend a hand shipmate, we've found our treasure... God's sake be careful!" he shrieked as Byron dropped the gas cylinder on the valve end, making a loud metallic clang, "it'll go off like a fuckin' torpedo if we crack that off!" He had seen an oxygen bottle explode at Laird's.

They dragged the bottle to the pedalo and lashed it to the boat with the rope that had secured it to the fence. They had a little difficulty re-launching with the extra weight on board, but with much shoving and cursing on Simmo's part, they got it back into the sea.

"Strike us a course for home Mr. Mate!" cried Simmo as they pedalled back along the shoreline to Gigolos.

They beached the pedalo, and dragged the gas bottle up the beach and into the back of the bar. The fluorescent light was a little harsh on their eyes after the moonlight, and was making Simmo squint. He fumbled a little with the fitting whilst connecting it to the line. He eventually made the connection tight, but not the mental connection that this bottle was a different colour from the others.

Byron and Simmo lurched back into the bar, where Rikki was frantic.

"Where you been? Ten minute you say!" she bollocked them.

"Gas," said Simmo, burping at the same time.

Ugh!" said Rikki, her face a mixture of disgust and bemusement.

"We've got a new bottle of gas for the pump!" Byron chimed in.

Rikki looked a little sceptical, but started to pour the beer. It took a minute or two to settle down but it looked good. The 'pirates' were looking rather smug, but jumped to as Rikki shouted "no bloody stan' there... give me hand, serve these people!"

The place was heaving, it must have been four deep at the bar. Simmo was busy pouring beer and handing it out, Byron busy mixing cocktails. Simmo thought that the cocktails had gone to his ears - the people at the bar all appeared to be laughing and giggling and talking gibberish. Simmo looked at Byron.

"What the fuck?"

"It's as though they have all been inhaling helium!" shouted Byron over the din.

Simmo paused mid pour, looked at Byron, then at the pump... helium? "Oh God," he groaned, the realisation dawning on him. He had seen kids on the beach coming up from Frankie's with balloons. And then he knew... they'd stolen a bottle of helium instead of carbon dioxide...

The helium was causing hysterics amongst the customers. A large fat American was saying something to one of the Don's boys in a high pitched squeal. Now Simmo had never seen the boys drink whilst on duty - or for that matter, thinking about it, had he ever heard them speak other than the odd grunt, so he was totally surprised when the boy replied in his own naturally high-pitched voice, "you takin piss?" making the Yank laugh louder, tears in his eyes.

The blow came as fast as lightning, striking the American square on the jaw. The juke box piped up with *C'mon Everybody* as the mother of all bar fights erupted with the vocals from the throng sounding like a single playing at 78 rpm. Within seconds chairs, bottles and tables were flying. Byron took shelter behind the bar as, Wild West style, two revellers high on helium-spiked lager went crashing through one of the new veranda windows.

"What the fuck?!" yelled Ally, returning from the bonfire. He began grabbing drunken pugilists by the arse and collar and propelling them through the door. The brawl had spread outside, but Ally was only interested in shoving the fighters out of the bar.

It took a good ten minutes to regain order. The Don was mopping his brow with a handkerchief. He shook Ally's hand, still laughing, and said in a very squeaky voice, "Dodge City had nothing on that one!"

In fact everyone left inside still seemed to be laughing, leaving Ally scratching his head.

Byron poked his head up from behind the protection of the bar. "Psst...psst!" he said, waving Ally over, "we've, err, had a little accident..." Ally scowled. "We, err, mixed the bar gas up with helium..."

"Helium?" quizzed Ally, raising an eyebrow.

"Err yes... it's mixed with the beer... made everyone a little light headed so to speak..."

"And whose bright idea was this then?" Ally was growling now.

Byron shifted his eyes to Simmo, who too had tried a pint of the helium enriched lager and could only nod vigorously for fear of bursting out laughing. Ally just shook his head and said "I might've known... it was all going too bloody well."

Ally set off for town early the next morning in the Land Rover to get some gas and order some more glass for the window. He intended to swing by the Don's on the way back to check on progress with the furniture.

Simmo was nursing quite a hangover. Byron reported nothing wrong with his head and put Simmo's down to mixing cocktails and high octane beer. The jukebox had miraculously survived the previous night's affray and was playing away in the background. Rikki was trying to look cross with them but couldn't keep a straight face. "What you two like," was all she could say, smiling.

Gigolos

Ally returned around lunch time. If he was pissed off about last night's events he wasn't showing it. He asked Sid and Byron to unload the gas.

"Hey wee man, I've been talking tae the Don" - Ally was positively glowing – "and he thinks he's got an air conditioner for us."

"Oh," said Simmo.

"Aye, it won't half make a difference tae us, much better than those ancient ceiling fans."

Rikki was observing the two of them. "How much cost?" She asked, narrowing her eyes.

"Err…" Ally shuffled a little, "two grand." Rikki cocked her head and raised an eyebrow. "Oh and then we will need the condenser and the pipe work…"

"How much all gether?"

"Two seven." Rikki stared even harder at him "All right, three tops then," said Ally holding out his hands. Rikki didn't look convinced.

"Can we afford it?" asked Simmo, who left all the financial stuff to Ally.

Rikki went to say something but Ally shut her up with a glance and a shake of his head. "Oh sure wee man, everything's fine."

In reality things were anything but fine. They had been spending money hand over fist. The building work and the cost of bribing the officials had consumed a sizable chunk of their savings. Ally had banked on pulling back some of the money as soon as the season really kicked off, but unfortunately the airport on the main island had suffered major devastation during the storm. Ally was putting a brave face on it, but no planes meant no tourists, and no tourists meant no money.

Later on Rikki said to Ally "why you no tell him?"

Ally shuffled a little before saying "och, you know how he worries."

Rikki did the banking so she had a fairly good understanding of their finances. "Why no leave air-conditioned for now?" she asked.

"Err..." Ally shuffled again.

"*Well?*" She looked at him.

"We, err, the Don that is ... we err... feck I think its Frankie's new one... och, should have been ten grand," he finally blurted out.

"Fluckin plick!" she exclaimed, "You no want trouble with Frankie."

Ally looked down.

"He go find out," said Rikki, shaking her head.

"Well, here's the thing," said Ally, "I've already paid."

Rikki swore at him in French and wandered back inside. Ally, after a few moments, followed her and took position at his spot on the bar, polishing absently and taking a deep drag on his rollie. Perhaps he had been a little hasty... "Bollocks... it was a feckin' bargain!" was all he could come up with.

Simmo and Byron cleaned off the pedalos and dragged them down to the beach. The yard was still in quite a state from the storm, the rain and the building work. With the help of the digger man they managed over a couple of days to get it into some semblance of order, although they could have done with a lorry-load of stones to finish it off. The drive was reasonably intact, although this too needed some stone to fill in the potholes.

"We're gonna need gravel and stones for the drive," said Simmo.

"Aye, but its gonnae have tae wait a wee while, just until trade picks up a bit."

Simmo nodded and went inside for a shower before the evening's trade kicked off. Ally had been busy re-glazing the window with Sid, and clearing out all the crap from the shed. He took numerous trips up to the bonfire site with the Land Rover, taking the broken bar furniture and the damaged loungers. Rikki was still a little frosty with him. Ally scratched his head and rubbed his chin, the shed roof was going to cost too. They had no insurance, so everything was coming out of their rapidly dwindling savings. God, he hoped the airport would reopen soon.

A few days later the Don arrived with the new furniture and a couple of loungers to boot. He and Ally stood on the veranda sipping ice cold beers. In the distance they could see trucks heading up towards Frankie's.
"Good news, Scotsman," said the Don, "my friends tell me the airport should be open again by the end of next week." The main island had taken the brunt of the storm.
"Thank Christ." Ally nodded up towards Frankie's. "How are they getting on?"
The Don followed his gaze. "Be at least a couple of weeks before he is ready to open again."
"Good...What's he said about the air conditioner?"
"Oh don't worry about him...I'll take care of it."
Ally just said "Mmmm...."
Simmo broke the silence with "where's the best place to put the couches?"
Ally shook himself from his thoughts. "Aye, under the windows is probably best." He shrugged to the Don before going back inside.

The letter came out of the blue. Simmo stood there holding it, staring at the envelope. There was no mistake recognising her small, neat handwriting.
"Well?" asked Ally, nodding at the letter, "Are you nae gonnae open it?

"I don't know."

Simmo bit his lip. He had hardly given her a thought in months. It was one of those blue air mail envelopes. As he stood there transfixed he couldn't help noticing how the ink from her fountain pen must have got damp at some point; it had seeped away from the letters leaving some of them a little faded, almost bleeding... Ally was still watching him. Simmo suddenly folded it and stuffed it into his pocket. "I'll open it later," he said and disappeared off out the door, leaving Ally scratching his head.

Simmo in his musings hadn't realised quite how far he had walked. "Christ," he said to himself. He was halfway to the ranch. He sat down on a rock and stared out to sea. He stood up again and pulled the crumpled letter from his pocket, then lowered himself back onto his perch to read it.

Dear Simon,

I trust this letter finds you well and in good health. I have had the devil's own job tracking you down. I have enquired of your solicitor as to your whereabouts, but it seems that they too have had no contact from you. It seems, apparently, that you haven't paid them for their litigation work. They were able to trace you via the bank account details I gave to them. No doubt you will be hearing from them shortly.

I am happy for my part not to proceed any further with the divorce. I must admit that I miss you and it is quite lonely here without you. I would love to talk to you face to face and maybe see if we cannot straighten things out. After all we have been married a long time.

Gigolos

I cannot imagine you and Alastair as landlords; I suppose he must drink a large proportion of the profits, if any. I hate to think of you out there with dodgy food and unsatisfactory sanitation. Make sure you cover your head in the sun, oh and use plenty of insect repellent as you know how badly you react when bitten.

Oh well Simon I guess that is all for now, look after yourself.

Love,
Sharon.

PS. according to Margi Stewart, Alastair's mother has not been too well.

"Well?" said Ally when Simmo got back to the bar. "The letter man, the bloody letter, what did she want?"

"I don't know," said Simmo taking the letter out of his pocket, "here, you have a read."

Ally read the first two paragraphs. "Well he said, it looks like Bob the Bidet has moved on to bathrooms new." He read on. "Cheeky bitch," he said, "drinkin' the feckin' profits... I wish I had the bloody time." He was stopped in his tracks with the very last line. "Mammy," was all he said, looking grave. He passed the letter back to Simmo. "I'd better ring mah cousin," he croaked. Ally had sent her a postcard when they had first arrived but that was - Christ - must be getting on for nearly two years ago. He rubbed his chin before he shuffled off to use the phone.

"I'd hang fire if I were you Ally, it will be stupid o'clock over there."

Ally looked back and nodded. "Aye," he said, "I was nae thinkin'."

Rikki watched the two of them slink back into the bar, Ally taking his usual position behind the counter.

"What wrong?" she asked Simmo.

Ally cut in before his friend could reply. "Simmo has had a letter from home. Bollocks really, but in it she mentions mah mammy's not been tae well, I'll give it a couple of hours then ring mah cousin. The old lady's nae got a phone."

Rikki looked concerned. "Hope she ok..."

"So do I," said Ally absently, gently polishing the bar.

Simmo wasn't sure how he felt. It was like the world had taken a lurch again, whipping up emotions that were all but forgotten...

Ally had managed eventually to get hold of his cousin. Apparently the old lady had had quite a bad fall and had been in hospital for a few weeks. The hospital suspected that she may have had some kind of minor stroke preceding the fall. She still lived in the same tenement where Ally had grown up. The social services would like her to move into some form of sheltered accommodation, but she was a tough old bird and was having none of it. This left Ally in a bit of a quandary. Did he fly home to see her now or wait until later in the year after the season when he would have more time and hopefully more money?

Business was picking up with the return of the tourists. Simmo tended to work the beach during the daytimes. He still did his Pedro act but wasn't entertaining the ladies of an evening, instead working on until late in the bar. Byron, amazingly, had acquired a lady friend: she worked as a cocktail

Gigolos

waitress in one of the big hotels on the other side of the island. Byron had taken the first night off that he had had since he'd been there, and spent it with the young lady, who had a VCR in her bedroom and had introduced him to Tom Cruise in the film *Cocktail*. Byron was fascinated by what he saw and started juggling with a wine bottle, cheered on by his new found love. He returned the next day, bumming a lift with the dray from town.

"Where the hell have you been?" Ally rebuked.

Byron just had a starry-eyed look. "I have acquired new skills, sir," he replied, "hopefully beneficial to our sales of alcohol."

"Go on," said Ally, "I have tae see this."

Byron lined up some shot glasses and took hold of a bottle of the local hooch. "Music maestro please!" he said to Simmo, who was standing by the jukebox with Rikki. Ally and Rikki looked at each other. Simmo pressed the switch and Eddie Cochran blurted out. Their jaws hung open to see Byron doing a very plausible Tom Cruise routine, with Simmo cheering him on.

"Well," he said to Ally at the end of his routine, "what do you think?"

"This will nae do," said Ally, shaking his head, "you've spilt half of it!"

"Yes, but it's only the local brew," quipped Byron.

"It's nae that," said Ally, "look! It's stripping the bloody varnish off the bar!"

There was indeed a faint effervescence bubbling away on the counter.

"Christ," said Simmo, "no wonder your cocktails are so bloody lethal!" Byron grinned and Simmo laughed. "It was a good show though mate. Hey Ally, you got to admit it was funny. How about letting him do his routine later?"

Ally pulled a face. "Aye, well...ok, as long as he waters the bloody stuff down. Wouldn't want anyone getting a splash of that in their eyes when he slaps it about like bloody Henry Cooper!"

Simmo shouted "Bar tender!" Byron snapped to attention.

"How could I be of assistance sir?" he replied, towel over his arm.

"Give us a hand to launch these bloody pedalos!"

Byron shook his head. "My talents are wasted here," he sighed, putting the towel down on the bar.

Simmo and Byron went off to the beach to sort the boats out. The minute they were out of the door Ally tried juggling the spirit, only for him to misjudge it and have a ricocheting bottle clonk him on the head before rebounding into the glass shelf, smashing the glasses and finally crashing to the floor.

Rikki was in fits of giggles. "You stick to polish bar...while we still have glasses!" Ally threw the bar towel at her before going off to fetch the mop and brush. Rikki looked at the jukebox. "Need some new tunes," she said to no one in particular before picking up the towel.

Rikki took the Land Rover to town the following morning, dropping Ally off at the Don's on the way in order to finalise plans for the floating platform. Ally was also in negotiation over prefabricating a new roof for the shed.

Rikki was a little concerned over their finances, with all the building work and the fact that at some point Ally may need a return ticket to the UK and all the associated cost that would go with it.

Still, she had managed to find some 70s and 80s singles for the jukebox, and giggled to herself when she thought about Byron's routine the previous night

Gigolos

- it had gone down very well with the customers. Even Simmo had joined in, managing to catch the bottle Byron threw at him, and even more amazingly managing to throw it back to Byron. She had been able to procure some of the singles from the *Top Gun* movie soundtrack and her *pièce de résistance* was the discovery of an old American officer's navel cap and epaulettes. "He look like proper gigolo now," she smiled to herself.

As she took the Land Rover keys from her pocket, she pulled out the shell as well, turning it over thoughtfully in her hand. She had tried to explain to Simmo about it... Well, there was only one way to find out for sure: she would have to dive. She drove back to Gigolos with flashbacks of her childhood springing to her mind.

The Don gave Ally a lift back to Gigolos. The two of them stood out on the veranda, usual beers in hand. It was that slack period, when the beach people and families went home prior to the evening people coming out. The Don had kept the minibuses coming despite Frankie's still being closed for repairs, although obviously the gambling crowd were going elsewhere.

Ally was a little awkward broaching the subject. "You see," he said, how do you think Frankie's gonnae react when he finds he has nae air conditioner?"

The Don studied him before blowing out cigar smoke. "He will be a little pissed."

"You're nae bothered then? said Ally, cocking an eyebrow.

"Let's just call it a little tax. After all, they can afford it."

"They?" Ally rubbed his chin.

The Don flicked ash from his cigar, then looked Ally square in the eye. "The Mob."

"The *Mob*?"

The Don nodded and mouthed the word "Mafia".

"Oh Christ," said Ally slowly.

"That isn't just a casino, Scotsman; it's a laundry, a great big Yankee laundry."

Ally was quite confused and scratched his head. "I nae understand."

The Don blew a smoke ring. "They launder money, Scotsman."

Ally felt sick to the pit of his stomach.

"Lots of money laundered here," he continued. "How do you think the colonials survive? They encourage it and then look the other way. But sometimes, Ally, we have to let them know they are on our turf; that they must respect us, too. So occasionally we may take a consignment of booze or a little something for ourselves. They know it's us, but what we never do is interfere in their main line of business."

Ally certainly didn't look convinced.

"If anyone asks, just tell them you bought it from me. They may even find it funny." The Don looked at his watch. "Time to go; see you tomorrow Scotsman," was all he said before heading off to his jeep.

Rikki presented Byron with his hat and epaulettes and he delightedly tried them on.

"You look officer an' gentleman," said Rikki, quite satisfied with his appearance.

"An orifice and a genital more like!" piped in Ally.

Byron thumbed his nose at Ally before going off to find a white shirt. "Give here," said Rikki, I sew them on for you." When she had finished Byron looked at himself in the bar mirror and nodded with satisfaction. Simmo gave him a thumbs up. "Way to go daddy-o!" he chortled. Ally just shook his head, but he seemed a little distracted.

Simmo had fitted the new singles into the jukebox; he had had quite enough of Pat Boon. Later in the evening he put *Halfway to the Danger Zone* on and Byron came in from the back to begin his cocktail routine. The crowd whistled and cheered, and afterwards Simmo, Byron and Rikki struggled to keep up at the bar; they had never sold so many cocktails. The extension and veranda were packed with dancing couples all fuelled on Byron's concoctions, and Blondie's *Denis* was rapidly becoming a favourite on the jukebox. Byron shouted to Simmo over the noise "I think that I may have found my true vocation in life!"

"Never mind that," yelled Ally returning to the bar with a fist full of empty glasses, "just keep the bloody things coming."

The next few weeks were crazily busy. The Don kept up the to-ing and fro-ing, while Ally and Simmo carried on with the reconstruction of the shed in the early part of the mornings, with Simmo taking up his post on the beach and Ally disappearing off to work on the platform later on. Byron and Rikki concentrated on running the bar during the day, with Sid coming over later for the evening shift. Ally had the digger man over to lift the new roof trusses in place and to give him and Simmo a hand getting the sheets up and secured.

No sooner was the shed roof finished than Ally turned his attention to building a plinth for the air conditioner and planning pipe work and internal fitting arrangements.

Rikki was worried. "He go kill himself if he no slow down," she said to Simmo. She was wringing her hands.

Simmo shrugged, sitting down on a beached pedalo. "That's just how he is. Once he gets his teeth into something there's no bloody stopping him."

"He worry about mother, he need go see her before..." Rikki didn't finish but Simmo caught the inference.

"I know," he replied, "but I think he wants to get all the jobs out of the way first."

"Simmo...he never marry?"

"No," laughed Simmo, "who would bloody have him, eh? Haha." Rikki punched Simmo in the arm. Simmo looked at her. "Seriously... I think there was someone, a long, long time ago, but it didn't work out."

"Oh," said Rikki, biting her lip. "Simmo," she continued after a short pause, "I wan' you take me out on pedalo."

"Hey pretty lady!" quipped Simmo, Pedro style. Rikki shook her head and punched him again in the arm for good measure.

"I wan' go out and dive in lagoon."

Simmo looked perplexed. "Erm, ok," he said, but why do you want to -"

Rikki cut him short by holding up her hand. "Jus' me an' you, we go early in morning, you tell no one."

"Ok," said Simmo, still confused. Rikki nodded, turned on her heel and walked back towards the bar leaving Simmo scratching his head.

Next morning Ally was busy laying the concrete for the air conditioner. Simmo gave him a hand with the mixing before saying he had a job to do on the pedalos. Ally just grunted and carried on.

Gigolos

Simmo poked his head inside the bar and nodded over to Rikki. "Byron," she said, "you finish stacking cooler, I go give Simmo hand with boats." Byron smiled. He was miles away calculating how many litres of beer they had sold last night.

Rikki disappeared into the bedroom and emerged with a rolled up belt. They headed off to the beach, where she clipped the belt around her waist. There was a sheath on the belt, from which Rikki pulled out a rather lethal looking knife and examined the blade before carefully returning it.

Simmo gulped "I hope that's not for sharks," he said, looking worried.

"No!" said Rikki laughing, "no sharks - open shells."

Simmo just nodded; he didn't have a clue what Rikki was up to. They launched one of the pedalos and pedalled out deep into the lagoon. Rikki stripped down to her shorts and bikini top and eased herself into the warm clear water. "I dive," she said, and with that she disappeared beneath the surface.

Simmo sat there staring into the water; he couldn't see the bottom. The minutes went by, but Rikki was still down there. Simmo was starting to get a little nervous; in fact he was becoming downright panicky. "Shit!" he said, and was starting to whip off his t shirt when SPLASH! Rikki's head appeared above the water. She coughed and spluttered a little, grabbing hold of the pedalo; Simmo grabbed her arm and helped heave her on board.

"Christ!" said Simmo, "I was getting worried."

Rikki just smiled. "Me out of practice; stay down much longer once."

In her hand she clutched an ugly looking shellfish. Simmo looked on as she prized it open. She prodded around inside the shell with the knife before reaching in with her fingers. "No good," she said.

Rikki took a couple of deep breaths before diving down again, and repeated this curious activity a couple of times more, but each time she returned to the surface empty-handed.

Heaving herself back on board once more, Rikki asked Simmo to move the pedalo a hundred yards or so further up. When she was happy with her location she dived again, but this time when she came up she was holding another lumpy shellfish. Simmo helped her back onto the pedalo and stared on fascinated as Rikki opened it carefully with her knife. This time she pulled something out. Holding it carefully between her thumb and forefinger she rinsed it off in the water beside the pedalo, dropped it into the palm of her left hand and held it out to Simmo.

"What is it?" He asked.

"It pearl."

"It's no bloody good though is it," said Simmo staring at it, "aren't they supposed to be white?"

Rikki eyed him. "You no know?"

"Know what?"

"Black pearl, very rare... very expensive."

Simmo looked at her dumbfounded; it didn't look black to him, more of a deep turquoise. Rikki nodded to him and then put a finger to her lips; Simmo pedalled them bemusedly back towards the beach.

It was getting near the end of the day and Simmo had dragged most of the pedalos up onto the beach. He was going to drag the last one up when a voice asked him "am I too late for a ride?" Simmo was about to say "sorry, we're done for the day," when he realised who it was.

"Pascale" he blurted. She smiled in that coy way of hers. "Where have you been? I mean, I've missed you! Sorry I thought you had gone away...for good, I- " Simmo was getting himself all tongue- tied.

Pascale held a finger up to his lips to stop Simmo rambling, before saying "I've been on an assignment."

"What, with the university?"

"No," she said shaking her head, smiling, "we've been doing a little independent snooping for Greenpeace."

"Oh," said Simmo.

"The French government are up to something. You know they tested nukes here years ago?"

"They're not about to nuke us, are they?"

"No, I don't think so," she was smiling again, "but they don't like us sniffing around. And," she continued, looking straight at him, "I wouldn't put anything past them... Our mission was to have been looking at the long term effects of the radiation on the environment here, but then we caught wind of some activity on one of the atolls. We sent in two ribs from one hundred miles away and managed to sneak in and out again, right under their noses! I think they've tried to keep their operations very low key so as not to attract any attention. After we returned Sven headed the ship back towards the island. It wasn't long before the French navy started harassing us, trying to force us out of the area."

"You're not in any danger, are you?" asked Simmo, now quite concerned.

Pascale smiled and looked down. "I don't know," she said softly. "We stopped once to try to survey a small reef but they nearly ran down one of our boats, they came straight at us; good job we had no one in the water or they would have been... what do you say in English... mincemeat, non?"

Simmo gulped; paradise seemed to be full of threats these days. "Give me a minute," he said, pulling the last pedalo up onto the beach, "I'll get us a couple of cold beers and you can tell me all about your adventures."

"You see her?" asked Rikki. Simmo was fumbling with the bottle opener. "Give here, take you all bloody night open them," she giggled. "I talk to her, tell her you been good boy, miss her plenty much."
Simmo nodded. "I have. Thanks."
He ambled back out and the two of them sat on the pedalo, sipping cold beer and staring out to sea.
"Where are you staying?" he asked.
"On the ship."
"Oh," said Simmo, scratching his chin, "are you here for long?"
"Probably a week or so, depending upon what we find. Maybe be a little longer."
Simmo looked a bit glum.
"Don't worry," she said, snuggling up, this assignment is almost over. Sven may want to return to New Zealand or carry on surveying for a little while longer, but my work is done now."
Simmo looked a little more relieved.

The bar was filling up with customers.
"I'll have to give them a hand," said Simmo reluctantly, looking at the throng in the bar.
Pascale smiled. "Well, I'll just wait until you have finished."
"You could stay here tonight...?"
"We will see."
Simmo disappeared off to shower and change before the evening shift. When he returned Rikki and Pascale were deep in conversation at the bar. Pascale was examining something that Rikki had handed her and the two girls were nodding and gesticulating.

Gigolos

"What are you two up to?" Simmo asked, but Rikki just tapped her nose. "Oh well don't mind me," he added, before going off on a foray for empty glasses.

Rikki left Byron behind the bar and disappeared outside for a few minutes with Pascale.

"What you think?" Rikki asked.

"Do you think there are lots more down there?"

"Everything look good, like when I was child. I thought all gone."

"I could borrow some scuba gear from the ship and we could do a proper survey... just me and you. But I haven't got a jeep anymore," she sighed.

"No problem, we got Lanrover. I take you back in morning?"

Pascale smiled. "Looks like I will have to stay."

Pascale, too, was impressed with the new extension and the air conditioning. Byron had recognised her as the girl from Frankie's, and they had chatted away in French during the brief quiet interludes. Pascale wasn't sure what to make of Byron's Tom Cruise routine, although he had it off pat. Some of the forty-somethings seemed to be going quite wild whilst Byron was performing - Ally picked a pair of knickers off the bar that someone had thrown at Byron.

"Who do you think threw them?" Byron asked.

Ally held them out, they were quite large. "Must belong to a Yank," he quipped, before tossing them at Byron.

The jukebox was bellowing away and a few couples were dancing. Minibuses were coming and going and the place was in full swing. Pascale thought it quite a transformation from the dilapidated shack it had once been.

Byron and Sid were talking, heads close together to hear each other properly. Sid was telling Byron about a root that was supposed to make you sexy.

"What, some sort of aphrodisiac?" Byron asked.

The word was lost on Sid. "Make you plenty horny," he said, "make you want boomy-boomy."

"Boomy-boomy?"

Sid made a thrusting motion with his hips.

"Oh," said Byron, "and it makes the ladies want...err... boomy-boomy too?"

Sid nodded his head. "Make everyone want boomy-boomy!"

Sid prattled on and Byron tried to make some notes in between serving customers and mixing cocktails.

"What you two up to?" asked Rikki eyeing the pair of them suspiciously, but Sid, who was stood to one side, shook his head and Byron just shrugged. "Oh, nothing."

Byron was already formulating methods and quantities in his mind's eye. He just needed that unpronounceable root to get started. Over the din of the later evening in the bar Sid was trying to relay an important detail that he had forgotten to mention - that this root had to be boiled for at least four hours - a fact that failed to make it onto Byron's note pad.

It was late when they shoved the last reveller out. Rikki and Sid had done most of the tidying up and the glass washer was bubbling away. Ally was unloading baskets of clean glasses onto the shelves as Simmo finished off with a quick tidy up and mop of the toilets.

He motioned to Pascale, who was sitting on a stool at the end of the bar. She sipped the last of her beer, depositing the bottle into the empties trolley before following Simmo towards the bedrooms.

Gigolos

Simmo held open the door. "It's going to be a little cosy," he winked, "Rikki and Ally have the big room now."

"I am sure we will manage," Pascale replied.

Simmo smiled, and then holding her hand he pulled her close, at the same time fumbling behind himself to turn out the light.

"What time is it?" Simmo asked.

"Early," replied Pascale, who was sitting on the end of the bed pulling on her boots, "Rikitea is taking me back to the ship."

Simmo sat up and rubbed his eyes. "Erm, you're coming back... aren't you?"

Pascale kissed him on the forehead. "Of course; I just need a few things from the boat.

Simmo, still half asleep, yawned "that's ok then", and settled back down on the pillow.

Rikki was waiting for her in the bar. "We go," she said. Pascale nodded, so they set off for the town and the harbour on the other side of the island.

Pascale's ship had once been a trawler, but was now painted a gaudy shade of green. Rikki parked the Land Rover on the quayside beside the ship and they climbed up the gangway.

"Hi Sven," Pascale said to a tall man with a beard.

"Hi, how's it going?" Sven replied.

"This is Rikki." Pascale motioned to her companion and Sven nodded hello. "Is it ok if I borrow a couple of scuba sets for a few days?"

"Don't see why not," replied Sven, "I don't think we will be using them."

Pascale disappeared below to collect some clothes and her camera. In the meantime Sven had one of the crew load the scuba gear into the Land Rover.

"When are we sailing?" asked Pascale on her return.

"Probably next week, Monday or Tuesday."

"I'll leave you a contact number so you can let me know."

Rikki wrote down the phone number on a piece of paper. Sven smiled at the name. "Gigolos? It's not a cat house is it?" He teased Pascale.

"No it's a bar, and a very good one at that."

Rikki chirped in with "there is minibus go to Frankie's casino from town, it stop there on way."

Sven smiled. "Maybe I'll bring some of the crew over to check it out."

Rikki nodded: "You do."

The girls set off back for Gigolos, Rikki stopping briefly in town for fuel.

"Have you told anyone else about the pearls?" Pascale asked.

"No, only you…oh and Simmo, but me no think he understand."

Pascale nodded thoughtfully.

Everyone was up and about their business when they got back. Byron was busy stocking the bar, Simmo was outside with the boats and Ally was mumbling and grumbling because he wanted to use the Land Rover to get to the Don's place. The two girls decided to leave diving the lagoon until early next morning and unloaded their equipment into the shed.

The platform was more or less finished. Ally had made a mooring for it out of an old oil drum filled with concrete, but would need a substantial boat to take it out into the lagoon, and as usual he was relying on the Don to come up with the goods. The plan was to launch the platform from the Don's and tow it around the coast, into the lagoon and into position.

The Don laughed when Ally told him about his mooring anchor. "No need, Scotsman," he said, pointing to the platform. It was already in the water and sat on its deck was a large concrete filled oil drum.

"Bollocks," said Ally, all that mixing for nothing."

The Don clapped Ally on the shoulder. "Never mind Scotsman, you could say it's a weight off your mind." Ally just moaned at the pun. "My friends will tow it around early next week, all being well. They will set off early to avoid the tourists on the beach."

"Aye, wouldn't be good publicity if we ran someone down in the lagoon." Ally climbed back into the Land Rover, the Don promising to call if there was any change of plan.

The Don's place was on the coast, not far from the harbour. Ally noticed the large trawler at the quayside. "Wonder is she Clyde built?" He said to himself as he drove past, his mind taking him back to a world he thought he had forgotten. Tied up a little further along the quay was a small military craft, a patrol boat or possibly a mine sweeper. It was flying a French ensign, gently flapping in the breeze. Ally didn't really give it much thought.

Pascale spent most of the day in and out of the bar, or helping Simmo on the beach. She was proving to be quite good at selling ice cream and the afternoon passed quickly and pleasantly, with Pascale helping to bring in the equipment during the early evening. They sat there on a beached pedalo; Pascale had brought them each a much deserved beer and they were watching the sunset, holding hands.

"It doesn't get much better than this you know," said Pascale, "cold beer and a handsome man."

"Tell me who he is and I'll kill him," joked Simmo.

"Are you ever serious about anything?" Pascale laughed.

"Nah," replied Simmo. "Well... maybe about you."

"Only maybe?" Pascale pouted.

"Come here," whispered Simmo, and pulled her close and kissed her.

There was a loud cough behind them. Simmo looked around and there was Jean Paul.

"Might I have a word Pascale... please?"

"There is nothing left to say is there, Jean Paul?"

"As you wish," he said dismissively, turning away. But then he paused, turned back again and spoke. "Concerning your things. Do you want me to send them here?"

"Pascale thought for a moment. "No, send them to the ship."

"Ah, so that's where you have been, hanging around with your hippy friends. Strange company you keep," he smirked.

"It's important work."

"What, being a busy body, poking your nose in where it doesn't belong?"

Jean Paul and Pascale locked eyes for a moment, before Jean Paul turned on his heels and headed towards the bar.

"What was that all about?" asked Simmo.

"His father works for the French government; he is the Deputy High Commissioner."

"Oh," said Simmo.

"He doesn't like my politics; I stand up for what I believe in."

"Well I believe in love," said Simmo, throwing his arms around her neck.

Gigolos

The bar was filling up rapidly. The minibus that had just arrived was packed to the gunnels, although they didn't look like your normal run of the mill tourists. A couple of them had guitars and one had what looked like a set of bongos. Pascale waved a tall bearded man over to the bar and he pushed his way through throng.

"Hi Sven," said Pascale, kissing him on both cheeks, "this is Simmo. It's his bar."

"And my partner's" Simmo added.

"Pleased to meet you," said Sven, shaking Simmo's hand across the bar. "When Pascale said "Gigolos" I wasn't sure quite what to expect."

Sven nodded "hi" to Rikki and Simmo smiled. "It's her fault, he said, "she came up with the name."

"You will have to tell me the story when you are less busy," shouted Sven over the noise.

Simmo nodded. He, Byron and Rikki were busy serving drinks whilst Ally and Sid were rushing round collecting and washing the empties. In a brief lull at the bar Pascale explained to Simmo that Sven was the captain of her ship, the Osprey. The rest of the party were crew and scientists.

Sven came up to the bar with a big order. "Is everyone here?" Pascale yelled.

"Everyone except Jimmy; he drew the short straw so we left him behind on anchor watch."

"That's a shame....but someone has to mind the shop."

Jean Paul was standing just behind Sven and Pascale and had caught most of their conversation, but instead of pushing forward to the bar he eased back through the crowd and headed towards the small foyer to the side door where the public telephone was. He made a brief phone call in French before disappearing off up the beach towards Frankie's.

The revelries continued. Pascale captured a photo of Simmo and Byron attempting the cocktail routine along with one or two more pictures of the evening, but she only had a few shots left on the film. As the evening drew on the instruments came out of their cases and the jukebox was switched off. The music and the beer flowed, and the evening turned into quite a sing-along. Even Ally managed to muscle in on the act, going through some of his usual repartee. Simmo was amazed when Pascale picked up a guitar and sang a solo, heart-rending performance of Donovan's *Catch the Wind* and Dylan's *Knockin' on Heaven's Door*.

"God," said Simmo admiringly, "I didn't know you could sing like that!"

"It usually takes a lot of beer before I can pluck up the courage, Pascale replied, blushing.

It was quite late when they bundled the last of the Osprey's crew onto the final minibus of the evening. Byron was admiring Pascale's camera. "An Olympus," he said inspecting it, "very nice." Pascale nodded in agreement, leaving it on the bar whilst she went to help Simmo collect the empties. Absently Byron put it under the bar out of the way, whilst he started to clean up. It took a further twenty minutes or so to eject the last of the diehards and the clearing up seemed to take longer than usual, despite having Pascale as an extra pair of hands. Eventually they finished and she and Simmo said their goodnights.

"Aye," said Ally, "it was a grand night," clapping Simmo on the back.

"Sometimes the impromptu ones are the best," replied Simmo, and Ally nodded in agreement.

Gigolos

It was Ally hammering on the door that woke them up.

"Pascale there's someone on the phone, says it's important!"

"OK, said Pascale, shaking herself awake and sleepily throwing a t shirt and some shorts on. She went next door, into Rikki and Ally's room where the other telephone was and had a brief conversation in French with Luc, one of the crew of the ship.

"What's up?" asked Simmo, following her into the other room.

"Jimmy's been hurt. Someone forced their way onto the Osprey last night, knocked Jimmy out cold and ransacked the ship; smashed up the lab and stole a lot of documents. Oh, and Sven thinks they have contaminated the fuel and fresh water tanks."

"Do you need to get back?" asked Simmo.

"No, not for now at least, it was a call to let me know what's happened and to check that I was ok."

"Who do you think did it?" Ally asked.

Pascale twirled her short hair. "Well, it is probably the French government who are behind it, they have had their navy harassing us."

Ally thought a little and then spoke up. "Aye, I saw a French warship at the quayside on mah way back from town. Patrol boat or something like."

"Sounds a little too coincidental if you ask me," said Simmo.

"Aye."

"Only one crew on board?" Rikki asked Pascale.

"Yes, everyone else was here."

"But surely whoever did it wouldn't have known there was only one bloke on board?" Simmo asked.

"Aye, would be a bit risky going ontae a ship with even half its crew on board," said Ally.

Pascale and Simmo looked at each other and at the same time said "Jean Paul."

"He must have tipped them off," said Simmo.

Pascale sighed before taking Simmo by the hand. "Come on, she said, "there's nothing we can do right now. Let's go back to bed."

Ally took a long drag on his cigarette before stubbing it out. "That Jean Paul's a shithouse," he said to Rikki before turning out the light.

Pascale was up early again the next morning. Simmo, barely awake, asked if she was going back to the ship.

"No; at least not yet. I promised Rikki we would dive the lagoon... but maybe this afternoon..."

She didn't finish. Rikki was ready to go and the two of them went out to the shed to fetch and check the diving gear. Simmo was wide awake now, so got up and dressed. He found Ally in the bar.

Ally looked up from his cloud of cigarette smoke. "Brew?" he enquired.

"Nah, I'm going to see what the girls are up to."

Simmo volunteered his services as pedalo crew. He launched the boat with the two girls sat on the side; it was sitting quite low in the water.

"You remember where we go last time?" Rikki asked.

"I've got a rough idea," replied Simmo as he pedalled them out into the lagoon. There was a large box of equipment piled into the other seat.

"It's not our standard dive boat," quipped Pascale.

Simmo smiled. "Pedro Pedalo Diving Tours at your service!"

"You know, that's not a bad idea!" Pascale laughed, "guided dives, especially as there might be treasure down there."

"Treasure?" Simmo's eyes lit up.

"Pearls," said Rikki.

Gigolos

"But they're no good, are they," said Simmo, "I mean, they're not white, are they?"

The two girls exchanged glances. Pascale spoke softly to Simmo.

"Black pearls can be any colour; they really fetch the most money depending upon the size and quality. These days on the other islands they are farmed... but it's every diver's dream to find a natural pearl. We need to study the lagoon properly to see what condition it's in, especially in the parts that a certain buffoon dredged."

Rikki and Pascale gave each other an 'ok' sign and disappeared below the surface. They were down quite some time, leaving Simmo twiddling his thumbs in the pedalo. When they came up they were carrying a string bag full of oysters. Pascale asked Simmo to pass her a tool from the box, but he wasn't sure what she meant.

"It's a bit like a clamp in reverse," she explained, "and it has a thread and a screw."

Simmo eventually found it. "What's that for?" He asked.

"Open shell," replied Rikki. Simmo didn't look convinced.

"Watch," said Pascale. She expertly inserted the tool between the bivalve's shells, wound the screw and opened it gently. She had a bit of a probe around. "Nothing," she said, closing the shell and easing the oyster back into the water.

Simmo looked at Pascale. "What's with the clampy thing?"

It's to open the shells, but it doesn't kill the oyster, so we can pop it back in the water to hopefully make another pearl. The commercial pearl farmers would plant a little piece of shell inside the oyster using one of these clamps, then thread strings of oysters on lines in the water."

"Oh," said Simmo, "I thought it was just bits of sand in them that caused pearls."

Rikki and Pascale studied him.

"Ok," said Pascale, "there are six oysters in that bag. Which one do you think contains a pearl?"

Simmo shrugged. "I don't know."

"Well, have a guess then."

Simmo looked. There were two nice, smooth looking ones, three a bit sort of lumpy and one really bumpy looking. Simmo picked the larger of the nicer looking two. Pascale nodded to Rikki, who immediately went for the old, gnarled one. Pascale opened Simmo's oyster first. "Nothing," she said and plopped the oyster back into the sea. On opening the one Rikki had chosen she produced a small but very fine light blue pearl. "See?" she said to Simmo, but Simmo didn't see; he shook his head.

"It is a common belief that it's sand that makes an oyster produce a pearl in the wild. But it's more probable that a parasite is responsible; so the older the oyster is and, I suppose, the harder life it's had, the more likely a pearl."

Simmo nodded. "Ah ha, I see now...then Ally should be full of pearls," he joked.

Rikki frowned and Pascale shook her head, smiling. She asked him to pass her a sample jar from the box; she thought she had spotted something else on the last dive. There was something down there in the lagoon that she really wanted to find.

They spent most of the early morning pedalling from one part of the lagoon to another. Pascale had a chino graph and waterproof notebook and would occasionally pause to make notes. They would have to get back to the bar pretty soon and get ready for opening so were going to have a last couple of quick

Gigolos

dives on the way back in. This time when Pascale broke surface she was almost ecstatic, she couldn't get her mouthpiece out quickly enough. She and Rikki were almost squawking in French before she cried out "Simmo, Simmo, it's true, and I've found a living specimen!"

Simmo looked perplexed. Pascale held out a jar with what looked like a whelk in it.

Oh, that's, erm, great," said Simmo, not sure what else to say.

"It's sinistral," she said beaming.

When they got back to the beach they found Ally sat on one of the pedalos, smoking.

"How'd you get on?" he asked.

"It good," replied Rikki.

Ally eyed the net bag that still had a few oysters in it. Pascale was going to take them with her back to the ship to do the usual environmental tests - if there was anything left of the lab to test them with.

Ally pulled a face. "Aye," he said. "Am nae fussy on oysters, I was working in Tilbury docks one time and had a few too many, was sick as a parrot."

"Was that a few too many drinks or oysters?" Simmo jibed.

"Feck you!" said Ally, before giving him the finger. "But I wouldn't mind some of them whelks, they're a different story," he added, putting his hand on Pascale's sample jar and inspecting the prized specimen. She quickly snatched the sample jar and put it behind her back.

"You can't eat that one, its left handed!" Simmo butted in.

Ally scratched his head before shouting "It's only got one foot!" as Simmo picked up the scuba tanks.

"All right then smart arse," Simmo retorted as he turned toward the bar, "it's a bleedin' left-footer then."

Ally raised his eyebrows. "You're trying to tell me now it's Catholic?"

"Yeah and it supports Celtic," said Simmo over his shoulder.

"I'll buy it a bloody drink then!" Ally shouted after Simmo, who had been joined by a laughing Rikki and Pascale.

Pacifists and Pugilists

Simmo loaded the diving gear and other equipment into the back of the Land Rover while Pascale and Rikki went inside to shower and change. On his return to the bar, Simmo found Ally standing at his usual spot, fag in mouth, absently polishing the bar and lost in deep thought.

The girls eventually appeared. "Gear's in the Land Rover," said Simmo.

"I'll drive Pascale back if you like," offered Ally, "I need tae go tae the Don's place anyway." Rikki nodded to Pascale.

"Are you coming back tonight?" asked Simmo.

"I should think so." Pascale smiled.

"Right," said Ally, stubbing out his fag, "off we go then."

Pascale was holding on tightly to the jar containing her precious sample and Ally was driving quite slowly so that they could speak over the engine noise and the flapping rag top. He was doing his party trick of rolling a fag with one hand whilst driving.

"D'you mind if I ask you something Pascale?"

"No...what is it?"

"What are you really up tae on that ship of yours?"

Pascale shifted a little uncomfortably before replying. "We're just taking a few samples, looking for any long term effects of radiation from the nuclear tests."

Ally stared at her. "That was a long, long time ago. I cannae see there being much - if anything - we don't already know about." He held Pascale's gaze. "And I cannae see them going tae all that trouble with you just for that." Pascale squirmed again. "So what's *really* going on lass?"

Pascale hesitated before asking, "Can I trust you Ally?"

"Aye, I can keep mah mouth shut."

Pascale bit her lip indecisively, and then spoke quietly. "We think that the French have been developing a new weapon, and that they have plans to test it on one of the atolls."

"Christ!" Ally spluttered. "What type of weapon?"

"Nuclear; Neutron possibly."

Ally rubbed his chin. "I thought they were trying tae ban all these tests now."

"And so they are, but in the light of other countries' development and testing... Look Ally, this would put the French right back at the centre of the world stage, a major player again. Plus with their missile technology..." Pascale let it hang in the air.

"Aye," said Ally thoughtfully, "we saw what their missiles did in the Falklands war."

"We... managed to get some photographs."

Ally swore as he took a corner a little too quickly. "Is that what they were looking for?"

"Presumably, although they couldn't know for sure we had them."

Ally puffed on his fag and let out a long sigh. They drove on for a while in silence, the Land Rover gently bumping and bouncing.

"Tell me," said Ally, staring ahead now, not looking at Pascale. "I keep meaning tae ask Rikki about..." Ally paused.

Pascale looked at him. "The bond thing?"

Gigolos

"Yeah, "said Ally, still looking ahead. "Was...err... she in some kind of trouble?"

Pascale glanced at him again before she too looked ahead. "No; not her at least... Look out!" she screeched, almost losing her grip on the precious jar as Ally momentarily lost concentration.

"Oops!" Ally laughed grimly as he swerved around a cyclist who was swaying precariously, carrying a large bundle on the handlebars.

"You know Rikki's father and uncle were builders?"

"Och aye, I gathered that." said Ally.

"They built a hotel but there was a big fire and a couple of people died. The backers blamed the architects, the architects and officials blamed the builders..."

"I get the score." Ally cocked his head. "Who were the backers?"

Pascale thought for a moment. "Not quite sure exactly, one of them was Dutch."

"Van Horen?"

"Yes, that was his name. After the fire he was finished as a developer on the islands." Ally nodded. "Anyhow, the builders took the blame; the story goes they needed money to stop her father going to jail."

"Ah," said Ally.

"They didn't have enough cash; you know how it works out here..."

"Aye, go on."

"So, that's where Chin Lee stepped in with his - what shall we call it - arrangement."

Ally had somehow managed to roll and light another smoke. "So she did it to keep her father out of jail then?" He nodded thoughtfully to himself. "You will nae say I mentioned anything will you?"

"No," said Pascale, "it is her business."

It took a further ten minutes to get to the dock. There was no sign of the French warship. As Ally helped Pascale carry the diving gear back on board, he pointed to a brass plaque below the bridge, *John Brown Glasgow*.

"Aye," he said proudly, "I could tell she was Clyde built from her lines."

Sven appeared around the corner. Pascale held the jar towards him and he took it, examining the creature within and smiling.

"I congratulate you on your discovery, mademoiselle," he said very formally, before laughing affectionately at Pascale's beaming smile. "So your hunch was right." Sven changed the subject. "Jimmy is still out of action, the bump on his head is ok but the bastards have broken his ribs and he can hardly move. The engine room is a mess." He looked at Ally. "With Jimmy laid up we only have one engineer and a greaser."

"Ally is a shipbuilder," said Pascale.

"Shipwright," Ally corrected. Pascale looked at him coyly.

"Would you be needin' a hand then?" Ally asked, smiling.

"If you wouldn't mind," replied Sven with relief. Ally nodded and Pascale gave him an unexpected peck on the cheek.

"Come on then," said Sven, "Pablo is in the engine room. I will introduce you."

Ally spent the rest of the morning helping out. The fuel and freshwater tanks had been contaminated with sea water. They pumped the water over the side, and then used water from the shore supply to rinse and refill the tanks.

Gigolos

"This will cost you a few bob," said Ally, but Pablo just shrugged.

The fuel was a little trickier. Between the two of them they worked out that they could just about squeeze it from the two smaller tanks into the main tank. They passed the fuel a couple of times between the two smaller ones before finally transferring it to the daily service tank. As they only had a small fuel separator to extract the water from the fuel the exercise took quite some time, and it was after lunch by the time they had finished.

Ally came up top for a smoke. Pascale and Sven didn't see him standing there in the engine room doorway.

"Are you sure they took them?" asked Pascale.

"Yes," said Sven, the prints and the negatives are both gone.

"I don't suppose we will get another chance...?"

Sven just laughed. "No, not now that they have another bloody warship here; dodge one maybe, but two? It was a miracle we captured the photographs in the first place." He shrugged. "And besides, they know now what we are really about."

Pascale thought for a moment before slapping herself on her forehead. "My pictures!" she exclaimed.

"What pictures?"

"When I was in the other rib, I took some photos." Sven grabbed her by the shoulders. "I mean, they won't be as detailed as yours but I used maybe twenty shots off a thirty roll film."

Sven still held her by the shoulders. "Pascale, do you know how important that film is now?" Pascale nodded slowly. "For God's sake we need to keep them safe. We need them to try and stop the French, but I am sure the Americans or Russians would be equally keen to see what they have been setting up. Where is your camera?"

"Pascale thought for a moment. "Merde," she muttered. "I think I may have left it at the bar."

"Can you give them a call and check?"

Pascale nodded. "Can I ring from here?"

Sven rubbed his chin. "Better not. They are probably monitoring our comms. Better ring from there." He pointed to a kiosk on the quayside before turning back towards the wheel house as Pascale headed for the gangway.

Ally took a long drag on his rollie. The cogs in his head had begun to whirr. "Aye," he said to no one in particular, returning to the engine room.

Pascale spoke to Rikki in French. The line clicked and crackled, but that was nothing unusual on the island's phones. Rikki couldn't find the camera at first, but Byron seemed to remember seeing it on the end of the counter, and after a bit of a search around Rikki found it there under a bar towel.

"Thank goodness," said Pascale, "there are some very important photographs on it." Rikki promised to put it in her and Ally's room for safe keeping.

With work finished on the Osprey, Ally and Pascale set off for Gigolos.

Ally pulled over at the garage on his way out of town. "Am just gonnae get some fags. D'you want anything? Pascale shook her head and Ally disappeared into the store. He came out clutching a pouch of tobacco but he had also bought something else. Stuffed into his shirt pocket was a roll of 35mm film.

The companions made idle chat on the way back, Pascale not once mentioning her camera. Ally kept his speed down so that they could talk over the engine noise, and prompted her onto another topic.

Gigolos

"Them oysters you had in that string bag the other afternoon... Aye, strikes me, the state of them, that they would be nae good for eating." Pascale couldn't help but smile. "Aye, the only other thing I know about oysters is that some of them contain pearls."

Pascale nodded slowly in agreement as Ally looked at her quizzically.

"It's true," she replied.

"So is there a fortune down there?"

"Pascale ran her fingers through her short hair. "There are definitely oysters containing pearls in the lagoon, but how many, and of what quality, who knows? I suppose you could dredge them all up and destroy the ecology of the lagoon, not to mention the habitat of one very rare snail."

"Aye," said Ally, "your whelk."

"And even then there is no guarantee of finding anything of real value. But I have a much better idea on how to make a regular, safe income without wrecking the place."

"Go on."

"Divers would love to find a pearl in the wild, so we could offer guided diving tours. They pay $100 up front, and we give them an escorted dive, allowing them to take, say, a couple of oysters. If they find a pearl they get to keep it. If not then they have a lovely dive."

"And you think people will pay tae do this?"

Pascale nodded. "I certainly do. We could put an air compressor in the shed, get some bottles and equipment and do equipment rental, even snorkelling and diving lessons."

Ally rubbed his chin. "Aye, I can see the attraction," he said after a while, starting a different set of cogs whirring.

Simmo waved from the beach as they arrived back. Pascale set off over the sand to him as Ally headed over to the bar. Rikki was serving and Byron was packing another batch of empties into the glass washer. Ally waved over to them. "Just getting changed," he said, pulling at his work shirt as if to demonstrate.

It took him a few minutes of poking around to find what he was looking for. "Ah ha," he said to himself, pulling Pascale's camera out of the wardrobe. Looking over his shoulder to make sure there was no one around, he wound the film on and removed it from the camera. He took the new roll from his shirt pocket and inserted it. He was about to replace it in the wardrobe when he paused and smiled. Dropping his trousers, he wound the film on and carefully began snapping pictures of his nether regions, clicking through the whole film before pulling up his pants and putting the camera back where he found it, stuffing the original film inside a pair of socks in his sundries draw. Feeling quite pleased with himself, he quickly changed and returned to the bar.

After putting the pedalos to bed together, Pascale and Simmo made an appearance. Rikki told Pascale that the camera was tucked away safe in the closet in her room, and Pascale nodded and tapped the side of her nose. Although it was early in the evening, the bar was already getting busy.

Jean Paul's father called him into the study.
"Close the door," his father said softly to him. Jean Paul obeyed and approached his father.
"Your suspicions were right, Jean Paul. Certain documents and photographs have been recovered."

Gigolos

Jean Paul smiled but his father held up his hand. "However..."

Another man was seated in the study with them, sipping cognac. "You know Philippe?" Jean Paul looked at the other man and nodded. "It seems that our mission on the Osprey may not have been altogether successful. The phone tap has revealed some information." He cut to the point. "Pascale has taken photographs of our -" he paused, "- business. I want you to take Philippe to Gigolos. You will make a distraction of some kind whilst Philippe retrieves the film. Would you recognise her camera, Jean Paul?"

"I think so...It's an Olympus, with a distinctive red strap embroidered with flowers."

"Are you sure?"

"Quite sure, I bought her that strap to go with the camera."

"Did you catch that Philippe?" Philippe nodded. "Then that is all, Jean Paul."

Jean Paul nodded and left his father and Philippe to their cognac.

The bar was filling up fast with early evening revellers, the season now being in full swing. Pascale checked on her camera, and deciding it was safest left in the wardrobe for now, went to help Rikki behind the bar. She was pleased to see Ralph, the boson from the Osprey, pushing his way through the throng. He ordered a beer and motioned to Pascale to come outside. "Back in five minutes," she said to Rikki, who nodded "ok". Ally watched the two of them go.

Ralph and Pascale walked down the beach, Ralph only speaking when he was sure they were alone.

"Sven intends to move the Osprey to the main island, discharge the dirty fuel and refuel."

"What then?"

"He wants to take the photographs you took to New Zealand."

"Why?" Pascale asked, pulling a face.

"He doesn't trust posting them."

"Oh I see…I was hoping to stay here…"

Ralph shrugged. "I don't see him having a problem with that. As long as we have the film on board, we can develop it and deliver it personally. Sven wants us to put about a rumour that we are having engine trouble and are heading to Oz for repairs; mission over. We need to get the film back on board. Are you sure no one else knows about it?"

Pascale paused, and then shook her head. Ralph studied her for a moment.

"Ok," he said. "How are we going to get it to the ship?"

"You could take it with you tonight, or I could ask Ally to run me back first thing in the morning. When is Sven planning to leave?"

"Probably the day after tomorrow, although once he has the film it may be sooner. Perhaps I might be better taking it with me tonight; there will be plenty of people on the bus."

Pascale shook her head. "You will have to walk across town alone. No, we will bring it back first thing. You can tell Sven tonight, and have the Osprey ready for sea. I don't want to ring the ship; Sven thinks that they are probably monitoring our comms."

A couple of the regulars recognised Ralph as the bongo man from the previous night's musical extravaganza. Ralph made a point of telling everyone he spoke to that they were leaving shortly for Australia as they needed to repair the engines. Customer-wise it was about three deep at the bar.

Gigolos

Ally was busy serving when he spotted the Don and gave him a wave, ignoring a couple of customers to serve him instead.

"Busy tonight, Scotsman," said the Don.

"Aye, there's been nae let up this evening." Ally was struggling with the pump; Byron had gone out back to change the gas. "Christ," he said to the Don, remembering the helium fiasco, "God knows what he will connect the bloody beer pump tae!"

The Don smiled. "I want to have a talk to you later, when it's quiet," he said, before backing out into the crowd. Ally nodded casually, and carried on serving.

Pascale was busy collecting empty glasses. Simmo had gone to fetch more mixers and to keep an eye on Byron, just in case. Midway through the evening Jean Paul, accompanied by his usual cronies and Philippe, arrived. Ally pretended not to notice, but watched them carefully. One of Jean Paul's party ordered the round, with Rikki serving him. The juke box was blaring away, with a fair number of couples dancing. Jean Paul's crowd had managed to procure the table nearest the juke box. Ally could see that every time Pascale went to collect their glasses Jean Paul kept talking to her, at one point grabbing her by the wrist. Ally could also see Simmo hovering around as if unsure what to do.

"Is he being a pain?" Ally asked Pascale as she came up to the bar clutching two handfuls of empties.

"I don't know what's wrong with him tonight," she said, "it's almost like..."she thought about it, "he is trying to provoke me."

Ally rubbed his chin. "Do ye want tae serve behind the bar? I can get Rikki tae collect glasses."

Pascale shook her head. "No; I wouldn't give him the satisfaction."

Ally shrugged and carried on serving, whilst keeping one eye on them. He could tell that Simmo was becoming a little agitated: every time he went near the group they would make some wise crack at his expense.

Ally watched the drama unfold. Philippe gave the slightest of nods to Jean Paul, before standing up and disappearing into the revellers. Jean Paul then suddenly grabbed Pascale, who was gathering glasses from the next table, and tried to kiss her, dragging her onto his knee.

Simmo saw his arse, screaming "Get off her you bastard!" Jean Paul shoved Pascale off his knee and she fell to the floor with a bump. Simmo threw a haymaker, which Jean Paul easily dodged.

Normally Ally would have been over the bar like a shot, but unusually he just stood there watching as Jean Paul stood up, raising his fists boxer style. No Marquis of Queensbury rules for Simmo though - he kicked Jean Paul squarely in the balls, kneeing him in the face for good measure as he slumped forward.

The momentum was still carrying Simmo forward when a chair hit him full in the face. Jean Paul's cronies were hurling furniture and glasses in all directions as Gigolos erupted into a mass brawl.

Ally still stood at the bar, observing. The Don stared hard at him, before turning his attention to the fight on the veranda, then back to Ally before nodding to his boys, who waded in immediately.

Ally in the meantime crept slowly around the bar. Jean Paul had picked himself up from the floor and was now standing over the prostrate Simmo. Pascale was punching him from behind as he backed up to take a kick, when suddenly Ally hit him on the cheek bone, right on the button, instantly stunning him.

Gigolos

"You had that comin' you bastard," said Ally softly as Jean Paul crumpled to the floor.

Ally caught sight of an unscathed Philippe pushing his way over through the onlookers, and beckoned him over.
"Get him out of here."
Philippe, scowling hard, remained motionless.
"Now! Get him out NOW!" yelled Ally.
Philippe looked like he might be about to throw a punch and then shrugged, stooping to pick up the stupefied Jean Paul. Pascale was fussing over Simmo, who had a large bloody wheal across his forehead.
"Get him in back," said Rikki. She helped Pascale move Simmo out of the bar, leaving Byron behind the counter.

Sid and Ally started cleaning up the mess. As bar fights went this wasn't a particularly large one but it had been quite savage, especially as the main protagonists were perfectly sober.
It didn't take the guys long to clear up. The bar settled down as the beer began flowing again. Ally took the broken chair outside, tutting and shaking his head. The Don followed him out.
"Scotsman."
Ally turned to face him.
"That Philippe; he's a French government man."
Ally nodded. "Aye, reckon he is."
The Don took a long pull on his cigar. Ally rolled a fag and the two of them stood in silence, smoking.
"Be careful, Scotsman, these are dangerous people and they are asking a lot of questions concerning the Osprey and anyone connected to her."
Ally nodded again. "Thanks for the warning. Come on," he said, clapping the Don on the shoulder, "I'll buy you a beer."

"Well, Philippe? Do you have the film?"

Philippe nodded. "I have switched it for a blank roll."

Jean Paul's father smiled. "Give me the film; I will put it in the safe for tonight and have it developed in the morning. Where is Jean Paul?"

"He is getting cleaned up. He took a beating."

Jean Paul's father cocked an eyebrow. "The Scotsman?"

"No, the other one."

He raised both eyebrows in surprise, and then shrugged. "Is he badly hurt?"

"No...only his pride."

"Tell me, Philippe, how were they allowed to get so close to the atoll?"

Philippe looked up from his cognac. "The whole idea was not to attract attention. To keep everything very low key, have everything prepared before anyone suspected. Technically the Osprey was chartered for a scientific survey, so we were not overly concerned at her presence. They must have got wind of our plan somehow and acted on their own initiative."

"Mmmm," mused the Deputy Commissioner, "any idea who tipped them off?"

Philippe paused. "I have my suspicions...and then again the Osprey may have encountered a fishing vessel or native fishermen."

"Sea gypsies?"

"Possibly."

"But where did the leak originate?"

"I suspect the pedalo man is probably mixed up in it somewhere."

The Deputy Commissioner nodded.

"Ouch! that hurts!"

Gigolos

Rikki pressed a cold wet towel to Simmo's forehead. "Sssh! It bring down swelling."

Ally came through from the bar. "How's his head?" he asked Pascale.

"Bloody sore!" replied Simmo, butting in.

"Aye, and it's made an awful mess of a brand new chair; I ought tae take the cost out of your wages." Simmo started to giggle. "Mind you I'm thinking Jean Paul has all the ingredients for a new cocktail."

"Uh?" said Simmo, not comprehending.

"Aye...Blue Bols!"

Simmo was laughing now as Ally continued, "Well I cannae stand here skiving," before going back out to give Byron a hand behind the bar.

Simmo was still soundly asleep. Pascale kissed him lightly on the cheek before dressing quickly and quietly. Ally was outside in the dark, smoking, when Pascale approached him.

"Hi," she said, "can I ask of you a small favour? Do you mind running me back to the ship?"

Ally nodded. "Aye," was all he said.

Rikki, too, was up and about, and after a brief chat with her, Pascale went into Rikki's room to retrieve her camera. She put it into her bag and fastened it carefully.

"I am ready to go," she said to Ally.

"Aye, come on then." He kissed Rikki before he and Pascale set off for the ship in the Land Rover. It was still dark, with just the faintest signs of sunrise. The two said very little. There was no other traffic on the road and Ally eased the vehicle round the twisty, winding tracks with little difficulty, so the journey to the dock didn't take them long. Ally parked on the quayside, near the phone kiosk, and accompanied Pascale on board.

The ship had all the appearance of a vessel ready to sail. The shore supplies were disconnected, the engines were running, the radar turning and everything was hove to. Sven and Ralph were in the wheelhouse, poring over charts. Pascale held out the camera to Sven.

"Phew!" he said, taking it and opening the back to check on the film before tossing it to Ralph.

"Here, put this somewhere safe till we're out at sea." Ralph nodded.

"Is it ok if I grab a few bits before I go?" Pascale asked.

Sven nodded. "Sure."

"Oh and I need my notes and my specimen."

"You sure you're not coming with us?"

"No, not this time." Pascale smiled.

Sven gave her a big hug. "I look forward to reading your paper; it may confirm your position as one of the world's leading conchologists!"

Pascale blushed. "Good luck guys," she said before going below to collect her things.

Ally was stood smoking by the gangway when she came back up.

"Ready?" she said.

"Aye...Here, let me give you a hand with your things."

Ally put Pascale's gear in the back of the Land Rover, and then climbed in. Pascale held her prized snail on her lap like a talisman as Sven waved to them from the fo'casle, breathing a sigh of relief as Ally put the Land Rover in gear and drove off.

"What now?" asked Ally.

"I guess I will carry on with my thesis..."

"No, I mean what will they do with the film?"

Pascale thought for a moment. "Develop it and take it to New Zealand."

Gigolos

"Why New Zealand?"

"The authorities are sympathetic to us there. The plan then is to publish the photographs and hopefully every nuclear campaigner and environmentalist will protest to the French government. Perhaps some of them may try to blockade the atoll with protest ships."

Ally rolled a fag, squinting into the sunrise as he drove them back to the bar.

Rikki was busy stocking the shelves when they got back. Simmo was sitting at the end of the bar with a coffee.

"All done?" he asked. Pascale nodded. "I see you've brought Brian back with you!"

Pascale looked confused. Ally went... "Boing!" Pascale shook her head.

Simmo and Ally looked at each other.

"You nae know your *Magic Roundabout*?" joked Ally.

Pascale shook her head again as Simmo and Ally simultaneously burst into a rendition of the theme tune.

"Time for bed!" Simmo laughed, grabbing Pascale, but Ally interjected.

"Nae time for that now, off with you wee man and get them bloody pedalos out."

"Up yours Zebedee," Simmo retorted, giving Pascale a kiss before heading out to the beach.

"It was a children's television programme," chipped in Byron, "one of the characters was a snail called Brian."

Pascale nodded slowly.

"Who Boing?" asked Rikki.

"Boing?" asked Byron, "Ahh, I think you mean Zebedee; strange character. Had a handlebar moustache and a giant spring rammed up his backside. Kept telling everyone it was time for bed. You only have to look at Alastair and Simon to see the effect this kind of television exposure had on children. I suspect the producers were spaced out on psychedelic sixties drugs."

Pascale burst out laughing. "Really? This was a kids' TV programme?"

"Without a word of a lie."

Pascale paused for a moment, a childhood memory creeping into her thoughts, and then cried "Ah, *Le Manège Enchanté!*" smiling and clapping her hands.

It was Byron's turn to look puzzled as Pascale continued excitedly. "I think this was the French version of the TV programme you are talking about, but I think the snail was called Ambroise!"

Byron considered this before saying "you may well be right, I seem to recall Ivor Woods' wife being French." He stood in silence, examining a glass for a while, before saying to Rikki "do you think it would be all right if I took this evening off? I was hoping to meet up with Chantalle; it's her evening off too."

Rikki looked over to Ally who was standing at his usual spot, polishing away.

"I cannae see why not, that is as long as Pascale does nae mind givin' us a wee hand." Pascale nodded. "Aye," said Ally, "but I still think Brian is the best name for yer snail."

Pascale just smiled and shook her head. "Better than 'Boing' I suppose!"

Pascale spent most of the day outside on the beach with Simmo, selling ice-cream and helping with the pedalos. Ally was inside pondering what to do with the film; he had contemplated hiding it in various places around the bar, including the lavatory cistern and the ladies' tampon machine. In the end he wrapped it in its container in plastic and took it out into the shed. He carefully emptied a jar full of nuts and bolts and inserted the film inside, concealing it with the nuts and bolts before putting it back on the shelf. "Safe for now," he said to himself, but he had a nagging doubt that it would not be safe on the island. He was thinking that maybe he would ask the Don if he could get it off the island and post it to his mother's; at least it should be safe there. That got him to thinking that he really ought to be paying her a visit after all; then he shuddered.

In an almighty flashback Ally lurched through time and distance back to Glasgow, back to the big grey tenement where he grew up, back to that huge drunken bear of a father, back to hiding under the covers and listening for... No that wasn't the word... dreading the sound of the key in the door, fearing the return of the "big man" with his wild rages and tantrums, back to the combined smells of cheap whiskey and cigarettes and sweat that would pervade everything; then the shouting would start. This was a mean bastard who took great delight in smashing up his mother's few meagre possessions just for the pleasure of breaking them, and then to further his enjoyment the belt would come off and he would beat the Jesus out of his mother and him too if he tried to intervene. Then one night a fourteen year old Ally, fearing that this was all there was, had had enough and after a savage brawl he took the belt off the drunken old sod before beating the old bastard half to death with it and heaving him over the tenement landing. No one was ever, ever, going to beat him anymore.

"Aye, the old bastard told the coppers I threw him off the block, but Mammy an' I said he fell; two against one."

They didn't see his father for a couple of years after that, then the old sod would come around when Ally was at work and put the arm on his mother for money for drink.

"Aye she was afraid tae tell me, in case I did anything daft, but she told mah auntie, so I had a wee word, just on the quiet like, elbows don't half make a sickening noise when you rip them out of their sockets don't you think? Anyways that put paid to his visits."

Eventually the drink got him, and the irony was that he was still married to his mother. She - or rather Ally - ended up paying for the bloody cremation.

"Aye," laughed Ally bitterly to himself, "I would nae have minded paying if we could have cremated him whilst the old bastard was still alive. Mind you, with the amount of booze inside him it's nae wonder we didn't blow the bloody crematorium up."

Ally had promised his mother he would place the ashes on his father's parents' plot in Kentigerns cemetery, but instead had flushed them down the bog in the public toilets in Argyle Street. A very fitting end, he thought.

"Aye, isn't that what you're supposed to do with shite?"

He was roused from his thoughts by Rikki asking sharply "What you do?"

"Ugh," said Ally, shaking himself from his daydream. Rikki had come into the shed quietly and had been studying him for some time.

"Och... I've been looking for a bolt for the generator."

She cocked her head slightly. "You ok?"

"Aye," said Ally, absently rubbing his chin. "Just been thinking about mah father."

"You never mention him, you miss him?"

"Christ no!" spluttered Ally, "he was an out and out bastard!"

"Oh," said Rikki, then quietly asked him, "You miss mother?"

"Aye," replied Ally.

"You go see her soon?"

"We'll see...Now come on woman I could do with a wee bite to eat." He gently slapped Rikki on the backside as they turned to leave.

Byron left with the early evening minibus. With him he had the concoction that Sid had given him the recipe for. He had told Chantalle all about it and she was up for trying it with him. Pascale and Simmo had finished with the beach and were busy in the bar. Trade was brisk and the evening passed quickly. Ally had kept an eye out; he was half expecting Jean Paul or some of his cronies to turn up, but much to his relief the night passed without incident.

Rockefellers and Moral Dilemmas

"Have the photographs brought in as soon as they are developed."

"As you wish, monsieur," replied the servant.

The Deputy High Commissioner and Philippe were seated in the high backed leather chairs in the plush office.

"I think, Philippe, that you have known me long enough to call me Charles." Philippe nodded. The two men were drinking coffee when the servant knocked and brought the photographs in. Charles was a little taken aback as he examined the first photograph. The servant remained po-faced as Charles dismissed him with a wave of his hand. Philippe observed the concern on Charles' face.

"Is the detail graphic?"

"Indeed," replied Charles, handing Philippe the photograph, "take a look for yourself."

Philippe's eyebrows went up and his jaw hung open. "What is this?" he questioned in disbelief.

"I believe 'bollocks' is the English term for it."

Philippe was holding a photograph of a large pair of testicles adorned with red hair. Charles was shuffling through the rest of the photographs, all of which seemed to be of the same ilk. He picked up the phone and asked for Jean Paul to be sent in to join them.

"Come here," his father said. "Do you recognise these?"

Gigolos

He handed his son the photographs. Jean Paul laughed at first, but soon stopped when he realised the other two men were far from amused.

"Do we know if any of the Osprey's crew had red hair?" Charles asked, looking from his son to Philippe. Philippe shook his head and Jean Paul hesitated, before speaking quietly.

"The Scotsman is quite grey, but I am fairly sure there is some red in his hair."

Charles nodded. "Of course, of course..."

"He must have switched the roll," said Jean Paul.

"Quite so, but he must also be privy as to what is on the photographs. The question is, is it all an elaborate hoax by the crew of the Osprey, or does the Scotsman really have the photographs?"

Charles mulled this over for a while before dismissing his son with a curt "thank you, you may leave us now."

As Jean Paul reached the door, his father added "one more thing, Jean Paul. Mention this to no one while we formulate our next move." Jean Paul nodded and went out, closing the door quietly behind him.

Charles poured two large brandies. Passing one to Philippe, he sat back in his chair with his eyes closed and his chin resting upon the back of his hands.

"It seems to me, Philippe," he reflected, "that only the Scotsman could have switched the film. We can assume by his actions that he knows the content of the photographs and also their value. Now he appears to me to be both street-wise and opportunist. I think we can safely assume that he is not an ecologist or nuclear campaigner. It will be difficult, but not impossible, for him to send the film off the island, unless of course he is not acting alone."

Philippe nodded in agreement. "So what does he want?"

"Why money of course. Is that not what makes the world go around?"

Philippe started to protest. "Our government will not pay blackmailers!"

Charles held up his hand. "Leave the politics to the professionals, Philippe. This may work to our advantage and solve another little problem into the bargain."

"In what way?"

"Give me a little time to make a few phone calls and then I will explain it to you. Also find out what is happening on the Osprey. See if they try to contact anyone here or deviate from their course."

"Very good."

"Oh, and have the post office and customs examine closely any UK or other overseas post."

Rikki complained to Ally when Byron didn't return the following morning, but by the afternoon she was getting a little worried. "Not like him be so late," she said to Pascale. Pascale suggested that she try phoning the hotel where Chantalle worked, so Rikki gave them a ring. The receptionist confirmed that the couple were both there but that they hadn't been well with a nasty stomach bug of some sort. She also explained in a long-winded manner that the Don had been there earlier and was planning on bringing Byron back with him when he came over later.

Rikki shook her head; she had her suspicions and said something to Sid in their own language. Sid mumbled something back at her, waving his hand before going off to collect more empty glasses.

The place was filling up nicely when the Don arrived in his jeep with a rather bedraggled-looking Byron in tow.

Gigolos

"What happened tae you?" asked Ally.

"Well, err, we tried Sid's recipe..."

Ally scratched his head. "Recipe for what? Disaster by the sounds of it."

"It was for an, err, well, an aphrodisiac I suppose you would call it."

Ally raised an eyebrow. "And does it work?"

Byron pointed down to his crotch and whispered "I've had a stiffy for nearly twenty four hours now!"

"Aye, and the side effects make you shit the bed I suppose."

Byron nodded, crestfallen. "But I'm sure that once this is researched properly... I think if I can extract the citrate..." he waffled on.

"Go on with you," Ally laughed, shaking his head, "you'd better take yourself off tae bed before you get arrested for having a concealed weapon in your trousers." Byron shuffled off.

"Thanks for bringing him back," Ally said to the Don, "and whilst you're here can you come outside a minute? I've a wee favour tae ask."

They walked out onto the veranda as Ally explained. "I've got a wee package I wish tae post tae mah Mammy. It's kind of personal and I don't want the local authorities going through it."

The Don scrutinised Ally sharply.

"I will make it worth your while."

The Don let out a long stream of cigar smoke and wiped an imaginary spec of ash from his sleeve.

"If you're sure you know what you are doing, Scotsman."

"Aye," said Ally, taking a long drag on his own cigarette, "I'll give it tae you before you leave."

Ally found a jiffy bag in the drawer with the other stationery. He carefully wrote the address on the envelope and, having retrieved the film from the shed, wrapped it in brown paper before sealing it up. He placed the jiffy bag in a towel before walking back into the bar. He spotted the Don sat at a table near the juke box, and in a manoeuvre the Artful Dodger would have been proud of he leant over the Don and deftly stuffed the jiffy bag into his inside pocket, all in the blink of an eye. The Don gave the briefest of nods as Ally shuffled off to collect some more empty glasses.

Frankie put down the phone and leaned back in his swivel chair. The Deputy High Commissioner wanted to see him.

"Like being called to the principal's office. Must be something important," he mused to himself. "Kinda funny he wouldn't discuss it on the phone."

He shrugged before picking up the phone again. "Hi sweetheart," he drawled, "have the car ready for one thirty, I've got to take a trip over to Charles' place; yeah, he wants a pow wow."

The servant showed Frankie into the Deputy High Commissioner's office.

"Sit down, Frankie." Charles went through the usual pleasantries before cutting to the chase.

"A number of years ago Van Horen wanted to develop the lagoon your casino stands on. He planned to build a hotel and a marina there."

"Go on," said Frankie.

Charles poured them both a drink. "At that time this was impossible, what with the fire and all that."

Frankie sipped his drink, interested but not wanting to give anything away.

"I - or rather the government - think that now would be a good time for the expansion of the tourist

Gigolos

industry on the island. Furthermore - and I think this would be particularly beneficial to you – they are proposing we build an airfield."

Frankie tried not to look surprised. "And where would you propose to do that?"

"On the land behind Gigolos, and allow you to replace Frankie's with a purpose built hotel and marina."

Frankie whistled. "That's a major investment. Why the change of tune?"

Charles looked him square in the eye. "I have my reasons... But my main concern at the moment is that I want that bar gone and the two idiots that own it out of here."

"So let me see if I've got this right. You want me to persuade them to sell their bar and land to me, and I take it you will be taking your usual commission."

Charles nodded. "I want you to offer them an exorbitant price for the bar."

Frankie frowned and then thought for a moment. "Wouldn't it be easier if I just had them killed? A little accident of some sort, a fire in their air conditioner perhaps?" He smiled at his own black humour, but Charles shook his head.

"No, no violence." Frankie shrugged as Charles continued "No...they have...what we shall call it...? Insurance."

The penny dropped with Frankie. "I see," he said. "They have something you want and you expect me to buy it for you." He started to laugh but Charles cut him dead with a stare. Frankie put his glass down. "Ok, so what's so important?"

"This goes beyond me," Charles said, leaning forward slightly, "it's a matter of national security."

"So what numbers are we talking?"

"Two million francs, plus my..."

"That's an awful lotta money!" Frankie spluttered, producing a handkerchief from his pocket and dabbing his partially bald head.

Charles nodded. "Indeed, but you get an airfield, a marina and a hotel, along with my lasting gratitude."

Frankie looked at his glass. "I haven't got the authority to sanction this, Charles. Gimme a couple of days; I will have to talk to the syndicate."

"Very well, but I can assure you that your little operation will be shut down by the end of the month should you not comply."

Frankie stood up. "Thanks for the drink; I'll be in touch." He knew better than to say anything else, and felt a little queasy stepping out into the bright sunlight after the relative gloom of the long hallway.

"Back to the bar, sweetheart," he said to the pretty young driver of the car. How in hell was he going to sell this one to the boys back East?

Mooring the platform had proved trickier than expected. They had towed it into the lagoon just after first light, and had positioned it twice before Ally was happy with its final location. Simmo had been pedalling around it like a nautical traffic warden, managing to keep the odd bather away. Pascale commentated on how smart it looked with its plate glass and stainless steel.

"It's a wonder it got here at all," Ally muttered - the tow rope had snapped bringing it into the lagoon and it had got caught on the reef – "Aye well, at least we were able tae drag it off with nae real damage done." He smiled at the thought of Byron and his yacht.

Gigolos

The Don arrived later that afternoon. The new attraction had immediately become popular with the bathers, and he stood on the veranda with Ally, admiring their handiwork.

"Your parcel was posted in LA yesterday." The Don didn't take his eyes from the platform as he spoke. "I had one of the stewardesses take it for me; shouldn't take too long to get to Glasgow from there."

Ally nodded. "Thanks."

The Don turned now, holding his companion's gaze. "As I've said, Scotsman, be careful."

Ally looked at the platform thoughtfully.

It was quite a formal invitation that arrived in the post. There was to be a meeting of all business owners on the island, to be held at the Deputy High Commissioner's residence. Ally and Simmo had been invited, and had been asked if they could be there an hour earlier than the other business men as there was something specific that the Deputy High Commissioner wished to discuss.

"What's it all about?" asked Simmo.

"I nae know," Ally replied, "am thinkin' that it may nae be a good idea if you come with me though, I nae want tae see any fisticuffs with that Jean Paul...I'll take Rikki with me."

Simmo shrugged. "Ok."

"And besides, wee man, I nae think you have anything smart tae wear."

"Cheeky git!" Simmo retorted, but he knew Ally had a point.

Rikki was suspicious. "Why you no want Simmo there?"

Ally shook his head. "Err, no real reason, it's just I can see there being trouble if him and Jean Paul are there. And besides he cannae speak French and you can."

Ally looked quite uncomfortable in a shirt and tie. Rikki was fussing over him straightening his collar. She had dusted off the seats in the Land Rover. Ally insisted on driving and Rikki sat thoughtfully in the passenger seat. It didn't take them too long to get to the ranch and being there early meant there was plenty of parking. Rikki spoke to Maurice in French who directed them to park by the manège. Ally had never been here before and was quite impressed at the place.

"Aye," he said to Rikki, "a few bob's worth of horse meat in them stables I'm thinking."

Rikki shook her head.

They made their way over to the house. The servant led them inside and showed them to the Deputy High Commissioner's outer office where his secretary was and they sat down. Ally, in Oliver Hardy fashion, fiddled with his tie uncomfortably. The intercom buzzed and Charles asked his secretary for the two men to be sent in. After a brief conversation in French, the secretary asked if just the gentleman would go in and if the young lady might wait outside.

Ally was shown in, leaving Rikki sitting in the outer office. Ally was surprised to see Frankie sitting with the Deputy High Commissioner.

"Hi Ally," he waved, "come in, sit down. Don't suppose you know Charles?"

"Cannae say I've had the pleasure," said Ally. He was going to offer Charles his hand but somehow he had the feeling that it wouldn't be accepted.

"Help yourself to cognac," said Charles, motioning to a tray with a decanter and glasses on the table. Ally took in the room as he helped himself. The ceilings were high, the walls lined with leather-bound books; there was an ostentatious desk in front of the window and a large fireplace with a picture depicting a French Napoleonic naval scene above it, which particularly caught Ally's eye. *Heroes* was the name on the back of the ship in the painting. In the centre of the room stood three high-backed, tooled leather chairs placed around a small ornate table. Ally sat down.

"Mind if I smoke?" he asked, producing the battered Golden Virginia tin.

Charles wrinkled his nose as Ally made a point of offering him one, which he declined with a wave of his hand. Frankie shook his head and produced a packet of Pall Mall. He lit his own cigarette before offering Ally a light, and began to speak through the growing haze of cigarette smoke.

"I want to talk to you about your bar."

"What about it?" said Ally.

"Well we think you've done a fantastic job with the place, but..."

"There's always a *but*."

"Sure is. Before your time here I wanted to buy your place, had some big plans to build a new hotel and a yacht marina. One of the major drawbacks to expanding trade on this island has always been its lack of an airport." Frankie paused.

"Go on," said Ally.

"At one time the government didn't want to see overdevelopment on the island, but everyone agrees that an airfield and marina is the way forward.

"And this everyone includes him?" Ally interjected, pointing at Charles, "and, err, your business associates?"

"You cotton on fast."

"Aye, well, I don't know whether I fancy selling."

"But you haven't heard my offer yet."

"Go on."

"Two million francs."

Ally sucked in his teeth.

"That is a very reasonable offer," Frankie added, leaning forward, "and you and I both know your place ain't worth jack shit, so I suggest that you take the money and run."

Ally paused for a moment, a little taken aback, absently producing another rollie from the tin. "I will have tae talk tae my partner."

Frankie smiled. "Sure. Oh, and one more thing, there are a few little terms and conditions, but Charles will tell you all about those."

Charles thanked Frankie. "Now if I may have a word with Alastair in private?"

"Sure thing Charles," said Frankie, getting up. "I think the others should be arriving about now."

He left the room and Charles poured himself another drink as Ally sat there impassively. Then Charles spoke quietly.

"I want the film, Alastair."

"What fil..."

"Bollocks," said Charles, "or to be precise, your bollocks." He produced a small pistol from his pocket. "I want the film you switched from Pascale's camera. Believe me I would have no qualms about killing you right here and now. My government wants it back and we will get it." Ally rubbed his chin. "On completion of this deal you will hand over the film, then you and your friend will leave French Polynesia forever. Understood? And if you have been foolish enough to develop it then I want all the negatives and prints as well. In the meantime you will look after that film as though your life depended upon it." Charles put the pistol back into his pocket. "Now I suggest you go out and join the other guests."

Ally downed what was left of his drink in one gulp and headed out of the door.

Gigolos

Ally took Rikki by the arm and led her away from the outer office. His hand was shaking slightly as he lit a cigarette.

"What wrong?" asked Rikki, as they entered the ballroom where the other guests were chatting and drinking around an informal buffet. "What *wrong*?" she asked again, more insistently.

"Err...nothing," said Ally hesitantly. Rikki stared at him hard. "Err...Frankie wants to buy the bar."

Rikki shook her head before replying determinedly. "You no sell."

Ally shrugged. "Aye...it's a very good offer."

"No sell Frankie! No sell anyone! We got good home here, bar make money now."

Ally squirmed a little under her pleading gaze, and let out a plume of cigarette smoke. "Come on," he said, "let's see what these bozos have got to say."

It was Jean Paul who thanked everyone for attending the meeting. He told them of the proposed new development, explaining that they had considered a number of options before settling upon this one. He emphasised the importance of having an airport on the island in this day and age, and also how the new marina would make it the number one sailing location in Polynesia. He explained that negotiations and planning were still at very early stages but that he hoped he could rely upon their support.

The speech was delivered in French, so Rikki translated this to Ally in short whispers. Ally slackened his tie off. He was quite relieved when Jean Paul finished and a small crowd began to applaud. He looked across the room to where the Don stood. He was not applauding. He looked at Ally, shook his head gently then looked away.

Ally hastily grabbed another drink from a passing waiter. "I could do with a piss," he said to Rikki, handing her his glass. He wandered off to find the toilet, asking one of the waiters for the bathroom. The waiter looked at him a little perplexed before pointing to a door at the top of the staircase. Ally nodded in a gesture of thanks and set off for the bog. When he opened the door and went inside, he realised what the waiter's confusion had been. This literally *was* a bathroom. It had no toilet, merely a bath and basin.

"Feck it!" said Ally, who was quite tall enough to piss in the sink. "I'll just open the tap and play the *Water Music*."

Having finished, he mooched around; in one corner a small closet was packed with aftershaves, deodorants, razors, shoe shine stuff and a hair dryer, all in unopened containers. An object on the shelf caught his attention. The writing on the box was mainly in French; the word *fuzzbuster* was all he could make out. He tipped it out and it fitted nicely into the palm of his hand.

"Aye," said Ally to himself, "might be a good time to change my appearance," at the same time dropping his trousers and pants. He was thinking that this must be one of those personal shavers and he proceeded to place the *fuzzbuster* against his hairy gonads. Almost simultaneously with flicking the switch, Ally let out an almighty scream as the device meant for de-fluffing garments gorged itself on his bright red pubic hair. Ally couldn't get the bloody thing off, despite the fact that in some places it had ripped patches of hair out by the roots. Rikki, standing at the bottom of the stairs, recognised the scream and charged upwards towards the source. The waiter had also heard the commotion and was already using a pass key to open the door. He couldn't help

Gigolos

but smile as he saw Ally with his trousers round his ankles wrestling the still hungry gadget. Rikki shoved the waiter back outside and closed the door with a clunk.

"Get it off!" screeched Ally. Rikki managed to cut the power but it was firmly entangled in Ally's pubes and beads of sweat stood out on his head. After a root in the closet Rikki found and opened a packet of razor blades and carefully started to cut the hair away from the fuzzbuster.

"Oh for Christ's sake be careful!" said Ally, looking at the glinting blade held between Rikki's dainty fingers. "It's bad enough being plucked but I nae need circumcising tae boot."

"You wanna do?" Rikki quipped back.

"No, err, you carry on."

It didn't take Rikki long to free him. She put the offending item on the shelf near the bath.

"That no razor," she said to him, "take fluff from trouser!"

"Aye, well, now you tell me! Come on, let's grab another drink and get out of here. I've had enough ball-ache for one day."

Ally was very quiet on the way back. There was an awful lot of money up for grabs. His mind got to thinking that if that was what the French were prepared to pay, then what would other interested parties be willing to part with? He shuddered, dismissing the thought and knowing deep down that he was in over his head.

Rikki, too, hardly said a word on her way back. Everything had been so good, but now it looked like things might be starting to fall apart again. What if Ally were to go away and leave her? She loved him. There were tears in her eyes as she bumped the Land

Rover over the last pot-holed patch of gravel in the yard at Gigolos. She pulled it up to a sharp halt, then jumped out and ran into the bar, tears welling up in her eyes. Byron and Simmo looked at each other.

"Seems upset," said Byron, stating the obvious to Simmo.

"I'll go see," said Simmo, but Ally followed her in before he had the chance and went straight into the back without saying a word.

It was some time later when Ally came back into the bar.

"Everything ok?" asked Simmo.

Ally grunted. "She's a wee bit upset."

"Why, what's wrong?"

"Och, it's just been one of them days. I nearly had mah balls chewed off."

"What?! They gave you down the banks?" Simmo looked confused.

"Nae I *literally* nearly had mah balls chewed off!"

Ally pointed to his crotch and relayed the tail of the fuzzbuster to a nigh on hysterical Simmo. After Simmo had calmed down again Ally said that he needed to talk to him about the bar later, after they had closed.

"Ok," said Simmo, wondering what all the cloak and dagger was about.

It was a little later that Rikki appeared. To Simmo it looked like she had been crying.

"You ok?" he asked.

Rikki nodded and tried to smile

"Sure?" he asked, more gently. Rikki nodded again but Simmo was not convinced.

Gigolos

Simmo hadn't seen much of Pascale; she had been spending most of her time in their room, catching up on writing her paper. But she was positively beaming when she came into the bar and waved Simmo over.

"I've finished it!" she exclaimed

"What?" said Simmo, "it's all done?"

"Not quite, but it just needs a little tidying up here and there before I submit it."

Simmo gave her a big hug. "Well done you!" Pascale smiled again. "So what's the next wonder of the deep to be solved?" he continued, "seven legged octopuses? Three breasted mermaids?"

Pascale giggled. "I am not sure," she said. "We will have to see how well my paper is received, but I still like the idea of the diving school in the lagoon."

Simmo laughed. "Real treasure hunting! Sounds daft enough to work, or perhaps you could charge snail fanciers to come and have a look at Brian's gaff! Do snail fanciers have an identifying trait, like train spotters wear anoraks?"

"Well, I suppose they might have little fishing nets."

"Mmmm, I wouldn't mind seeing you in fishnets."

"Ooh la la!" Pascale shook her head and pulled tongues at him, then headed out onto the veranda to collect some glasses.

The evening trade was picking up. Unusually, Ally wasn't at his usual spot at the bar; in fact he was nowhere to be seen.

"Where is he?" Simmo asked Byron.

Byron shrugged and then said "I thought I saw him go into the back...with a bottle, earlier."

Alarm bells began to ring in Simmo's head. He would get Sid or Pascale to mind the bar for him if there was any sort of a lull. Eventually there was a bit of a let up and he went out back to find his friend.

Ally was sitting on the bed, a rather large scotch in one hand and the inevitable rollie in the other, staring absently at the old photograph of his uncle in the IRA. Simmo closed the door. Ally motioned to a glass on the chest of drawers, and Simmo picked it up and held it out to Ally, who poured a measure equal to his own into the glass.

"What are we drinking to?" asked Simmo

Ally rubbed his chin and thought for a moment. "The Titanic." Simmo looked puzzled. "Aye, cos one minute it's all plain sailing and the next a bloody iceberg comes out of nowhere."

"Are things that bad?" asked Simmo, not wanting to push Ally but still not knowing what the problem was.

"Aye, well, in a manner, or maybe not."

Simmo could see another bottle on the table, only that one was empty. "You're not making much sense," he said.

"Well, wee man, what would you say if I told you we were rich, or potentially rich – Rockefeller rich?"

Simmo was lost. "Sorry Ally, I don't follow."

"That Frankie, right? He once had big plans, and now it seems he has got 'em again."

"What plans?" Simmo was now becoming exasperated.

"He wants what's ours," said Ally, pouring himself another extremely large one.

"What? He wants to buy the road?"

"Nae, not the road, the whole bloody lot. The bar, the lagoon, the land, the road, everything."

Simmo started to laugh.

"I tell you man, I'm being serious."

"So what's the deal then? Come on, what's he offering?" said Simmo, slightly bemused.

Gigolos

Ally sighed and then said, slowly, "two million francs."

Simmo sat down slowly on the bed next to Ally and then he, too, poured himself a generous glass. "Jesus!" He swallowed a large gulp of scotch. "Are you sure it's not some kind of a wind-up?" Simmo noticed that the rims of Ally's eyes were showing red.

Ally shook his head. "Nae wee man, this was nae wind-up."

The two men sat there in silence for a few moments until it was broken by Byron hammering on the door.

"Simmo, help, quick!" he shouted, "I was trying to change the gas but I've got the connector stuck!"

"How many times have I told you?!" shouted Simmo through the door, "lefty loosey, righty tighty!" He stood up, shaking his head. "I'd better go and have a look," he said to Ally, "the last thing we need is him snapping the fitting off in the bloody gas bottle."

Ally nodded. "Icebergs; bloody icebergs," was all he said, with a slight slur to his voice.

Simmo found Byron, who had somehow cross-threaded the fitting and the gas was hissing out. In the process he had also managed to give himself a small freeze burn on his hand.

"You go back and give them a hand in the bar," said Simmo, "I'll sort this out. Tell them I will have to knock the gas of for a few minutes."

Byron nodded and shuffled off, moaning about his hand. Simmo shook his head before concentrating upon the icy fitting. Luckily enough the thread wasn't too badly damaged. He fetched a small file from the shed, and after a little fettling with the file he was able to repair and tighten up the fitting and returned to the bar with a sigh of relief. It was chaotic inside, with customers in ranks three deep and all wanting beer. It took a good fifteen minutes or so to clear the backlog. Rikki was unusually quiet but Simmo was far too busy to pay her much attention. Ally was conspicuous by his absence, but with Pascale's help they were coping. It proved to be one of the busiest nights of the season and it was well into the early hours of the morning before anyone went to bed.

Despite the hour, Simmo found that he couldn't sleep. "All that money," he thought to himself. Eventually he drifted off with thoughts of Mrs C surrounded by brochures and salesmen... ordering an endless stream of new kitchens and a new Bentley which was duly consumed by a giant sea snail that spoke French... it had been a long day...

Simmo woke up to find Pascale smiling at him.
"You were restless last night," she said, "you were talking in your sleep."
"Was I?" said Simmo, rubbing his eyes.
"Yes," she giggled, "at one point you were yelling "don't eat the car Brian!'"
Simmo started to giggle too. "Must have been something I ate!"
"Have Rikki and Ally had a row?"
Simmo shifted around to look at her, getting tangled up in the sheets in the process and almost falling out of bed. He thought for a while. "I'm not too sure. Apparently when he went up to that shindig at the ranch, Frankie offered to buy the bar."
"*What*?!" Pascale raised both eyebrows.
"Apparently he wants to buy us out."
Pascale started to laugh. "Competition got too much for him!" she giggled.
"No, seriously, he wants to buy the lot - the bar, the lagoon, the land. He wants to build a new hotel-come casino, a marina and - get this - an airstrip."

Gigolos

"But you can't! It would destroy the ecology! I thought the local government was totally against overdevelopment, particularly here."

"I don't know," said Simmo, now wide awake, "but you won't believe this: Frankie offered Ally two million francs."

Pascale's jaw dropped. "You wouldn't sell, would you?"

Simmo didn't know what to say. "Erm…I haven't thought about it; it's just starting to sink in."

Pascale stared at him, hard.

"I need to talk to him properly, he was quite drunk last night and much of what he said wasn't making sense." Pascale didn't look too sure but Simmo took her hand. "If I could buy you anything you wanted, what would you have?"

Pascale squeezed his hand and looked down. "Nothing," she said. "I have you and everything I want right here." Simmo felt a big lump rise in his throat. He pulled her close and kissed her.

Pascale found Simmo on the beach sorting out the pedalos.

"Hi," she said to him, "have you had a chance to talk to Ally yet?"

Simmo shrugged; he had tried that morning but Ally had been evasive and ill-tempered."

"I tried," he said, "but he just kept avoiding the questions. He took the Land Rover and went off to town."

Pascale gave Simmo a hand to launch the last pedalo. Simmo straightened up, and then sat on the boat, deep in thought.

"If I didn't know him better I would think he was hiding something, or at least holding something back."

"You know him better than me."

Simmo shook his head. "And I haven't seen him hit the bottle like that since God knows when, Glasgow maybe. Christ, how long ago was that?"

Pascale sat down next to him. "Rikki thinks he will take the money and run away."

"Run away where? I can't exactly see him as an international playboy in Monte Carlo, can you? You know, grubby vest and a knotted hankie on his head." Pascale started to giggle. "I'll tell you one thing though," Simmo continued, "I am one hundred percent certain he loves Rikki, although I don't think you would ever get him to admit it. I just can't figure out what's going on." He changed the subject. "Have you heard anymore from Sven?" Pascale had mentioned the brief phone call she had had from him.

"No," she said, "other than what he implied about the holiday snaps being ruined."

"What will he do? Will he have another crack or return to New Zealand?"

Pascale pursed her lips. "I really don't know," she said, sighing. "I don't think there will be another opportunity like the last one again. If only we could have published those photographs! I think the public outcry would have put an end to it."

Simmo held her hand. "You can't win them all you know," he said softly.

Ally had taken himself off into town; he had parked up and found himself wandering around the quay, absently looking over the various craft tied up alongside. God! He wished he could just get on one and bugger off somewhere - anywhere. Why had he been such a smart arse? He should have just taken the film, but he hadn't been able to help himself giving the bastards the finger - or a load of bollocks -

Gigolos

the thought of which brought him the briefest of smiles. He needed someone to talk to, but he didn't want to talk to Simmo. A thought crossed his mind: the only person he could talk to was the Don. He might be able to help, or at least give him some advice.

He drove up to the Don's place, but he wasn't there. He managed to communicate a message to one of the workers for the Don to get in touch with him and, that done, he took the Land Rover and headed back to the bar.

Ally bumped the Land Rover over the gravel and into the yard. The Don's jeep was there. Byron was standing at the end of the bar, engrossed in a book.

"Where is the Don? Ally demanded.

Byron looked up. "In the back," he replied hesitantly. "He is with Rikki I think."

Ally went into the back. The Don and Rikki were still talking as Ally slipped silently into the room. Ally coughed.

"Ah, Scotsman," said the Don. "Rikitea and I were just talking about you."

"Nothing bad I hope."

"Not at all." The Don said something to Rikki in her own language and she nodded, smiling a little at Ally as she left the room. "I've asked her to fetch us a drink; I think we need to talk."

Ally shuffled a little before popping the inevitable rollie into his mouth. The two men stood in silence as Rikki came back with a bottle of scotch on a tray and two glasses.

"Thank you," said the Don, taking one of the glasses. He sat down on one of the small chairs and Ally sat on the bed. Rikki poured them both a drink before putting down the bottle on the dressing table and scuttling out of the room. The Don produced a cigar and Zippo and the room soon began to fill with a hazy miasma.

The Don focused on a faded photograph on the wall. "Who is that?"

Ally regarded the picture. "It's mah uncle."

"Ah yes, the Irish freedom fighter; I remember you telling me about him."

"Aye."

The Don let out a long stream of smoke. "A brave man standing up for what he believed in. Let me tell you, Scotsman, about our struggles for freedom. The French occupied this region in the 1840s. In Tahiti there were big battles between our people and the French soldiers. We have been resisting them in our own way ever since. King Pomare led the resistance back then. He waged a bloody guerrilla war against them from his mountain stronghold. Believe me, Scotsman, we have long sort our independence; many of us fought for the free French during the Second World War, the French promising us independence in return."

"Aye, the British did the same with the Irish during the First World War."

The Don nodded. Pouvannaa was our leader after the war. He organised the resistance but he and many of his supporters were arrested and held for several months after a large dockside demonstration in 1947... But that," the Don paused and took another long puff on his cigar, "just made us more determined.

"In 1949 our leader, Pouvannaa, was elected to the French lower house with a huge majority. Again, Scotsman, in 1952, he was re-elected and then two years later won an overwhelming majority in the Territorial Assembly. We tried in early '59 for a secession from France, but De Gaulle was trying to

Gigolos

bring about a referendum for a fifth republic, and with the ongoing struggle for Algerian independence he saw a 'no' vote in any of France's colonies as a vote for their own freedom. He made it quite clear that, if such a thing were to happen, they would pull out instantly and, of course, cut off all their aid and support, which would have left us destitute and unable to function. Then as now they controlled the entire infrastructure."

The Don took a sip of whiskey. "We also got wind that they were to move their nuclear testing from Algeria to French Polynesia."

This was Ally's cue to take a drink.

"The French resorted to dirty tactics, economic blackmail and pressure on individuals; they even managed to force a split in the party."

"Aye, I can well believe that."

"You know, Scotsman, that there are 118 islands spread out over an area the size of Australia? So, what did they do?"

Ally shrugged.

"They banned him from the radio."

Ally nodded. "The British government did the same to Jerry Adams, the Sinn Fein leader."

Both men nodded, and sat in silence for a moment.

"After that," the Don continued, "the French tried to silence Pouvannaa. They arrested him on trumped up charges and sentenced him finally to fifteen years in exile. His party was banned in 1963 because we protested about the nuclear programme and the influx of French troops and personnel flooding the islands. Many people left their traditions - farming and fishing - and went to work for the French. Our children weren't even allowed to speak their own language at school." The Don paused. "I, too, spent many years in exile."

Ally looked up from his drink and stared at the Don.

"I had to take a stand, Scotsman; I considered it was a small price to pay. The question is, will *you* take a stand?"

Ally gulped.

The Don looked at Ally hard. "I have heard about your entanglement."

Ally spluttered. "I did nae know it was a fuzzbuster, I thought it was a shaver!"

The Don laughed. "No not that, although I heard about it too. The photographs, Scotsman; it took me a little while to figure it all out."

Ally lowered his head. "They threatened to kill me," he said slowly, again looking up from his drink.

The Don took another cigar from his pocket and lit it, a small tendril of smoke drifting into the air.

"If you go public, Scotsman, with the photographs in all the newspapers, it would be very difficult for them to kill you."

Ally looked confused.

"It would reflect very badly on them."

"Aye, but it's not your arse in a sling."

The Don smiled. "It might be all our arses."

They were disturbed by Simmo crashing through the door. "Sorry," he said. "Ally, can you give me a hand? Bloody Byron has only gone and got himself stuck in the glass washer."

Ally sighed.

"Yeah, the soft git went to take the glasses out while it was still going... with a towel. It's got wrapped around his wrist and the spindle. I don't think he is too badly hurt but he is squealing like a stuck pig."

Ally got up. "Duty calls," he said to the Don, raising his eyebrows and downing his drink in one before heading out after Simmo. The Don stared at the photo on the wall for a short while before he too headed back out into the bar.

Luckily enough for Byron he was just a little bruised. Rikki had the foresight to pull the plug out as soon as Byron had started screaming. Ally had to hold him still whilst Simmo cut the towel away with a Stanley knife.

"What possessed you to reach in with a bloody towel in your hand?" Simmo asked, exasperated.

"The glasses were hot," replied Byron in a shaky voice.

"It's a good job it's buggered and the belts slip," replied Simmo, "it could have twisted your arm right off."

Ally started singing "come on baby, let's do the twist." Rikki gave him a dig in the ribs.

"Och," said Ally, "he'll nae do that again in a hurry." Simmo didn't look convinced.

Pascale was positively beaming when she came into the bar.

"Someone looks happy," said Simmo.

"I am!" she said, throwing her arms around him and giving him a kiss. "My paper has been very well received."

"Fame at last," said Simmo.

"No - not fame, but recognition."

"Well that deserves an even bigger kiss," said Simmo, folding her into his arms.

"Put her down!" shouted Ally, "and bring some mixers in. Our mate here cannae lift with that arm."

Pascale raised her eyebrows quizzically.

"Don't ask," Simmo explained, "he managed to get himself caught in the glass washer. He's all right though, just twisted his wrist a little."

Pascale shook her head and laughed.

"Honest to God," said Simmo, "if you ever need a human guinea pig to safety test something, he's your man. I've never known anyone so clever and so stupid all at the same time."

"Oh well, as long as he wasn't hurt," replied Pascale, stifling her giggles.

Simmo smiled and then quipped "I dread to think what would happen to him if the phone rang whilst he was ironing."

The season was drawing to a close, and although the bar had been relatively busy that evening, most of the customers had gone, just leaving the old boys and a couple of diehards to send on their way. Rikki knew that the rains were coming soon and was making plans with Sid and Ally to tidy the shed in readiness for bringing in the loungers and tables.

"Aye," said Ally, we dinnae want tae get caught out like last time." He was absently rubbing the scar on his head.

Simmo was waiting for an opportunity to get Ally on his own. He needed to find out what was going on. What had he and the Don been talking about? He had only caught a brief snippet of their conversation, and Rikki definitely wasn't her usual self.

They had kicked the last of the customers out and the tidying and cleaning up was all but done. Pascale had made them all a brew and, unusually, everyone was munching away on biscuits.

"Where did we get these?" said Ally, stuffing a whole Jaffa cake into his mouth.

Gigolos

"You ordered a case of them," replied Byron.

Ally tried to speak through a mouth full of biscuit. "I nae ordered Jaffa cakes!"

"Oh but you did," Byron replied indignantly, you wanted supplies before the rains, I remember you distinctly asked me to order them."

Ally scratched his head whilst dunking another one into his coffee. Suddenly he slapped his forehead, sending a shower of biscuit in all directions.

"It wasn't Jaffa cakes you daft shite; I wanted gaffer tape, not bloody Jaffa cakes!"

Simmo burst out laughing. Ally shook his head and Byron just shrugged.

"I'm just glad said I did nae ask you tae order the inflatables... The lagoon would have been full of bloody blow up dolls by now."

"Oh I don't know," said Simmo, "we could have put a red wig on one and stood it at your place at the bar..."

They were all still laughing when the phone rang. It was Byron who answered it, Simmo giggling at the thought of an ironing Byron singeing his ear. "Who is it?" he asked.

"I don't know," replied Byron, "I can't understand the accent."

"Here, pass it to me. Hello?" replied Simmo to a female with a very board Glaswegian accent. "Hang on a minute, I'll get Ally... It's for you," he said, motioning to his friend with the receiver. I think it's your cousin."

Ally went into the back to use the other phone. When Simmo heard them talking he placed the phone back on its cradle with a click and returned to join the others. Byron offered him a Jaffa cake, but Simmo didn't feel hungry any more.

It was some minutes before Ally came back in. With the inevitable rollie hanging from his lip, he looked at Simmo. "It's Mammy," he said quietly. "She's in a bad way."

They were lying there in the dark, arms around each other.

"Will you go with him?" Pascale asked Simmo quietly.

Simmo thought for a moment. "I ought to, I just don't know if we can afford for both of us to go."

"I think Rikki has that one covered."

"What do you mean?"

"You remember the pearl she found?" Simmo nodded, although Pascale couldn't see him in the dark. "She sold it, for a very good price."

Simmo smiled. "Oh...and to think I thought it was worthless..."

Pascale leaned on her elbows. "I have a little money you can have."

Simmo started to splutter. "No, I couldn't..."

Pascale smiled, a brief glint of moonlight reflecting on her face. "Simmo, my father is a professor of economics at Lyon University. I have my own savings and he sends me quite a generous allowance."

Simmo frowned a little. "Erm, ok, but I will pay you back."

"Settled then!"

"But what about this place? Simmo wrinkled his brow in the darkness.

"Well I'll be here - Byron, Sid and Rikki, too. I am sure we will be able to cope, and anyway the rains will be here soon."

Simmo thought for a while. "Are you sure?"

"Of course I am my darling."

Simmo pulled her close and drifted off into a dreamless sleep.

Old Faces and Familiar Places

Ally was in a bit of a daze. Mammy had had a massive stroke, his cousin had said, and it was only a matter of time...

"Shit," he muttered, pushing himself up out of the chair and forcing himself to think. "Come on," he said to Byron and Sid, who had come in early, "let's get the loungers and the furniture into the shed. We'll take the shutters out first."

Simmo came in from outside. "Can you call the Don?" Ally shouted over to him, "tell him we will be bringing the pedalos in early. I want everything shipshape before the rains, and besides you won't be able tae do the beach and run the bar whilst I'm away... Aye, and I would rather bring them in whilst there is a gang of us here tae do it. It near killed us last time." Ally again rubbed the scar on his head.

"I'm coming with you," replied Simmo. Ally looked surprised. "Don't worry, it's all sorted."

Ally frowned, knowing that the bar and the building work had eaten most of their savings.

"Pascale is lending me a few quid, and I've got a little bit squirreled away."

Ally said nothing. He just put his arm on Simmo's shoulders and nodded, then looked around the bar. Rikki and Pascale had both been up and about early and he hadn't seen them for some time.

"Where are the girls?" he asked.

"They've taken the Land Rover and gone off into town to organise things." Ally lit a fag. "Don't worry," said Simmo, trying to reassure his friend, "everything is in hand."

"Aye, well we'd better crack on then."

It was a busy morning. They placed the shutters in the yard and crammed the loungers into the shed. Sid phoned round a couple of the old boys to come up and help drag the boats into the yard. They left Byron in the bar to serve the odd customer coming in for an early drink.

The afternoon was just as busy, hanging the shutters and trying to get the rest of the clutter back into the shed. Ally was occupied with the generator, checking the batteries and the charger. He had been meaning to service it for a long time. He changed the fuel tank, the fuel filters and the engine oil. On the second try of cranking it over, it fired. "Thank Christ for that," said Ally to himself. He was happy that the batteries were ok and were charging properly; he shuddered at the thought of Byron trying to hand crank it if the batteries failed. He made a mental note to himself to show Sid how to do it. He just had visions of Byron getting a mouthful of starting handle.

Simmo stood in the doorway looking on. Ally certainly had the knack with machinery.

"How's it going," he asked?

"Ok...still blowing smoke like a bastard though." He still needed to do the piston rings but stopped short in his thoughts. If they were still... he shook the thought away.

"Erm, I've been meaning to talk to you," said Simmo cautiously. Ally wiped his hands on the rag Simmo had passed him and looked at him, but they were interrupted by the sound of a car crunching on the gravel. Ally came to the door to see Frankie getting out. It looked like he had a large brown envelope in his hand.

Ally shoved past Simmo. "I want tae have a wee talk tae him," he said hurriedly. This time it was Simmo's turn to stand scratching his head.

Ally put his arm around Frankie and steered him down the drive, away from the bar.

"You guys look busy," Frankie drawled.

"We are... trying to get the place in order before the rains."

Frankie looked up at the sky. "Won't be long now." He turned to look at Ally. "I've brought some papers for you to look at."

"I've got a problem."

"You can get a cream for that," cracked Frankie.

"No!" Ally was exasperated now. "It's mah Mammy, she's had a stroke; she's not expected to live."

"I am sorry about that." Ally looked at him hard. "No, really, we all love our moms."

"I'm going back tae Glasgow tae see her before..." he didn't finish.

Frankie shifted on his feet a little uneasily. "Take this" he said, handing Ally the envelope, "you can study it on the plane."

Ally straightened himself up to his full height, towering over Frankie.

"Look," said Frankie, "this wasn't my idea, and in fact the boys back east ain't too happy, no sir-ee, not happy at all." Ally shrugged. "Whatever you've got on Charles he wants it back, pretty badly, right? So maybe we could do a deal?" Again Ally shrugged, giving nothing away. "Ok," said Frankie, holding up his hands, have it your way." He nodded toward the envelope. "Read through it and let me know one way or the other when you get back." He paused, studying Ally's body language.

There was the briefest hesitation before Ally nodded, saying "aye, we'll be back." Frankie cocked an eyebrow. "Simmo is coming with me."

Frankie nodded slowly. "Good luck –"it was Ally's turn to cock an eyebrow "- with your mom."

Frankie held out his hand and Ally shook it slowly. He watched Frankie walk back to the car; he climbed in and said something funny to the pretty young thing behind the wheel. They pulled away smiling, Frankie giving Ally the briefest of waves before the car turned off down the drive.

Ally stared down at the brown manila envelope in his hands. There was a slight tremor there. Simmo walked out to join him.

"What's that?" he asked, pointing to the envelope.

"Well it isn't from the feckin' *Readers Digest,* replied Ally, glaring. Then he clapped Simmo on the shoulder. "Aye, come on wee man, I've got a bottle of old paddy gathering dust..."

Simmo's world took a lurch, a sudden flashback to the bottle he had once been saving. Ally spluttered a little before saying, "och, come on wee man, I need a drink," and for the first time in a very long while Simmo thought that he needed one, too.

Ally disappeared into the back to get the bottle. Simmo noticed that he didn't bring the envelope back into the bar with him. Ally had just poured them a large one each when the two girls returned from town. Not only had they sorted out all the travel but they had also been shopping. Pascale held up a pair of jeans against Simmo and nodded, pleased with herself.

"You can try these on later," she smiled.

Gigolos

Simmo looked at her, puzzled.

"Well you have made all your jeans cut-offs," she replied to his odd look.

Simmo smiled. "Yeah," he said, "cut-offs and flip-flops are no good in the Glasgow rain."

"Aye at least it will be summer over there," Ally chipped in.

"That's good then," Simmo retorted, "at least the rain will be a bit warmer."

Everything was set for the boys to catch the morning ferry to the main island, then a quick flight to Tahiti and from there to New Zealand.

"New Zealand??" asked Ally.

"Much cheaper go this way," said Rikki, nodding, "no flight from Tahiti." Ally rubbed his chin.

"Trust us," said Pascale, "it might take a little longer but this really was the least expensive way of doing it... From there to Paris, Paris to London, then a quick hop to Glasgow."

"We could get the train tae Glasgow," suggested Ally, who in all reality was still scared shitless of flying.

"Plane quicker," replied Rikki.

Ally started to *um* and *err* but Rikki shut him up with a wave of her hand.

"Already paid for!" she said firmly with her arms folded.

Ally knew there was no point arguing. Pascale handed him an envelope containing the tickets and a hand-written schedule of flight times and departures.

"Pretty efficient," said Simmo. Pascale did a mock curtsy.

Rikki handed Ally another envelope, quite a fat envelope at that. He opened it, his eyebrows raising slightly. It was stuffed with notes.

"I cannae take this," he mumbled, but Rikki closed her hand around his.

"You go see mother, tell her business is good, and tell her you found love."

Ally couldn't get any words out. He pulled Rikki close and held on to her. He wanted to tell her he loved her but could only manage to say "Rikki, Rikki," over and over again.

That night in bed Ally was restless, dreaming and mumbling in his sleep. At one point he called out to his Mammy and awoke with beads of sweat running down his face; he still didn't know what to do. He thought about praying for the first time since he was a child, but dismissed the idea; even if God was real he probably wouldn't listen to the likes of him. "Oh God," he said to himself in the end anyway, "the least you could do is tae send me a fecking sign."

They were all up early the next morning. Pascale was fussing over Simmo, making sure he had everything. There had been a brief scare the previous evening as Simmo had misplaced his passport. He and Pascale had ransacked the room and had just about given up when Rikki came in holding a very dusty passport; it, along with his driving licence, had fallen down the back of the drawers in the big room, which once of course had been his.

As they went out of the door the sign buzzed menacingly. They all looked up at it but, unusually, it seemed quite benign, just spelling *tail*. Ally studied it for a while. A sign! he thought to himself and then said to Simmo "I guess we do have a tale tae tell."

They bundled their gear into the back of the Land Rover, Simmo giving the door an almighty slam that made Ally cringe. He revved up the engine and they set off. Both Rikki and Pascale went with them, bouncing around in the back with the bags.

Ally looked worried. Pascale asked him if he was ok.

"Aye I'm fine," he replied, "just wondering how safe it is leaving Byron there on his own. He burnt a lab down once you know." Pascale laughed.

It didn't take them long to get to the quay, where a small ferry was tied up alongside. The sky was darkening rapidly as they unloaded the gear. Simmo now stood holding hands with Pascale, whilst Ally had his big arm around Rikki's shoulders.

"Looks like the rains are coming," said Simmo.

"Aye," said Ally.

They were disturbed by the sound of a jeep arriving. It was the Don. He waved Ally over.

"I am sorry to hear about your mother, Scotsman."

Ally shuffled a little before stuffing a rollie into his mouth; he nodded and splurged out "thanks."

The Don passed Ally a small piece of paper through the open window of the jeep. Ally looked down at the neat small writing, and then slowly looked back to the Don.

"This is the number of a friend in London," the Don explained. "He is a newspaper man..." he paused "...and he's sympathetic to our cause." He emphasised the *our*. "It would be best if you could memorise the name and number, or at least disguise it in some way if you can't."

Ally looked back at the paper, wrinkling his forehead slightly. "A wee bit cloak and dagger, isn't it?" he said.

"The daggers may well be drawn," replied the Don with an expression resembling Marlon Brando. Ally took a long drag on his fag and the Don smiled.

"Well good luck, Scotsman...and don't worry about the girls, Ally; I will watch over them."

The conversation was interrupted as the ferry fired up its engines. A plume of thick black diesel smoke curled into the air. There was just time for some final kisses and goodbyes as the crew made ready to bring in the gangway, then the two men climbed aboard, Simmo a little awkward in the now unfamiliar cowboy boots.

Within a couple of minutes the gangway was hauled on board and the mooring ropes cast off. Simmo shouted "I love you!" to Pascale, but he wasn't sure that she could hear him over the engine noise. Ally and Simmo leaned on the rail, waving, the boat pitching slightly as it turned from the quay. The engine note changed as the boat sped up to full speed, spray breaking over the bow, quickly leaving the island behind. The boys waved until the girls were mere dots upon the quayside.

As the boat proceeded on its short journey to the main island, the first drops of rain began to fall. Ally and Simmo sat there in relative silence, lost in the moment. Ally studied the Don's piece of paper - he was very adept at remembering things when he wanted to. *Paul Smith*, he read, wondering whether that was an alias or a genuine name.

Simmo woke him from his musings. "Come on Ally, were getting off here."

Ally gathered his bags and his thoughts. The boat tied up quickly and they were soon off. Simmo seemed to be walking a little strangely.

"What's up, wee man?" asked Ally.

"It's the bloody cowboy boots - I think they have shrunk!"

Gigolos

Ally scratched his head. "More likely yer feet have spread from wearing flip-flops all the time."

Simmo nodded, and with a familiar sense of *deja vu* he wished he had packed a pair of trainers.

They dived straight onto the waiting bus, anxious to get out of the rain. Pascale had given Simmo a sensible sized holdall and had carefully helped him pack it. He could smell her evocative perfume on it, and found it comforting and somewhat unsettling all at the same time. God, he thought, he was missing her already. Oh well, too bloody late now. He just hoped that they wouldn't be away too long.

Ally was staring wistfully out of the window, the view obscured by the driving rain on the glass. His thoughts were everywhere but he was desperately trying to concentrate on the name and phone number...

"This *is* the right bus?" asked Simmo, suddenly flustered.

"Aye," said Ally still gazing through the window.
"How do you know?"
"It said airport on the front," replied Ally, dryly.
"Erm, ok."

Simmo was feeling a little out of sorts. He couldn't define it, but he was starting to get a little panicky. Glasgow was an alternative universe where a very different Simmo had once lived. He looked around the packed bus, which contained a curious mix of tourists and locals. There was a gentle murmur of cosmopolitan conversation going on in the background. Simmo tried his best to engage Ally in conversation a couple of times, but his companion remained glued to the window abstractedly, and after a couple of terse *ayes* and *naes* Simmo finally gave up.

The journey passed uneventfully and they arrived at the small airport in plenty of time. Ally, two strides ahead of Simmo, checked them in at the desk. He had thought it prudent to keep hold of both passports along with the tickets.

Simmo took himself off around the few small shops. He was looking for a book to read on the flight. After examining a couple, he finally settled on a story about the Hindenburg, with a picture of a blazing airship on the cover.

Ally frowned and cringed when he saw the book. "Could you nae find one about a bloody shipwreck or something for a change?" He scolded.

"Well, erm, it's not actually about planes," said Simmo uncomfortably.

"Aye, but it's the next best bloody thing!"

Simmo looked at the book's cover. Perhaps, on reflection, it had been a poor choice.

Ally, too, looked for something to read, but there was little choice and nothing there particularly tickled his fancy. In the end he picked up a copy of *National Geographic* simply because it had an interesting picture of an erupting volcano on the cover.

It wasn't long before their flight was due to be called. Ally took the precautionary measure of visiting the gents' before the announcement, but instead of heading for the urinal he chose one of the traps and, having finished his pee, he took the piece of paper the Don had given him, and with a final look he threw it down the pan. During the bus journey he had been silently repeating the name and phone number over and over to himself like a mantra, and now had it firmly placed in his head. He repeated it to himself one last time and then, like a Japanese submarine commander, he said "fire one!" at the same time pulling the lavatory chain and watching the paper

Gigolos

swirl a few times before it disappeared around the s-bend.

"Come on Ally!" shouted Simmo urgently as he emerged from the toilets, "the flight's been called!"

Ally was shaking going up the steps onto the small plane. He had to duck to get through the door, but at least this was a more modern looking aircraft than the last one that they had been on. He put both their bags into the luggage compartments, shouting slightly at Simmo over the noise of the engines and the rain.

"You sit by the window!" I can stretch mah legs down the aisle."

Simmo nodded.

The rain was verging on torrential now. Ally hoped all the instruments were working, because he couldn't fathom how the pilots would be able to see very far...His heart skipped a beat as a maintenance truck approached. He could see its amber flashing lights silhouetting Simmo in the window, but luckily enough it drove straight past. The seat belt and no smoking signs went on and shortly afterwards the plane began to taxi.

Ally shut his eyes as the engines began to roar, but the take-off was smooth and it wasn't long before the signs went off again. Relieved, Ally stuffed a rollie into his mouth. Whether it was the fact this was a more modern aircraft or just that he had an awful lot on his mind, he wasn't quite as jittery as usual. The flight to Tahiti was a relatively short one and it wasn't long before the seatbelt sign went on again, but landing was a different story for Ally. As the plane banked sharply he could feel himself gripping the seat. A luggage locker door on the other side of the plane came open and something fell from it, making a large bang in the aisle, and it was all he could do to keep himself from screaming. Fortunately for him this was the final approach, and within a couple of minutes the plane was safely back on the ground.

"Come on, wee man," said Ally a little shakily, desperately looking around for a bar, "I need a drink."

"I thought you were sickening for something," replied Simmo. Ally looked at him oddly, cocking one eyebrow.

"Well you haven't had a drink up to now, so I...erm..."

Ally nodded in understanding. "I was doing alright till that bloody thing fell from the luggage locker."

"I think it was a book..."

"Well I shit mah pants, wee man! Sounded more like a bloody bomb tae me...Come on, bar's open," said Ally heading into the lounge.

"Shouldn't we check in?" asked Simmo falteringly.

"First things first," said Ally, ordering a large *Red Label*.

He motioned to the bottle but Simmo shook his head." Just a coke for me, thanks."

It was Ally's turn to look surprised. "Are *you* sickening for something?"

"No, I just think I'll wait till we get on board."

Ally finished his drink in one gulp and they went to check in.

As they were walking away a customs official called out to them, beckoning them over with his finger. He asked them to come with him, and led them into a small drab room vaguely smelling of disinfectant, where they were questioned about the purpose of their trip. They were then taken into separate rooms, their baggage was given a thorough going over and both of them were ordered to strip.

Gigolos

Ally didn't like where this was going when he saw one of them putting on latex gloves.

Simmo was already waiting outside when Ally came out, rubbing his backside.

"Aye well next time find someone who hasn't got fat fingers tae do that!" he spat out right in the face of the senior official. The pan-faced man handed him his passport back without saying a word. "Is that it then?" Ally continued angrily, "Can we board the bloody plane now?"

The official shook his head slowly. "You two stay there till the flight is called."

"Well can I nae at least get a drink then?"

Again the official shook his head, before turning away and saying to another customs man, "If they move, arrest them."

"What was all that about?" whispered Simmo, the cogs beginning to turn, "they must think we have something."

Ally laughed. "Have you ever thought of becoming a copper?"

Simmo studied his friend for a moment. "You know, don't you? You know what they are looking for!"

Ally gave him the briefest of nods. Simmo tried to continue but Ally shook his head and put a finger to his lips. "Not now, he whispered, "wait till we're properly alone and out of earshot." He nodded towards the customs official.

They had to wait in uncertainty for about an hour before the flight was called. The customs official followed a few paces behind them until they were almost on the flight. Ally turned and glared at him.

"You'll have tae stick your thumb up your own arse now pal," he growled, before turning back to board the plane.

It was a wide-bodied Air France jet they boarded for New Zealand. They were quite literally the last two to board so there wasn't much delay between their getting seated and the plane taking off. Ally had a fag in his mouth, lighter in hand, just waiting for the no smoking sign to go off. The stewardess came around and asked them in French what they would like to drink. Ally ordered the inevitable and a beer for Simmo.
"You know," said Simmo, we must have learned something whilst we've been out here."
"What do you mean?" asked Ally.
"Well, the stewardess asked you in French and you ordered and answered in French... albeit with a Glaswegian accent."
"Aye, well, you cannae work in a paint factory without getting splashed." Ally was smiling.
"Très bien," said Simmo, laughing.
"Merci, mon petit homme," replied Ally, laughing too. "I suppose we have had to learn the hard way."
"No other way with us two," said Simmo.

For the life of him Ally still couldn't work out why it was cheaper to fly to New Zealand, but in the scheme of things he supposed the extra travelling didn't really count. He just hoped that they would get there before... he shook the thought away and tried to settle into the crappy in-flight movie but gave up in the end, closing his eyes and drifting back to his childhood in Glasgow as he quietly slipped into a deep, distant sleep.

Gigolos

Simmo smiled at Ally's rhino-style snoring. The woman opposite looked a little annoyed so Simmo gave him a slight dig in the ribs, which curtailed the din, at least for a little while.

Simmo settled down into his book. Whilst it was a novel it was quite factual about the events, and he was pleased about that as he had once done a project about the Hindenburg back in the dark ages when he was at school.

The flight passed smoothly and quickly, with only the occasional snore from Ally to acknowledge he was there. When he awoke with a jolt, to learn the flight was almost over, he scratched his head in bemusement.

"You've been out like a light," said Simmo.

Ally stretched, yawned and then motioned to the book. "Any good?" he asked, noting that Simmo had made some serious inroads into it.

"Not bad so far."

"So what do you think really happened to the Hindenburg?"

"Dope." said Simmo.

"There's nae need tae be like that!" rebuked Ally, "I was only asking."

"No!" Simmo was laughing and shaking his head. "*Dope*... it's what they coated the outer skin with - I think it contained aluminium dust; they reckon it built up a static charge. It landed in a thunder storm and when they dropped the mooring lines down - BOOM! - a static discharge, a spark, set the whole bloody thing off."

Ally shuddered. "Sounds like a bloody great flying capacitor." Then he grimaced, adding quietly, "this thing is made of aluminium." He pulled an unlit rollie from his mouth and looked at it before stuffing it back in.

Simmo nodded. "Yeah, but we've got rubber wheels."

Ally didn't look convinced. "Aye, and I'll be needing rubber underpants if we have tae land in a thunder storm." He was going to order another drink when the captain announced that they would be landing shortly and the seatbelt and no smoking signs went on. "Bollocks," said Ally putting his lighter down, having failed to light his fag and leaving it dangling from his bottom lip.

"Come on, wee man, we have tae get across the airport."

"Just give me a minute, my feet are killing me!"

Ally ploughed on ahead, Simmo hobbling behind trying to keep up, clutching his holdall and book at the same time. They checked in without any problems. The flight was on time and, all being well, they wouldn't have too long to wait.

Simmo had nearly left his holdall behind, having put it down to try and wiggle some room in his boots, but Ally was on the ball. "Aren't you forgetting something?" he said, nodding at the bag.

"Oh Christ!!" said Simmo; that would be typical. He was amazed at how many people could be coming and going all at the same time. It must be a logistical nightmare running this place, he thought to himself.

Simmo was getting a little peckish, but decided he would wait until they were on the plane. Whilst they were sat waiting, he tried to tackle Ally again.

"What's going on Ally? What were the customs men looking for?"

Ally shushed him. "Keep your voice down," he whispered, sparking up a rollie. He looked down at his feet and thought for a while before speaking.

"Do you remember, Simmo, that Pascale lost some photographs?"

"What?!" Simmo looked at him. "The ones she took with Sven?"

"Shush!" hushed Ally, trying to calm Simmo's rising voice. He was trying to think how to play this. "Well I did nae trust that Jean Paul; I thought he was up tae something that night in the bar, you know the night he started the fight with you? I had an inkling it was something tae do with the photographs... so I, err, switched the film in her camera, just for safe keeping mind."

Simmo started to splutter. "You stole her film?!" he squawked.

"SHUSH!" said Ally looking around frantically, "shush." He put his big arm around Simmo's shoulder and pulled him close, "let me tell you what happened..."

Ally repeated the tale, explaining how he had overheard the conversation on board the Osprey and worked out that the French were planning to test a new weapon - a nuclear bomb or maybe something even worse. Pascale's friends were going to publish the evidence and hopefully create enough public outrage for the French to renege. Then of course the film went missing, or so everyone thought. Simmo listened intently.

"Aye," said Ally, "unfortunately Jean Paul's father got wind that I had the film."

Simmo's jaw dropped. He went to speak but Ally shushed him again.

"Dinnae worry, wee man, the film's safe. Anyhow, you remember that meeting Rikki and I went tae at the ranch?" Simmo nodded. "Charles, Jean Paul's father, got Frankie tae put the arm on me." Simmo looked a little confused. "Charles leant on Frankie,"

Ally explained, "tae make us the offer for the bar... on one proviso... that I hand over the film."

"Christ," said Simmo, "what did you tell them?" His stomach was turning summersaults.

"I told them I would have tae talk tae mah partner."

Simmo went ashen. "What are we going to do Ally?" he whispered.

"As I see it, we can sell the bar, take the money and run, or we can tell them tae stick it up their arses, hand the film over to the newspapers and hopefully survive the fallout."

Ally laughed at the pun but Simmo just sank down in his seat. "What about the girls?" he said, still reeling from the revelations.

"Och, the Don's looking out for them." But that wasn't what Simmo meant.

The tannoy sounded. "That's our flight," said Ally, "come on." He downed his drink while Simmo fumbled for his bags and followed him out.

They boarded another Air France jet for Paris, via Tahiti (again!) and Los Angeles. Usually Simmo would have been disappointed at not having a window seat, but the whirring cogs in his mind were in full-time overdrive. A large American lady sat to his left was trying to draw him into conversation but Simmo, normally congenial, was having none of it, instead choosing to hide his head in his novel.

When the hostess came around with orders for food and drink Simmo found that his hunger had passed, and settled for a beer instead. Ally, too, only ordered a sandwich and a scotch. Simmo still had some more questions but realised now wasn't the time. Ally could see that Simmo was worried but there wasn't much more he could do to reassure him.

Gigolos

Simmo found he was reading the same page over and over again so in the end gave up, and he tried to switch off by watching the in-flight movie. Ally settled down to his *National Geographic*. It not only covered volcanic activity, but earthquakes and tsunamis. He hadn't realised quite how seismic Polynesia was.

The flight to Tahiti passed relatively quickly and they were soon refuelled and airborne again and off to L.A. Ally was deep in his musings, wondering whether they would get to Glasgow in time... Simmo had calmed down enough to enable him to continue with his book, which was now reaching its climax.
"How are you doing, wee man?" asked Ally suddenly.
"Erm, ok I think; it's been a lot to take in." Ally just nodded.

Simmo finished his book and fell asleep in the middle of another dreadful in-flight movie. Ally, too, succumbed to the drink and the boredom, having read his magazine from cover to cover. He wondered to himself whether, if he had had the chance of a university education, then perhaps he would have liked to have been a volcanologist. He too dozed off with thoughts of volcanoes and earthquakes stalking his dreams.
The flight passed between bouts of drinking and sleeping, the captain finally announcing that they were on time and would be arriving in L.A. shortly.

They had quite a while to wait before the flight to Paris. Simmo decided to go and get a shower, whilst Ally unsurprisingly opted for the bar, first making a brief phone call to Gigolos and speaking to Rikki...

"The girls are ok," he told Simmo. "Byron hasn't managed to burn the place down yet, just caught his hand in one of the shutters."

Simmo just smiled and Ally shook his head; Simmo had managed to get the cowboy boots off, but had the devil's own job getting them back on.

They grabbed something to eat from one of the fast food joints, and then went back to the bar. Ally looked at his watch. "They should be calling our flight soon," he said, and almost on queue the tannoy sounded.

Another long journey loomed ahead of them. Simmo normally liked flying, but the constant travelling was wearing him out. They boarded the plane and settled down. He had meant to look for another book, having finished the Hindenburg story, but couldn't be bothered in the end to hunt for one.

It was dark when they took off, but with no hint of maintenance men. It wasn't long before the cabin crew dimmed the lights and most people turned in for the night.

Ally's rollie shone like a small red beacon in the darkened aircraft. It was a couple of hours into the flight and he was growing impatient. "Come on, come on," he said to himself over and over again, but there were still many hours to go.

Simmo was pondering over what was going to happen when they got back to Glasgow - not so much about Ally's poor mum, but the bar. It had become his world... and what about Pascale? He couldn't see her being too pleased about Frankie turning Brian the snail's home into a boating lake for the rich and famous. But the thought that frightened him the most was what would happen to them if they didn't sell. He also knew that, despite his bravado, Ally was scared too.

Gigolos

The flight had almost passed without incident when Simmo needed to answer the call of nature. The toilet he had been using for most of the flight was now out of order, which meant using the one on the other side of the aisle.

"Let me out!" said Simmo to a disoriented Ally, "I need a pee!"

He made his way to the toilet, went in and did what he had to, but when he came to open the door there was a problem: it wouldn't budge. "Here we go again," thought Simmo with a sigh. It appeared to be catching on the bottom, so he grabbed it under the lock, and by a combination of lifting and shoving the door opened. "Phew!" he thought.

Outside, a young French woman was waiting. She looked a little nervous. In broken English she explained to Simmo that she was scared of small spaces and, having just witnessed the incident, was worried about getting locked in.

"Ah," said Simmo, "claustrophobic. No problem, you just have to lift and push at the same time."

Now a tired Simmo who has been drinking isn't a rational being.

"Tell you what, he continued, "I'll come in with you and show you how to open the door."

The woman didn't look too sure.

"No, no," said Simmo hastily, "I don't mean I will stay in there with you, just show you how to open the door then leave, erm, *je pars*?"

The woman nodded in reluctant agreement. Simmo closed the door and proceeded with his demonstration, only the door wouldn't open again despite his best efforts, and the woman now was starting to panic; she was hyperventilating and making heavy breathing noises. Simmo, very flustered now, tried to calm her down but was only making matters worse.

Outside a small queue of passengers was waiting. Simmo was yanking heavily on the door now.

"I think it's coming" he said but his fellow inmate didn't seem to comprehend, so he gave it another almighty heave and yelled "IT'S COMING!!" Simmo could see that a rubber strip at the bottom of the door had come loose and was wedging it stuck.

"If I can get it up, you pull it off!" he shouted. The conversation echoed through the door to the people waiting in the small queue outside.

The woman finally seemed to understand and pulled while Simmo shoved.

"Oh thank God for that!" he cried with relief, "it's come off at last!"

The pair of them collapsed onto each other and the toilet door swung slowly open. One of the ladies waiting outside gave them a filthy look and tutted as they filed out. The man at the back winked at Simmo.

"Lucky bastard, eh?" he leered. Simmo looked confused. "You know, the man continued, "the mile high club."

Simmo was going to try and explain but in the end it was just easier to wink and smile back.

"You've been a while." said Ally.

"Erm, yeah," said Simmo "I had a problem with the bog door."

Ally shook his head. "You know something, Simmo? If... aye, and this is a mighty big if... if we ever get to heaven and you see St Peter stood there...just promise me you will keep away from those fecking pearly gates!" Simmo laughed.

Ally was just about to spark up when for the final time the no smoking sign went on.

Gigolos

"Shit," he said.

"We're nearly in gay Paris," said Simmo.

"We got intae enough trouble in bloody gay Amsterdam I seem tae remember," said Ally grimly.

Simmo nodded his head.

It didn't take long before the captain had them back on the ground. It was a smooth landing but it still didn't stop Ally digging his fingernails into the seat.

The customs men gave their bags a thorough going over, asking Ally repeatedly the purpose of their visit.

"At least they didn't strip search us this time," said Ally, absently rubbing his arse, "but we will have tae get a move on if we're going tae catch the Glasgow flight."

He led the two of them across the terminal, Simmo still hobbling. They went through the rigmarole of checking in once again.

"Hurry!" said Ally to Simmo.

They made the gate just as it was closing and once again they were the last two to board the plane. It was a much smaller jet this time and it was only full to half capacity. Simmo moved to a window seat and Ally sat next to him in the aisle.

"Hopefully this one won't take long," he said.

"Yeah," said Simmo, "soon be there... I tell you what, though, if I thought lorry drivers had a square arse, God knows what an airline pilot's must look like!"

Ally smiled. "Aye, I dinnae know how many hours we've been sat on ours."

"True," said Simmo, yawning, "and when you think about it we spend our whole working day stood up."

"Nae wonder mah bloody back aches then." Ally groaned.

The flight passed smoothly and without incident, the time measured by whiskey and cigarettes. Simmo sighed at the approaching lights of the city as the plane touched down in a gentle Glasgow drizzle.

The men grabbed their bags and vacated the plane. Ally was fully expecting to get stopped at customs but no one bothered with them this time. They were just walking out of the airport when a familiar female voice from behind stopped them in their tracks.

"Alastair, Simon, there you are! I thought I had missed you."

Both men paused and turned, open mouthed as there, walking towards them, was Mrs C.

Newspapers and Crazy Capers

The whirlwind that she was ushered them out of the terminal into the carpark. Ally had a job squeezing into the back of the two door Golf, Mrs C insisting that the stunned and silent Simmo should sit in the front.

Simmo could see her lips moving, but like a man going under anaesthetic his mind couldn't register what she was saying.

"Don't worry Alastair, we will fetch you back to our place." Simmo shuddered at the 'our,' as she continued. "There you can freshen up, and then I will take you straight to the hospital."

"Aye," said Ally, "err, it's just that I was planning on staying at mah Mammy's."

"Oh, no, no," said Mrs C "That's out of the question. You *must* stay with us, *insist*; we can't have you there in that grotty –" she stopped short. "Can't have you all alone in her flat at a time like this."

Ally mumbled something but, like a scene from *Star Trek*, resistance was futile.

Simmo felt cold despite it being summertime. The rain was running down the side window; to Simmo, the drops looked like tears.

Ally started to roll a fag but both he and Simmo nearly jumped out of the seat as Mrs C yelled, "not in the car Alastair!" Ally finished rolling it, looked at it longingly and put it back in the tin, with the lid making a metallic click.

"Filthy habit," she admonished, with a slight shake of her head.

Simmo felt he was suffocating; it was like he couldn't get enough air into his lungs. The roads were familiar yet not so, all at the same time. He pinched himself...just in case... but to no avail, this was real!

"Christ," he muttered to himself, not realising he had said it out loud.

"Everything ok, Simon?"

"Erm.." was the only thing Simmo could splutter.

This was the tone, then, for the journey home. Mrs C Spoke and Simmo and Ally just sat there with an occasional "err "or "erm" escaping their lips. It didn't take more than half an hour but to Simmo it seemed longer than the entire flight from L.A. to Paris.

She eased the car into the driveway; there was a sudden silence as she turned off the ignition. She climbed out of the car and Simmo followed suit, managing to exchange glances with Ally in the back. Ally just pulled a forlorn face and shrugged as Simmo let the seat go so that he could climb out. He slammed the door, making Ally cringe. Mrs C had disappeared off to open the front door.

"We cannae stay here," he whispered

"I know, I know," Simmo hissed, "but.."

He was cut short as Mrs C appeared from around the back of the house. "I've opened the door for you, bring your bags in." With that she turned and went back inside.

Ally grabbed the holdalls from the boot and nodded to Simmo. "Come on wee man, she's opened the tradesman's entrance for us."

Gigolos

She made them both a coffee which came with the obligatory two rich teas.

"I expect you will want a shower and change after the flight, Alastair, then I'll run you to the hospital."

Ally nodded, heading for the back door. "I'll just have a wee smoke with mah coffee."

"If you must," replied Mrs C, tight lipped with disapproval.

Simmo bolted for the door, still hobbling slightly. "I'll grab a quick shower while he's having a fag," he said hastily. Not giving Mrs C time to answer, he was up the stairs in an instant, grabbing a towel from the airing cupboard on the way past and causing the neat pile to topple over. He shut the bathroom door with a mediocre clunk rather than the usual slam. He stared at the bidet and wondered whether it was the same one that they had hurled through the Provost's windscreen - it didn't appear to be even slightly damaged.

He sat on it, whilst he prised his boots off. "Fuck," was all he could say, hoping the hot water from the shower might help with his dilemma. He didn't want a scene.

"Are you going tae be long?" Ally disturbed his thoughts.

"... erm, finished now... be out in a minute."

As he passed him on the landing, Ally nodded towards the bedroom.

"She's waiting for you," he whispered.

Simmo's mind reeled as "come into the parlour said the spider to the fly," sprang into his thoughts.

She appeared at the door. "I've put you some clothes on the bed."

"I don't know whether they will still fit me," said Simmo, "I've lost a lot of weight since..." The sentence just hung in the air.

"I can see that," she replied, "and it looks like you have streaked your hair."

"I'm not the same."

"I can see that too." Her arms were folded now.

"No, really...I'm just not the same."

She studied him for a little while then nodded to the basket in the corner. "Put the dirty towel in that when you have finished. Oh, and I think I have a belt you can borrow hanging up in the wardrobe." She turned on her heel and headed back down the stairs.

It didn't take Ally long to shower and change. Simmo waited for him to come out of the bathroom then followed him down the stairs. They shuffled into the living room like two naughty schoolboys called into the headmaster's study. The loose fitting jeans folding over the top of Simmo's cowboy boots, along with the baggy shirt and wide, big-buckled belt, gave him a pirate appearance.

"Those boots," said Mrs C, shaking her head. Ally was trying hard not to smile. "Come on, get in the car," she sighed.

The traffic was light and it didn't take them too long to get to the hospital. Simmo wasn't sure why but he felt spaced out in a way he hadn't felt since... when? Amsterdam, he supposed. He put it down to lack of sleep and jet lag. They twisted their way along corridors and went up in a tatty lift. Mrs C appeared to know where she was going.

"Margi Stewart said your mother was in the stroke unit," she said, to Ally, as though reading Simmo's thoughts.

Ally said nothing, just nodded grimly.

Simmo hated the smell of hospitals; it was a smell he had come to associate with death... he shook himself, trying to drive morbid thoughts from his

Gigolos

mind. Mrs C rang the bell and they had to wait a few minutes for a nurse to come to the door. Ally went to speak but Mrs C butted in, that this was Alastair come to see his mother. The nurse nodded and explained that there was someone in with her and that they had a policy of no more than two visitors at a time, so Ally went in alone.

Simmo and Mrs C had just sat down on two chairs opposite the doors when Margi Stewart came out. She looked from one to the other, then smiled at Simmo.

"I would hardly recognise you," was all she said.

Without looking at him Mrs C opened her purse and handed Simmo a five pound note.

"Three coffees Simon, we passed a WRVS canteen before we got in the lift."

Simmo went to speak but nothing came out, so he shuffled off instead.

"And no sugar for Margi!" Mrs C shouted after him, the echo reverberating in the quiet corridor.

When he returned with the coffees the two women were sat deep in conversation. Simmo silently handed them their drinks before sitting himself down on a rickety plastic chair a little further along the corridor. He'd only been there a few moments when he made the fatal mistake of closing his eyes and soon drifted off into a deep, deep sleep, the untouched styrofoam cup making a gentle splosh onto the floor.

Ally had barely taken in anything Margi had said to him. He was looking at his mother. She was in a small room off the main ward and looked very pale and wizened to him. A sign hung over the bed - *Nil by mouth* - and there was a drip in her arm.

"I'll leave you alone then," Margi had said as she made her exit.

Ally mumbled something incomprehensible and sat on the chair next to the bed. He fumbled with the cot side, letting it drop so that he could hold his mother's hand.

"Mammy, Mammy," was all he could say at first. He looked down at her and took her small hand in his; the skin was tough after a lifetime of hard work. He was unsure what to say. There was no point in asking her how she was or anything, was there? So he just started talking about the island and reeled off the whole story of how he and Simmo came to buy the bar. He left nothing out, telling her about Rikki and how he had found love... It seemed very odd to him to say *love* out loud, but his mother let out a little sigh. Had her breathing become more laboured? More shallow? It felt like she was slipping away.

He sat there for a while in relative silence, the sterile white light from the fluorescent tube making him squint slightly. He could vaguely hear medical machinery pinging from the ward. She was definitely slipping away; Ally had seen it all before. He told her quietly that he loved her and he was sorry he hadn't been a better son, and felt a very faint squeeze on his hand.

"What should I do?" he asked her "I've nae done the right thing ever in mah life. Should I take the money and run or make a stand for the things I love?"

For the first time since he had been there his mother twitched slightly.

"Aye" said Ally, "I know what you would do."

There was again just the slightest of squeezes on his hand, then nothing. Her breathing became shallower and shallower and then, not with a gasp but almost one last sigh, it stopped. She had seen her boy.

Ally sat there in silence for some time, tears rolling down his cheeks. He helped himself to a tissue

Gigolos

from the box on the locker at the side of the bed, and pulled the cord for the nurse. He kissed his mother lightly on the forehead.

"I think she's gone," he said to the nurse who was now examining his mother.

The nurse nodded. I'm sorry for your loss," she said gently.

Ally left the room with one last glance. He knew now what he had to do.

Ally was lost in his own thoughts in the car on the way back from the hospital to Mrs C's. He mused over what it had been like before the old man really started hitting the bottle. His early childhood had been quite a happy one, but then...what? He supposed it was after the old man had got the sack - aye, that was when, he thought to himself. His father had been a shop steward; he supposed he must have been blacklisted or something. Whatever happened, the old git never worked again...

Mrs C pulled up sharply, the sudden jolt rousing Ally from his thoughts. Simmo let him out of the car, an as yet unlit rollie hanging from his lip. Simmo said something, but Ally was still miles away.

"I'll be in in a minute," he mumbled; "I'll just have a wee smoke."

Simmo nodded and shuffled off. Ally went to reach into his pocket when he realised he was still holding something in his hand. It was a small bunch of keys, the keys Margi had handed him. The keys to his Mammy's flat.

A movement in a car parked a little farther down the road caught his attention. As Ally looked the driver started up and pulled away. There was something familiar about...

"Ally!" shouted Simmo, "come on in, I've made you a brew. Come on, you're getting wet..."

Ally shook himself. The rollie was soaked and the gentle Glaswegian drizzle was running down his neck. He shuddered, then with a glance tossed the sodden rollie away and followed Simmo inside.

Mrs C made some idle chit chat then spoke softly to Ally. I've had a good long chat to Margi. Apparently your mother long ago sorted out the arrangements for her..." she trailed off for a moment before continuing. "There is an endowment policy...paid up; she wants to be cremated and the ashes scattered on her parents' grave. The policy etc. are all in the bottom draw in the –"

"Aye" Ally interrupted, "I know where she keeps her stuff."

"That's good Alastair," she replied.

"It's Ally," he said tersely.

"Yes, I know, sorry Alastair - err - Ally. Also Margi is down as her next of kin because we didn't know if you would be back."

Ally looked affronted. "I would nae miss mah Mammy's funeral!" he spluttered.

"Quite, but we didn't know how long it would take for you to actually get back home."

Ally nodded a half apology, his eyebrow rising slightly.

"Anyhow, Alastair, this enables her to deal with the death certificate and the arrangements. She is also your mother's executor - not that she had anything much to leave, but what little there is, is all for you, with the exception of a gold St Christopher that she promised Margi."

Ally nodded, and Mrs C patted his hand reassuringly. "Margi is going to take care of things. Also, your mother wanted a piper and a requiem mass, and has chosen hymns, oh, and a song for her final send-off at the crematorium. Are you happy - sorry, happy is a very inappropriate word... would you like Margi to carry on with the arrangements?" Ally nodded. "Ok," said Mrs C, "I'll give her a ring."

She left the room. Ally stared at the slight indentations she left in the lush shag pile.

"I could do with a drink," he announced suddenly, rousing himself.

Simmo nodded. He went into the kitchen but his hand froze on the cupboard where he had once gone to fetch a bottle of scotch. He opened it with a shudder but no skeleton fell out; instead, like Mother Hubbard's, it was bare.

"Shit," said Simmo. "I'll have to nip out and get a bottle"

Mrs C, who had just come back into the room, frowned. "Bottle?" she asked.

"Aye," said Ally "I could do with a wee dram."

Simmo looked in his wallet. "Shit," he said again.

Ally fumbled in his pockets and pulled out a tenner.

"You will have to be quick, Simon," she said, "it shuts at ten."

Simmo took the tenner and nodded. It was a good ten minute walk to the shop.

"Would you like me to drive you?" she asked. Simmo shook his head. "Would you like to take the car then?"

Simmo looked aghast. "Erm, no, it's ok." He didn't like driving at the best of times but he hadn't driven a car in Christ knows how long.

"You are still on the insurance." Simmo looked perplexed. "It keeps the cost down," she explained.

"Oh," said Simmo, not comprehending. "I think the walk would do me good."

Ally asked if it would be all right to use the phone. "Tae, err, ring the bar and let them know we arrived safely." He wanted to tell Rikki that his Mammy had gone; he shuddered at the thought.

Mrs C frowned slightly, then nodded. "You can use the one in the hall," she gestured with her hand before going out into the kitchen.

Ally followed her through the door, and studied the receiver before picking it up and dialling.

Mrs C shouted in "Would you like a coffee, Alastair?"

"Aye," mumbled Ally, fumbling with the piece of paper that Pascale had written the international dialling code on. The line crackled and buzzed before finally connecting.

Mrs C stood by the kitchen door. She wasn't exactly eavesdropping but could hear most of the conversation. It sounded like Ally had a girlfriend by the way he spoke to the female voice on the other end of the phone. As he began describing his mother's death to the voice on the end of the line, Mrs C started to step away towards the kettle. The conversation was a little more muffled when suddenly her ears pricked up.

"Aye," Ally was saying, "he's fine, there were nae any disasters on the plane –" he started to smile. "Well, err only one but I'll tell you about it next time." There was a pause while he listened and responded with "Nae, no she cannae speak tae him, he's nipped out to get us a wee drink…Aye, I'll pass that on tae him…"

She? Mrs C was really frowning now, but she shook the thought away and turned to the coffee, pushing the plunger down on the cafetière and absently putting three spoons of sugar into Ally's coffee mug.

She returned with two coffees and sat primly in the white leather chair opposite Ally.

Gigolos

"Just the way I like it," he said, holding up the mug in thanks, "strong n' sweet, a bit like mah women."

Mrs C fidgeted a little uneasily in the chair. "There's something I have been meaning to ask you, Alastair."

"Go on," said Ally.

"Is this bar of yours a success? I mean, well, that was an awful lot of money the two of you invested."

Ally took a sip of his coffee. "We get by."

Mrs C's face again set into a frown. "It seems to me that you've squandered all your redundancy on it."

Ally spluttered on his coffee. "It's been a great investment!" he retorted.

Mrs C shook her head. "That money should have been spent here. Simon would have found another job and we would have almost certainly patched things up."

"*What?!*" said Ally, thumping his mug down on the table, splashing drops of coffee onto the white leather, his face flushing in agitation. "Him, you and Bob the Bidet? Two's company and three's a bathroom suite."

Mrs C didn't rise to the bait. "That was just a little fling, nothing more." She lowered her voice. "A woman has needs, Alastair. And anyway, judging by your appearances the two of you, well, you don't look like you have a fucking pot to piss in."

Not once had Ally ever heard Mrs C swear. He tried but he couldn't get his words out.

Oh, and I know all about Amsterdam - gay bars, drugs and my husband getting duped out of his redundancy. I felt a laughing stock when Margi explained it all to me."

Ally looked perplexed.

"Oh come on, Alastair it's a very small grapevine around here and plenty of people have had a good old laugh at my expense."

"Well," said Ally indignantly, his eyes narrowing "for your information smart arse, not only is he doing well, he's potentially very rich."

This stopped Mrs C dead in her tracks. "What do you mean, Alastair?" The fine lines at the side of her mouth twitched a little.

"The bar is worth two million francs!" he exclaimed, blurting it out.

"Don't be ridiculous! It couldn't possibly be," she scoffed.

With the agility of a cat Ally leapt angrily out of the chair and took the stairs two at a time. He dragged socks and clothes out of the holdall before grabbing the manila envelope and storming back down to the living room.

He thrust the envelope into her hand. "Aye, there, if you dinnae believe me!" she stared at him, somewhat taken aback. "Go on, read it!"

Mrs C slowly picked up her reading glasses from the small wooden coffee table next to her chair. She took the document out of the envelope and at first was glancing at it nonchalantly, but as she started to read her expression changed.

"My God, Alastair," she said, gently sliding the contract back into its envelope. "Is this real?" She didn't say any more, she could recognise the truth in the angry expression on Ally's face. The word *she!* Suddenly jumped into her mind but Ally had deftly slipped the envelope from her hand and was heading for the stairs, leaving Mrs C feeling somewhat stunned.

As he came back down the stairs she stepped aside. "Tell Simon I have gone up for the night. He knows his way to our... room," she paused, then shrugged, "or if not, then the bed is made up in the box room."

Ally heard the door go, or rather the slam; he must have nodded off. Simmo came in with two very large scotches. Ally took his and the two men sat there in silence, each lost to their own thoughts. Eventually a snore from Simmo disturbed Ally's reverie and he took the glass from his friend's hand. "Just like the old days," he said wryly, leaving Simmo asleep in the chair. Christ, how long had it been since either of them had slept in a bed? Ally didn't know; all he knew was that he was very, very tired.

It was nearly noon when Ally came down the stairs. Simmo was up and about. Brew?" he asked.
"Aye," said Ally, mah mouth feels like the bottom of a parrot's arse."
"Don't you mean cage?" laughed Simmo.
Nae, not with the taste I've got in mah mouth." Ally stuffed the first rollie of the day between his lips and went to spark up.
"No!!!" screeched Simmo, "if she smells that..." Ally cocked an eyebrow at his friend, who was a nervous wreck.
"Calm down, wee man, I'll take it outside."
Simmo flopped down into the white leather armchair, the cushions emitting a gentle hiss-cum-farting noise. His insides were churning - he had very nearly climbed into bed with her. He had woken up and, still half asleep, had been guided by some sort of ancient autopilot into her room. He had started to undress before realising where he was. Fumbling in the dark, he had picked up his clothes and backed out sharply, teetering on the top step, grabbing the curtain and narrowly avoiding falling down the stairs.

He would have to remember to re-attach the couple of curtain hooks her had dislodged before she noticed...He had spent the night on the sofa, his face sticking to the leather cushions.

A sharp voice shouting "Simon!" had woken him up. "I thought you would have spent the night in our bed but if you're not going to then at least have the decency to use the bed in the box room." She tutted and shook her head. "You're going to wear out the leather. I'll be home five-ish by the way. Oh and don't forget it's bin day."

Ally laughed at Simmo struggling with two large black waste bags, desperately trying not to snag them on the back gate. "Not like the old days," he said, "when the men used tae come up the path and collect the bin."

Simmo nodded. There was a sea of fag ends around the back door, so he went in and came out with a dustpan and brush.

"Very domesticated," said Ally. Simmo just shook his head. "I'll get you a pinnie," he joked.

"Fuck you," replied Simmo, disappearing back inside. He was muttering and spluttering because he couldn't find a fresh bag for the bin.

"She's getting tae you, wee man."

"I know...what are we going to do, Ally?"

Ally just took a long pull on his rollie and shrugged, holding his palms out.

The phone, when it rang, made the pair of them jump. Simmo picked it up. It was Margi. He handed Ally the receiver before taking the mugs out to the kitchen to do the washing up.

A couple of minutes later Ally followed him out. "Arrangements made for next Tuesday," he said.

"Oh," said Simmo. "What day is it?"

Gigolos

Ally scratched his head. "I think it's Thursday."

"I've lost all track of time." Ally nodded. "That's quick then," Simmo continued after a pause.

"Aye...there is no need for an inquest and Margi's second cousin is an undertaker... I think she may have called in a few favours... At some point I need tae go tae Mammy's flat, Margi has been over and picked up the insurance policy and her St Christopher but there are a few things I need tae pick up. Aye," said Ally putting his arm around Simmo's shoulder, "there's also a *Dubliners* album with the song for the crem on it."

"I suppose we'd better go over tae Mammy's," said Ally.

"Ok," said Simmo, straightening the cushions before they left, and carefully locking up.

They were about three or four houses down when Ally realised he had forgotten his lighter. As he turned around, a car a little further down the road was pulling off - a blue Peugeot saloon. The driver ducked down as though he was adjusting the radio as they walked back onto the drive. Simmo was fumbling for the keys so hadn't noticed anything, but Ally had recognised the face.

"Tell you what, wee man; I've had a bit of a change of mind. I'm going tae need a shirt and a black tie for the funeral..."

Simmo couldn't understand Ally. He had pushed them off the bus two stops before they needed to get off and was scanning the place like he was lost - or had lost - something. He started to complain that his feet were hurting and that he would have put on the old trainers that were still in the house if he thought that they were going bloody walkabout.

"Aye," said Ally, "do you good tae burn off some of the calories she insists on feeding you."

They wandered in and out of various shops and Ally found a shirt, a tie and a new jacket. Simmo was pretty sure that his own suit would still be in the wardrobe. "Good job we didn't ransom the lapel," he smiled to himself.

"What's so funny?" Ally asked sharply.

"Nothing," replied Simmo, but he was still smiling.

He was somewhat overwhelmed at being in amongst throngs of people, and was glad when they finally set off for home. Simmo was a bit perturbed again when Ally insisted that they get off a stop before theirs.

"Are you training for a marathon or something?" he asked exasperatedly.

"Err...nay, I just fancied walking after all that sitting."

Simmo shrugged. His feet were getting sore now. The cowboy boots, once he had broken them in, had been very comfortable, but his feet had swollen badly on the plane and the boots were pinching his toes.

As they turned onto their road and were approaching the house a grey Peugeot saloon pulled slowly away from the curb. Ally wasn't surprised. Grey car; blue car; but the same driver.

Simmo looked a little confused when they got in.

He scratched his head. "Could have sworn I tidied the cushions before we went out."

Ally shrugged. "I cannae remember."

Simmo straightened the cushions. He looked around, but everything else appeared to be in order.

"It's just the jet lag," said Ally.

"It's more likely that I'm going insane from hanging around with you all these years!"

Gigolos

Ally picked up a cushion from the chair and threw it at Simmo, making him squeal "for God's sake don't break anything!"

Mrs C was on fine form that evening. The table was set immaculately and the smell of cooking from the kitchen was fabulous - Steak Diane and all the trimmings.

"Ten minutes boys," she said before disappearing off upstairs.

Simmo's jaw dropped when she walked into the room. "She must have lost a few pounds whilst I've been away," he thought admiringly. She wore a little black number with black high heeled sandals. She really did have a pair of shapely legs. Simmo looked at her feet. He had always had a thing for women in high heeled sandals, which was a bit of an idiosyncrasy considering his height.

"I take it you approve then Simon," she said. Simmo could only blush.

The table was set for four, the guest being Margi, who had come to discuss the final arrangements with Ally. She was a little taken aback when she saw Mrs C.

"Will you look at the state of me? When you said a little supper...I would have made the effort if I'd known."

Mrs C waved her hand dismissively. "Oh, it's nothing special. Simon, take Margi's coat."

The meal was as good as it looked. Mrs C chatted away merrily and the wine flowed freely.

At the end of dinner she suggested that Margi and Ally go into the lounge to finalise things whilst she and Simmo did the washing up.

"Do you mind washing, Simon?" She held out a hand with beautifully crafted nails.

Whilst Simmo was elbow deep in the sink she sidled up behind him, putting her hands right around his waist and squeezing gently.

"God I've missed you," she said.

Simmo could feel his stomach muscles tensing.

"Mmm" she said, "you've gone all muscly."

She was giggling; she raised her hand and started stroking his hair, whilst her leg rubbed on the back of his.

"Erm," was all Simmo could splutter. Was there just the slightest hint of a slur? She had been topping the glasses up all evening. Once upon a time two or three glasses of wine and he would have been anyone's... Simmo smiled at the thought, but now, well, he had had plenty of practice. He turned, and in a move practised on numerous forty somethings he slid her arms gently down by her sides. She closed her eyes and licked her red lipstick, awaiting the kiss. But the kiss didn't come as Simmo, in a move somewhat similar to a basketball player, dodged to the side and picked up a tea towel.

"All done," he said, nodding at the dishes, "I'll help you dry."

Mrs C teetered backwards a little on her heels. Her mouth opened and closed but she was too flabbergasted for words... this was a proven formula, it never failed. As she momentarily pondered her predicament the phone in the hall began to ring. She looked towards it, and then at Simmo.

"Aren't you going to get that?" he asked.

She paused for a minute, still stuck for words, before nodding and teetering out into the hall. She gently closed the door, glancing over her shoulder before answering and neither seeing nor hearing Simmo as he, too, gently opened the door.

He stood in the kitchen doorway. Her voice was hushed but at the same time agitated.

Gigolos

"No Gary I couldn't come over. I've got something on... Well I'm sorry you waited at the gym for me... What about our little arrangement?!... Fine then, if you are going to be like that... you're not the only fitness instructor I know... What do you mean I won't find one with one as big as... Listen Gary, I've had more than you've had hot dinners, and you know something Gary? Yours isn't even average! Good bye Gary." The line clicked, and then buzzed as she replaced the receiver. She was startled to see Simmo standing in the doorway, arms folded.

"Leopards and spots," he said.

She went to say something but Simmo had turned his attention back to drying the dishes. Mrs C darted up the stairs; he couldn't be sure if it was a snuffle or a sob, but either way he didn't give a flying fuck. He tossed the tea towel onto the floor, poured himself another large glass of red and went back into the lounge to join Margi and Ally.

"What was up with her last night?" asked Ally.

"Dunno," replied Simmo, shrugging.

She had come down in her dressing gown, made some excuse about feeling unwell and had gone to bed, and Margi had left not long after.

Simmo looked at the drain in the bottle of Red Label.

Ally nodded. "We made some serious inroads into that last night."

"Erm," said Simmo, slightly distracted.

"You ok wee man?"

"Never better; I just want to go home.... Sorry Ally, I didn't mean... it's just that there is nothing here for me."

Ally nodded, then opened the bottle and drank down the last drop. They heard Mrs C rummaging in the hall. She poked her head into the lounge.

"Err, I have to pop into town," was all she said.

Simmo nodded to the empty doorway. "I suppose we'd better tidy up," he said, gesturing to the glasses, but then thinking again. "You know what? Fuck it, let's fuck off into town; the pubs will be open soon."

Simmo smiled as the bus took them past Barrowlands. He had seen Stiff Little Fingers there, and Christy Moore. He remembered Ally at the Fingers gig pretending not to enjoy himself and then propelling himself right to the front. Christy Moore's *Ordinary Man* popped into his head.

I'm an ordinary man, nothing special nothing grand
I've had to work for everything I own

"Too bloody right," he thought. Simmo was missing Pascale.

The afternoon passed pleasantly enough and, despite starting early, the beer had no effect on Simmo.

"It's nice tae be this side of the bar for a change," said Ally, "although even Byron could pour a pint quicker than this shower."

An old lady seemed to be struggling with the cap on a bottle of Mackeson.

"Here," said Simmo, let me."

He snatched the bottle and with the opener he always carried in his pocket he deftly opened it.

"What have you done?!" cried the woman behind the bar. Simmo shrugged. "She was taking that home!"

"Shit," said Simmo, who ended up buying her a large scotch and another bottle.

"Aye," said Ally afterward, "you pulled there."

Gigolos

"Hey pretty lady," quipped Simmo in his Pedro accent, and the two of them burst out laughing at their own private joke, leaving the woman polishing glasses behind the bar smiling and shaking her head.

Ally clocked the Peugeot again when they got back but said nothing to Simmo. Mrs C had tidied up and there was a note on the kitchen table: she was with Margi, they had taken some clothes to the undertakers for Ally's Mam. They were going to watch a Tom Cruise video, and that if she had a few glasses of wine she would probably stop over, and there was a homemade shepherd's pie in the freezer.

"All joking apart," said Ally, "she has been pretty good, your Mrs."

Simmo nodded.

"And Margi too."

Simmo nodded again. He smiled at the thought of Byron's Tom Cruise routine, then wondered what Mrs C would make of him.

After they had eaten Simmo put the telly on. That was one thing he hadn't missed at Gigolos. There was some inane shite on about some geezer who loved himself trying to get a blind date with three of the stupidest women he had ever seen.

"Serves him right," said Ally, he's bagged off with the ugly one."

Simmo's response was a snore. The shepherd's pie and the second can of McEwen's had acted as a general anaesthetic. Ally took the half empty can from his hand and put it on the table. "He must have Rip van Winkle blood in him somewhere," he thought.

Ally let himself out quietly. Fifty yards or so down the road he heard a car start. He didn't look back.

There was no cloak and dagger with the buses this time. Ally made a point of bending down to fasten his shoelace after he got off the bus at his Mammy's stop. He wanted the man in the car to see exactly where he was going. As he entered the tenement he couldn't see anyone following him, but he was sure someone was. He produced the key and after a little fumbling he let himself in.

It was quite gloomy in the late evening, but Ally was quite familiar with the old place. It smelt of sixty years of woodbine smoke - she never liked those filthy tips, as she called them. He went into her room; neat and tidy as ever. The carpet and curtains were threadbare but clean, her dressing gown hung on the back of the door. Ally held out the sleeve and sniffed it. It smelt of tobacco and cheap perfume.

Ally was keeping an ear open as he opened the bottom drawer of the clothes chest. He knew that was where she would put it. He removed the neatly folded cardigans and then he reached for the shortbread tin. A picture of a piper was on the lid. He placed it on the bed. His package was on the top. He put it to one side before removing the other contents from the tin: Some old letters tied with a thin faded red ribbon - love letters he presumed - and an envelope stuffed with ten pound notes. Ally thumbed them, and then whistled softly. "There must be well over a grand," he thought to himself.

Under the letters was a package wrapped up in brown paper and tied up with faded string. It felt weighty. There was also an old cardboard packet with reinforcing on the sides. Ally picked up her nail scissors from the dressing table and cut the string. Inside the package was an ancient revolver; it had been his uncle's. He rattled the other packet, fished around inside with his finger and pulled out a cartridge. He tipped the packet out onto the bed: there were six cartridges in all.

It took a couple of attempts to break the revolver open; he wasn't pushing the leaver hard enough. He loaded the chambers and snapped it closed, putting his package containing the film into his inside jacket pocket along with the envelope with the money.

Ally paused. He could hear a sound coming from the front door. Moving stealthily, he stood behind it. Sure enough, the lock clicked and a figure entered the room. Ally had the advantage: this guy was coming into the gloom. He had a pistol in his hand but Ally, with his usual speed, stepped out from behind the door and brought the barrel of the revolver down on the man's head with a dull thud.

Ally went through the interloper's pockets: his wallet contained the usual money, credit cards, a French driving licence - and some sort of diplomatic ID pass. Ally stuffed the wallet into his pocket, picked the pistol up with a doyley and with a bit of a struggle managed to put it back into the shoulder holster, dropping the unconscious man back down on his face. He then started pulling the furniture apart to make it look like the place had been ransacked. Just to add the final touch, he poured what was left of a cheap bottle of scotch over the comatose body and butted the door frame producing a lump and a little blood. He then balled the unconscious man's hand into a fist and punched his own face with it, leaving blood on the man's knuckles. Ally went back out into the hall. He gently closed the door before kicking it back open and then started shouting and kicking things before staggering out into the hall.

Bridie Mac's door opened a crack. "What's going on?" an elderly voice called. "I've called the police!"

"It's me Bridie, Ally."

The crack opened a little more. "Ally? I was so sorry tae hear about your Mammy, we were good friends you know.

"Aye, I know. I've just been around tae get a few bits for the undertaker and I found some low life ransacking the place."

"But the woman is hardly cold yet!" Bridie spurted out, appalled. "Are you hurt Ally?"

"Nae, not at all. Bastard had a pop at me so I gave him the good news." He rubbed his chin.

"You always were a canny lad, Ally," Bridie replied.

Two large policemen appeared and before Ally could speak Bridie started to tell them the tale. One of the coppers had a look at the man, spreading him roughly into the recovery position and not noticing the small pistol and shoulder holster. Ally had given the other one a short statement and Simmo's address, with frequent interjections from Bridie.

Ally asked if he could go. "It's her wake you see."

"Sorry for your loss," said the copper. "Is there anything of any value in there?" Ally shook his head. "Ok then, I'll get someone to ring the council and sort out the lock."

Ally thanked him and left leaving Bridie bending the policemen's ears.

"The coppers are getting younger," he thought, "or is it just me getting older?"

Two ambulance crew passed him on the stairs. Ally walked up to the main drag, taking the Frenchman's wallet from his pocket and removing the money before slinging it over the wall and hailing a cab.

The paramedics started to pick the unconscious man off the floor when one of them jumped, dropping him down on his face a second time. He shouted to the coppers, who couldn't get away from Bridie, "he's got a gun!"

Ally was just in time to catch the overnight train to London, and was lucky enough to get a seat by the window. He had stuffed the revolver down the back of his pants. It was uncomfortable sitting there; he could feel it digging in. He would wait till later, when most people were asleep, then go to the toilet and swap it into his jacket pocket.

The 'burglar' had eventually come around in the hospital, but he wouldn't answer any questions, only giving them a phone and ID number. It was a good hour or two before anyone actually rang it, after which the local nick was awash with rumour when it transpired he was some sort of diplomat. There was even speculation that he could be a spy.

Simmo was awoken by a loud knocking on the door. He was half asleep when he answered it, to see two detectives standing there. They were looking for Ally.

Simmo invited them in. "No, he's not here. Have a look if you like," he said. He was a bit surprised when one of them actually did.

"Do you know where he is?"

Simmo shrugged and shook his head. "Is he in some kind of trouble?"

"We don't know. Can you shed any light? We found an unconscious man in his mother's flat. There had been some sort of fight."

"Burglar?" Simmo shrugged again.

The other detective returned. "All clear," he said, giving nothing away. "We want to speak to him as soon as he gets back."

"Erm, yes," said Simmo, "sure." He sat there scratching his head after the men had left. He just hoped Ally had gone on a bender and was lying there pissed somewhere.

The train rumbled on through the night. Ally had managed to shift the revolver to his jacket pocket, thinking it prudent to pack it with toilet roll to disguise its shape. He wanted to sleep but the jolting of the train kept waking him up. He reeled off the phone number in his head a couple of times... it was still there.

He must have nodded off; he was awoken by the man next to him who accidently caught him with a rucksack he was getting down from the luggage rack. A few minutes later the train pulled into London Euston. Ally waited a few minutes before joining the throng. He could see two coppers at the barrier.

"Always in twos, like bloody buses," he smiled. Despite the early hour there was a group of young lads who had been on the piss. Ally sidled into the middle of them, and as they were passing the coppers he put his arms round two of them, pulling their heads close to his to shield his face and disguise his height.

He was only wearing a light Harrington and was feeling a little chilly as he left the station, despite the morning sunshine. He walked for a couple of hundred yards, stopping occasionally and crossing back and forth across the road. He went into a tobacconist and purchased a block of Golden Virginia and papers, and asked for change for the phone. The man asked him did he want a card.

"Why?" said Ally, "whose birthday is it?"

"No, a card for the phone." the man explained.

Gigolos

"Ahh."

Ally emerged from the shop clutching a one pound phone card. He found a booth and eventually figured out how to use the phone. He rang the number; it rang and rang.

"Shit!" he said, replacing the receiver on its cradle. "If that's an office number then fuck it!"

He gave it another go, and this time a groggy voice on the other end of the line replied.

"This better be good at this ungodly hour on a Sunday morning."

"Is that Paul Smith?" asked Ally.

"Who is this?" the reply was drawn out, suspicious.

"Mah name's Ally."

"And?" the voice asked.

"I've just got in from French Polynesia... a mutual friend sent me."

There was a pause. "Ok," said the voice, "meet me in the Punch Tavern on Fleet Street, about twelve. Tell the barman you are looking for Roger, he will point me out. You've got that, err, Ally isn't it.?"

Ally nodded before replying yes and replacing the receiver. He had some time to kill, so pausing at a small kiosk he bought a street guide to London and set off for Fleet Street. The walk was doing him good after the long train journey. He caught his reflection in a shop window. God, he looked rough. He piled into a Wimpy Bar and freshened up as best he could but he didn't want to take the Harrington off. He grabbed a coffee and something masquerading as a burger before setting of again, the so-called hamburger giving him a little indigestion, He pondered on its name; he hadn't understood why a beef burger was called a hamburger till Simmo had explained about Hamburg steak... "Bloody smart arse," said Ally to himself. He studied the map again; another twenty minutes he reckoned.

He knew he would be a little early so stopped every now again for a fag, using this as an excuse to glance behind. Despite the fact there were a lot more people milling around, he didn't think anyone was following him.

The pub was a fine looking old place with fancily tiled and mirrored walls Ally ordered a double before a little sheepishly telling the camp barman he was looking for a Roger.

"Aren't we all, darling?" came the reply. The barman studied Ally, who was standing with his arms folded. "He doesn't usually come in of a weekend," he added. "I'll point him out to you if he arrives." Ally nodded.

Ally sat in a corner nursing his drink. A couple came in, followed by two smart looking gents... Eventually a large man with a big red nose and a walking stick arrived and Ally clocked the barman nodding over towards him.

The man was clutching a very large pink gin, and wheezed as he sat down. "Gout," he said.

Ally just looked. The man must have been at least eighteen stone. "Roger?" he quizzed.

"That is correct." He squeezed Ally's hand in the bear's paw of his own.

Roger dabbed his sweating face with a large handkerchief. Ally started to explain but Roger held a finger to his lips. "Do you think you could pass it to me subtly?"

Ally gave the slightest of nods, pulling the packet out with his tobacco tin and putting it on the table, where Roger casually covered it with his handkerchief before pocketing it.

Ally finished his drink. "What now? he asked.

Gigolos

"Well, I need to be somewhere before three."

Ally went to speak again but the man smiled. "Watch this space, as we say in the trade."

Roger got up, but before he left he leaned in close and whispered in Ally's ear. "And do get rid of the gun. Ta-ta."

Ally was left sitting there. It all seemed...what? *Anti-climax* was the word he was trying to formulate. "Feck it," he said to himself. He ordered another drink and sat down to study his route back.

He headed towards Blackfriars Bridge, which was totally the wrong direction for Euston. There was a smell of chips wafting on the breeze and this gave Ally an idea. There was a small café-cum-chip shop on the right.

"Eat in or take out dear?" the woman on the counter asked.

"Err...eat out," Ally replied, transfixed by a faded sign on the wall for luncheon vouchers, whatever they were; his mind elsewhere.

The women took a couple of attempts to get an answer: "S-a-l-t a-n-d v-i-n-e-g-a-r dear?"

"Aye, err, yes please."

The woman handed him the chips the way a psychiatric nurse may hand out a placebo. Ally asked if there was a toilet he could use and the woman pointed to the illuminated sign at the back of the café beside the fish range.

"Do you want me to put them on top of the range dear? Keep them warm while you go?"

Ally shook his head and set off for the bog still clutching the chips.

"I blame the government myself," she said to the man in the back who was pouring a sack of spuds into the chipper.

"What?" he said

"Turning them out...out into the community!"

Ally tipped half the chips down the pan. He placed the rest on top of the cistern, putting the revolver in the middle and packing the chips around it. Before wrapping it up again, he stuffed a few chips into his mouth and folded the papers back around it, making it look a very presentable portion of chips. He threw the rest of the toilet paper from his pocket down the pan and gave it a flush, the chips and tissue blocking the pan and the water overflowing.

It was some minutes later when another customer complained that the toilet was flooding. The woman from behind the counter came out tutting and shaking her head.
"'ere Burt," she shouted to the bloke who had previously been making the chips, "I told you he was one of those bloody lunatics!" He's just blocked our toilet with the chips he bought and half a loo roll!"

Ally walked onto Blackfriars Bridge. He stood roughly in the middle with the chips on the rail and, checking below, he gently eased them over the edge. That done he headed for the tube to take him back to Euston, but he was in no particular rush.

Forgiven Mistakes and Seismic Quakes

"Where the hell have you been?!" spluttered Simmo. "The bloody funeral's tomorrow! Mrs C is right pissed off. She and Margi have been checking out the hospitals, and the morgues. Not to mention the bloody coppers - they've been here twice!"

"I know," said Ally. "They banged me up last night when I got off the train, only let me go about half an hour ago."

"Where have you been then?" asked Simmo again.

Ally tapped his nose. "You'll see, wee man."

"And where's the bloody Dubliners album you were supposed to collect?"

Ally slapped his forehead. "Sorry, I forgot," he apologised.

They were interrupted by the front door opening.

"Oh so you're back, are you? Poor Margi is at her wits' end."

Ally went to speak but Mrs C's glare shut him up. She was clutching an album. "Here," she said, thrusting it into Simmo's hands. "I have had to go all the way across town to collect that." She was not amused.

"Those coppers," said Simmo when they were alone, "the ones that came back the second time, they didn't look like ordinary dicks."

Ally shrugged. "Feck 'em," was all he said.

Ally and Simmo finished off the last of the McEwen's. Tea had been sparse, Mrs C's way of making Ally do penance.

As Simmo tidied up, Mrs C poked her head in and spoke. "If there is anything you want ironing, Alastair, now would be a good time. There will be plenty of things to do in the morning."

"Thanks," said Ally, rubbing his scar and leaving the lounge to fetch his things from upstairs.

Simmo was slumped in the lounge when Mrs C came in, closed the door silently and sat down opposite him. He looked up from the telly. Mrs C picked up the remote control and put the TV on mute.

"Simon," she said. "Is there someone else?"

Simmo looked blank for a moment, looked down at his feet and then straight back at Mrs C.

"Yes," he said. Mrs C leant forward.

"Is she a local girl?" Mrs C's mind was leaping ahead of her.

Simmo thought, then answered, "Erm, not exactly."

Mrs C tried to prompt him. "Go on, Simon."

"She's French."

"Oh...and does she work in the bar?" She was starting to flush a little.

"Not exactly."

"What do you mean, not exactly?" This time Simmo didn't falter under her gaze as she exclaimed "Oh for Christ's sake Simon what does she do? A croupier, a chambermaid, *what*?!"

"She's into snails," he blurted out.

"*Snails!*" laughed Mrs C. "What, she sells cockles and mussels around the pubs like Molly Malone?"

"No, sinistral snails."

"Now you're talking nonsense!" she was becoming exasperated.

He paused for a moment. "Left handed snails."

"And what? she sells these? Are they some sort of a delicacy out there?"

Gigolos

"She has just written a very well received paper on them. They're as rare as rocking horse shite and she has discovered a whole colony of them in our lagoon."

Mrs C was just starting to cotton on, but Simmo stole the lead. "She is a doctor of marine biology and a leading light in the field of cockles and mussels alive alive oh."

Somewhat taken aback, she paused for a little while before asking "You don't think, Simon, that we could..."

Simmo interjected. "Women like you come into the bar every night... and I've had my fill..." all of a sudden he was Pedro again. "Hey pretty lady," he tensed his arm, flexing his muscles and rippling his biceps, "you like my big muscle? I take you out on my pedalo, give you lovely ride."

She was aghast. In his face she saw the face of Gary, then Bob and then every other flyboy she had ever encountered. As she fled from the room, Simmo shouted after her, "most pretty ladies like you leave me a tip!"

In London, across the city, lights were starting to come on: in the Foreign Office and the French Embassy and all the way downriver to the new premises, where the presses for the morning edition were already rolling.

In Whitehall, a very weary undersecretary was having his ear bent. Yes, Ambassador, I can see your point..."

The ambassador rattled on. "Well perhaps if you had kept us informed... a matter of national security..."

In the end the undersecretary had had enough. "Well I'm sorry Ambassador, but we have discussed this at the highest level... no we are not prepared to issue a gagging order... you will have to deal with your own fallout, if you pardon the pun."

The Ambassador had one last go but to no avail.

"What did the PM say?" asked the civil servant on the other side of the desk.

For the first time that evening the undersecretary smiled. She quoted Winston Churchill to me... in his very own words... fuck 'em."

Mrs C was up and about early. There wouldn't be a lot of people at the funeral. Margi, obviously, and one or two others. The hearse was coming here first although they would stop briefly outside the tenement. Any other mourners were to meet them at the church. There was a limo for Ally and Margi. Ally thought this was a little extravagant, but Mammy had planned this like a military operation. He wanted Mrs C and Simmo to come with him in the limo, but Mrs C insisted that he and Margi were family and that it should be just them.

Simmo put the suit on. It still fitted fine; he just needed a belt for the trousers. Hanging up with the suit was a brand new M & S black tie. The shoes were a little tight, a consequence of wearing flip flops all the time. Other than the first night that they had stayed there, this was the only time he had been in their... NO!... it wasn't their room... her room. The decor and the units were different but it smelled the same.

He had a stomach-turning burst of something akin to a melancholy nostalgia. There in a plastic case was the cuddly teddy with the UR18 number plate, the one he had bought her. He didn't hear her come in but he felt her presence as he was sitting on the bed. She put her hand on his shoulder.

Gigolos

"Are you ok Simon?"

"Yes... I was just thinking... reminiscing..."

She placed both hands on his shoulders now and squeezed them gently. "I'm sorry, Simon."

Simmo nodded and put his hand on hers.

"Still friends?" she asked.

Simmo nodded and she gave him a peck on top of the head, and left the room. Simmo stood in front of the mirror. The figure that stared back was no longer the man that the suit had been made for.

"Simon," said Mrs C, "you haven't done the tape for the crematorium.

"Shit," said Simmo, "what track was it again?

"*I'll take you home again Cathleen*!" Ally shouted in.

"Ok." He rooted through the drawer but couldn't find a blank cassette.

"Sod it," he said, snatching up one of Mrs C's home-made C90s instead. It just had *sixties* written in her own neat writing on the case. It took him a little while to master the new stereo but after a couple of attempts he sorted it.

"All done?" asked Mrs C.

Simmo gave her a thumbs up. He had taped over the Kinks and had made sure that the rest was blank.

Margi arrived. "It will be here in about fifteen minutes," she said, before filling the silence with idle chat. Ally was into his third large one and was unusually quiet. Simmo supposed that was only to be expected.

"Have you got the tape, Simon?" asked Mrs C.

"Erm, no, I'll go and get it." Simmo put his jacket on and slipped the tape into his pocket.

Ally came in from outside; he still had a rollie in his mouth but for once Mrs C pretended not to notice.

"It's here," he said quietly.
"Ok," said Mrs C. "You and Margi go on and Simon and I will lock up."

There was a simple wreath on top of the small coffin. Simmo locked the door as the cortège slowly pulled away, and he and Mrs C followed behind the limo. There were no other cars.
"At least it's a nice day for it," said Mrs C.
"I don't think any day is nice for a funeral," Simmo replied.
"You know what I mean, Simon."
Simmo nodded, the sunshine making him squint. They stopped for a minute in the bus lay-by, opposite the tenement. The next stop was the church. There may have been one or two people he recognised out of the ten or so standing outside. Ally managed a quick fag before they took the coffin in.
It was a full requiem mass given by a priest who was old enough to have personally known St Patrick. It went on and on, interrupted by an occasional hymn. The smell of incense was choking. Towards the end Simmo could hear shuffling from the back of the church. He turned to see the piper getting ready. As the coffin was being led out he followed and began to play; Simmo recognised the tune but didn't know what it was called.
It was a sombre moment, but as the piper went down the steps the actual pipe part of the bagpipe came out and fell to the floor, leaving the bag making a whooshing noise. Simmo couldn't help himself and started to grin, only for the piper's kilt to flop up over his back as he bent down to pick it up. Simmo burst out laughing at the site of a red hairy arse and bollocks. Then the thought of Ally with a split head and one big brown eye almost escaped his lips, only to be stifled by an elbow in the ribs from Mrs C, who

Gigolos

too was trying desperately not to laugh. In her efforts to silence Simmo and stifle her own laughter she went over on her ankle in the high heels.

"Ouch!" she cried. Simmo put his arm round her. "I've twisted my ankle."

"Ok," said Simmo, "sit down for a minute." She sat on the steps and Simmo started to massage it for her.

Margi came over after talking to the undertaker. "We're getting pressed for time," she said.

Simmo nodded. "I thought it was never going to end."

"Me too."

Mrs C interrupted. "You and Alastair go on; we will meet you there."

The piper, who had now regained his composure, resumed playing whilst the cortège set off once again.

Simmo helped her to the car.

"I won't be able to drive, Simon." Simmo started to panic. "Deep breaths," she said to him.

"But I haven't driven for years!"

"You'll be all right," she said, none too reassuringly.

Simmo fumbled, trying to move the seat forward and adjust the mirror at the same time. As he settled into the driver's seat Mrs C asked him for the tape – she wanted to have a listen just in case. Simmo patted his jacket frantically before remembering he had moved it to his inside pocket. He put it into the cassette player and after a couple of attempts found the play button.

"That's good," she said.

Simmo stopped the tape and pushed what he thought was the rewind button. As he pulled out into the traffic Mrs C cried "look out Simon!" A taxi narrowly missed them.

"You're driving on the wrong side of the road!"

"Shit," said Simmo.

With much kangarooing from Simmo and extra vigilance on the part of Mrs C they eventually arrived. He pulled the car onto the verge, there being nowhere else to park. As he was about to get out Mrs C snatched the cassette, and gave it to Simmo to put in his pocket. He got out, slammed the door, helped her out and started to guide her over to a small open grave. Mrs C was hobbling quite badly.

"No Simon," she said, "not this one."

Simmo looked at her. A couple of the mourners glared.

"This is a burial," she whispered. Simmo looked perplexed. "Mammy is getting cremated."

"Shit," said Simmo, the word resonating in the relative silence, causing one mourner in particular to give him a filthy look.

Simmo half smiled, half nodded an apology as they backed away before turning towards the chapel building with an industrial chimney. The priest was still droning on and on. He could see the undertaker anxiously looking at his watch. Mrs C managed to grab the attention of the usher. She waved the tape. He nodded, came over and stooped to whisper what track number?

"It's the first one," she whispered back, "it's all ready to go."

The usher nodded and disappeared off with the cassette.

They were sat at the very back. As the priest concluded, the red curtain behind the coffin began to open. There was a slight hiss of static and the music started. Mrs C and Simmo slowly looked at each

Gigolos

other. This wasn't the Dubliners... Simmo was trying to recognise the words...

You know that it would be untrue
You know that I would be a liar...

Mrs C put her hand over her mouth as Jim Morrison bellowed out *come on baby light my fire!* just in time to see the curtains closing. Ally craned his neck around. He was shaking his head but for the first time that day he was smiling.

Then it was done. The old priest shook Ally's hand and said something to Margi which made her smile, before cadging a lift with the limo. The next funeral was already on the launch pad.

The original plan was for Mrs C to take them back. Ally had a quick word with the small group that was still there then they shuffled off for the car, Simmo supporting Mrs C. She asked Ally if he didn't mind driving, looking down at her foot and then across to Simmo, gently shaking her head.

"Rough ride?" smiled Ally.

Mrs C smiled too. "Like being an extra in *Death Race 2000*. I had to remind him we drive on the left!" She nudged Simmo gently with her shoulder, causing her to wince by putting extra pressure on her leg. "Give Alastair the keys Mr Molehusband and we can all go home."

Ally poured them all a drink before going out of the back door for a smoke. He was gone about twenty minutes. Simmo was just starting to panic when Ally returned clutching tobacco and a newspaper. He flopped the paper down on Simmo's lap, the whack making him jump. His eyes widened and his jaw dropped as he read the headline:

*International condemnation of French
secret weapon.*

The report went on to say that there were fears of triggering a new international arms race and an urgent meeting of the UN Security Council was being called. The photograph confirmed that it was a weapon and various experts speculated upon the consequences of its use.

Mrs C and Margi laid out a buffet and afterwards they settled down in the lounge. Ally asked to use the phone: he wanted to check the availability of flights. There was no direct flight from Glasgow to Paris, but there was one from Heathrow the following day, and after an almost incomprehensible conversation with a man from the railways, neither being able to understand the other's accent, he confirmed that they could catch the overnight sleeper with just enough time to connect for the airport.

"As soon as that?" said Margi after Ally explained his plans. He looked to Simmo for confirmation. Simmo nodded. "We will have to get our act together though, if we're going to get back before Byron burns the bar down!"

"Byron?" asked Mrs C, and Simmo promptly reeled off some of their adventures. Margi had tears of laughter in her eyes, especially when he told her the tale of the *boomy boomy* juice. Mrs C asked whether they had any photographs? Ally said they didn't have them on them right now, and gave Simmo a conspiratorial wink. Simmo promised to send some when he got back.

Margi looked at her watch. "It's time I was leaving", she said.

Gigolos

"No," said Mrs C, "I'll call you a cab."

As she was leaving Ally tried to stuff a couple of hundred quid into her hand but she wouldn't take it. After she'd gone Ally poked his head through the door. "I'll just have a wee shower," he said.

They could hear him bumping about upstairs, then a gurgling from the pipes.

Simmo and Mrs C sat there in silence, with only the slow, gentle tick of the clock in the hall to disturb their thoughts.

"I'd better start packing," said Simmo. Mrs C looked at him. "I guess this is it," he added.

She shrugged. "I suppose so."

Simmo went out into the hall, then poked his head back in. "Don't mind me asking, and I know it's none of my business but... "Simmo paused. "Is there anyone special in your life?"

Mrs C smiled, then laughed. "God no! I mean, I have plenty of male friends but having one around the house on a permanent basis... well ... they make the place so untidy." She stared hard at Simmo. "There is one, but apparently he is in love with a fishmonger." There was a brief silence, then the two of them burst out laughing.

Ally was a man on a mission: he wanted to get back home. Mrs C had called them a cab - although her ankle had gone down a little she didn't want to drive, and besides she had had a few drinks. Ally thanked her and offered her some money for the phone. "Don't be daft," she said.

She held Simmo by both hands. "Good bye, Simon."

Simmo looked at his feet and then back up to her face. "Good bye, Sharon." He gave her a peck on the lips and then they were gone.

After closing the door she went upstairs. The suit was neatly folded on the bed. She picked it up and hung it in the wardrobe. The bathroom looked like a bombsite with Ally strewing towels everywhere. The waste bin was filled with torn up paper. It was the manila envelope and the contract Ally had shown her, ripped into four quarters. She hoped they knew what they were doing. Then, remembering one of Simmo's mum's expressions, "the good lord looks after drunks and small boys", she smiled.

Simmo wore the dated pair of trainers, the boots stuffed into his holdall.
"Wise move wee man. At least I will nae have tae put up with your moaning about your bloody feet!"
Ally was hoping that they wouldn't get another pull off the coppers, but they would have to wait and see. He relayed what had happened in London.
Simmo pulled a face. "So what happens now?"
"We go home."
"Do you think they will have a pop at us?" Simmo looked a little worried.
Ally thought for a minute, letting out a long stream of cigarette smoke.
"Nae," he said at last, I think they were only interested in getting the film back. The damage is done now, aye; with all this publicity it would look too suspicious.
Simmo looked at him blankly.

The train rattled on through the night, getting in on time.
"Feck it," said Ally, looking at the tube map, "let's jump a cab."
They made their way back outside and hailed a black cab from the steady flow of traffic.

Gigolos

"Heathrow," said Ally to the taxi driver. Again they made good time out of the city and were soon at the terminal. Ally gave the driver a generous tip.

"You sickening for something?" asked Simmo.

"Err, nae, wee man." Ally scratched his head.

"Not like you, Ally, such a large tip."

"Aye, I could nae be arsed waiting for the change."

They checked in with no problem and were soon bound for Paris.

"I reckon if we're going tae get any hassle its coming now," said Ally, but again they breezed through customs as they boarded the plane for the first leg of their journey.

Simmo had a window seat, but he pulled the blind down. The take-off was smooth and Ally was soon puffing away. The events of the last few days had caught up with the both of them and they spent most of the flight with one or the other of them asleep.

They had a couple of hours' stopover in LA, which was mainly spent in the bar. Ally had phoned Rikki and Pascale had grabbed the phone to speak to Simmo.

"You did it!" she said, "I am so proud of both of you. Sven and the boys are heading for Tahiti - they are going to join the protest." She also went on to say that Jean Paul's father had been recalled to Paris in disgrace for his mishandling of the situation.

Ally gave him a dig in the ribs. "Come on Casanova, we've got a plane tae catch." He just had time to tell her he loved her before Ally dragged him off.

They boarded the flight for New Zealand. Ally was quite chatty but Simmo was reflecting on the last few days. He felt free at last. He had exorcised his ghosts...

Ally was a little agitated as the seat belt light came on. The captain expected a little turbulence, but this only lasted for about fifteen minutes or so.

"Aye, I'll never get used tae flying." He had been all right up to that point and it was a great relief to him when the plane touched down in Tahiti.

Simmo was looking out of the window. "What do you make of this?"

There were claxons going off and people running around.

"Shit," said Ally "you dinnae think the bloody plane is on fire?"

Their speculation was interrupted by the captain. A small tsunami wave of about forty centimetres had just struck the island. As a precaution, the passengers were to leave the plane and coaches would take them further inland until the danger passed.

Ally and Simmo looked at each other.

"Shit," said Simmo.

"Aye," said Ally, "but it could have been worse: it could have been a bigger one."

Byron was perplexed; it was like someone had pulled the plug out of the lagoon. He went back into the bar, shaking his head.

"Strangest thing," he said to Rikki, "all the water has gone out of the lagoon."

Rikki and Pascale looked at each other in panic, then simultaneously looked towards the sea. There was a terrific roar as a two metre tsunami crashed through the bar, sweeping it away.

Gigolos

Simmo was starting to panic; another wave had struck. This one was about a metre high but as far as he could gather it hadn't done any real damage. Ally was frantically trying to ring the bar but the line was dead. He tried the Don, and even the High Commissioner's office; nothing.

"I'd nae worry wee man, it might just be the phones here." But there was no conviction in what he said.

The hours passed and speculation grew. There was a rumour that bigger waves had hit the outlying islands - their islands. The airport in Tahiti had reopened and Ally was trying to get a local flight, but the main island airport was still closed to all but military traffic. Information was very garbled and Simmo was now in full blown panic, but Ally had a plan.

"Let's go down tae the docks, see if we can find the Osprey."

The harbour master's office was in chaos. There had been a little damage, mainly to small boats, but the harbour was still functional. There was a lot of military activity as the relief effort got under way. Eventually Ally got hold of an official, but the Osprey wasn't in port.

"Shit," said Simmo.

Ally had another plan. He asked the same official if he could contact the Osprey, but the man started making excuses. Ally produced the wad of money from his Mammy.

"English pounds," he said, "worth a lot of francs."

The man took the money and went into an office at the back. Ally was just starting to think he had done a runner with the cash when he came out again and beckoned Ally over with a finger.

"Osprey on radio." Ally went into the back room and the man handed him the receiver.

"Sven," said Ally.

"Yes?"

"It's me, Ally."

"I thought it was the harbour master's office." Then Sven realised who it was. "Is Pascale with you?" he asked urgently.

"Nae," replied Ally. Sven was silent. "Simmo and me are in Tahiti, the girls are..." he didn't finish. "We cannae get in touch."

"No," said Sven, "I hear it's been pretty bad out there."

"We cannae get a flight or anything, we need tae get back." The desperation in his voice was palpable.

Sven was again silent for a moment. "We are about a day's steaming away. Where are you staying?"

"We're not."

"Ok, I suggest you hang around the International Hotel and as soon as we're close enough I will send a rib to pick you up."

Simmo was like a cat on a hot tin roof, he couldn't sit still. Ally was nursing a beer. They didn't have a lot of money left. Ally had given the man at the harbourmaster's office the envelope from Mammy's, and the couple of hundred from it that Margi hadn't accepted was rapidly dwindling. After what seemed like an age Ally had eventually got through to Margi to let her know they were all right.

The hours passed but both men were silent. The hotel manager let them have a room at a knock-down price after Ally explained their circumstances. Ally suspected it was one of the staff's. Simmo couldn't sleep so Ally took the bed and Simmo dozed in a chair.

Gigolos

There had been some French military personnel in the bar earlier and Simmo had fished for information, pointing to their island on a map. In his pigeon French he worked out that their island was only about forty kilometres from the epicentre of the undersea earthquake that had formed the tsunami. The waiting was torture, and being Simmo he could only think the worst.

The hammering on the door made Simmo jump out of his skin, his vivid dream vanishing like mist. It was Pablo from the Osprey and another of the crew who Pablo introduced as Mark.

"We've come to pick you up," said Pablo.

It didn't take them long to gather their things together. Simmo was cursing because he couldn't find his trainer under the bed and managed to stub his toe at the same time. Normally Ally would have laughed his head off and taken the piss, but his good humour had left him. He had already paid for the room and was heading towards the door when Simmo came down.

"Sven sent us as soon as we were in range for the rib," Pablo explained. "We refuelled before coming to the hotel to fetch you, so put these on and we'll get going."

He handed them all-in one suits and lifejackets. Simmo's legs looked like a concertina in the large bright orange suit.

"Have you had any word from Pascale?" asked Simmo. He was twitching a little and there was a tremor in his voice.

"No," said Mark, "sorry."

Simmo was trying to place Marks's face. Ah, he thought, he had been the guy with the bongos the night the crew had come to the bar.

"We pick up bits n' bobs on the radio, snippets really, but your side of the island took the brunt of it." Mark hesitated and sighed. "I believe there may have been lots of fatalities."

Conversation in the rib was virtually impossible over the noise of the outboard. Despite the heat and the waterproof suit Simmo felt cold - cold on the inside. He'd had that feeling once before, after... after... he shook the thought away.

Ally, despite the constant buffeting and spray, could still manage to produce rollies and marked their passage in a plume of cigarette smoke. Within a couple of hours they had rendezvoused with the Osprey. The rib was quickly hauled on board and they were soon changed and taken to the wheelhouse.

Sven sat in a large chair, staring out of the wheelhouse window. As the ship took a gentle roll he looked at the two men.

"Guys," he said, "I'm sorry, it doesn't look good."

"Have you heard anything?" asked Simmo.

"Nothing official." Simmo's face fell. "There is a French warship co-ordinating the operation. They are trying to account for tourists and islanders. I think because of the island's close proximity there was no warning."

Sven had altered course as soon as the rib was on board and Ally could feel the thrust from the engines. Sven wanted to congratulate Ally for taking the film to the newspapers but now wasn't the moment.

The Osprey ploughed on through a squall. It was still the rainy season; spray was breaking high over the bow and the Osprey was going full speed. The crew tried to make conversation with their passengers but it was obvious to all on board that Simmo and

Ally were both in a state of shock, as were they all. Pascale, after all, had been one of the crew.

As the island drew nearer, Sven asked Ally, "which way do you want to play this? I don't know if we can get in the dock. We may have to anchor off and send the rib in."

"Oh," said Ally, Simmo style.

"Or we can sail around to the other side and see if... "Sven didn't finish. He thought for a while before quietly concluding "I think it's best if we send the rib into town. They might have a casualty list, or I imagine there will be makeshift camps for survivors."

Ally agreed. When they were close enough Sven had the Osprey heave to and they launched the rib, Sven coming with them this time.

It took about an hour to get into the town. The quay was still ok, but the tin sheds along it had taken a mauling. Further along, a fishing boat was high and dry, keeling over and lying on its side. The French minesweeper was tied up alongside the quay.

The rain was intermittent with sudden, sharp downpours.

"Shit," said Ally, looking at the debris strewn everywhere. You could see where it had piled up along the narrow streets. Rivulets of brown water were running down the slope, as what little drainage there was had been blocked.

Sven approached the mine sweeper, and after a heated conversation the sailor on the gangway summoned an officer, who came out to speak to them. The rough estimation was twenty percent loss of life, he said, but that figure could still rise as another roughly twenty percent of the population were still unaccounted for. Simmo asked nervously what the east coast was like. The officer looked down. "That was where most of the casualties were," he said, explaining that almost all the waterfront properties had been washed away.

The officer took their names. "Who else lived at the bar?"

Ally reeled off Rikki and Pascale's names but he couldn't remember Byron's surname. "Do you know?" he asked Simmo. Simmo just shook his head.

Sven suggested they wander through town, just to see if there was anyone about that they recognised. Looking dazed, there was one old boy that used to come into the bar.

"Pascale? Rikki?" Simmo asked him, but he shook his head.

"Tous partis." He said in French.

Simmo looked blank. "It means all gone," said Sven softly.

"What about the Don?" asked Ally. The old boy looked at him oddly. "The Don, you know." He slicked his hair back and stuffed a hand in his pocket in a Marlon Brando pose, pretending to smoke on a cigar with the other hand. Simmo saw recognition on the old boy's face but then it began to fade; he shook his head and repeated "tous partis." The three men turned on their heels and headed back for the quay.

It took about twenty minutes in the rib to get to the other side of the island. As they headed for the lagoon they could see Frankie's, or rather what was left of it. There was only half of one wall left standing, and a couple of hundred yards on there was a heap of twisted, painted metal, presumably whatever had been parked in the car park. The black strip of asphalt, too, had gone, other than for a few dark patches here and there.

Sven slowly guided the rib up the lagoon. There was a lot of debris and trees in the water and he

Gigolos

didn't want to hole her or foul the screw. He beached the rib on the only relatively clear patch he could see.

As Simmo and Ally stepped ashore the heavens opened again. Further up the beach, Simmo could see some sort of megalith sticking up out of the sand. Stood on end and half buried there was a pedalo.

"A fitting epitaph," said Ally bitterly.

There was nothing left of the car park or the road on which Simmo had toiled so hard. As for the bar, there was nothing save a couple of sheared off foundation posts. The shed had gone, too, except for the old Lister generator, its concrete foundation pad now facing the sky.

"Never did get around tae changing the rings," said Ally.

About two hundred yards up the slope where the tank had been was a pile of twisted corrugated sheets, and from there they could hear the staccato of the rain on the metal. Once a comforting sound, and now what? A lament, thought Simmo.

Sven and Mark had caught up with them.

"Listen," said Sven, trying to be subtle, "let me and Mark go up there and see if..." but he couldn't finish.

Simmo's mouth opened and closed but nothing came out, though his brain was screaming.

"I nae think so," said Ally.

Between the four of them they managed to sift through the tin. It was more spread out than they first thought, but after an hour or so it was obvious there was nothing to find.

They spent the next couple of hours searching but the light was starting to fail and the persistent bursts of rain didn't help. Mark had discovered what was left of the Land Rover, but again there was nothing to be found.

"Why are we all so afraid to say the word *bodies*?" Simmo thought to himself. "Scared of jinxing I suppose." But he had little hope left.

"We have to go," said Sven, "I don't want to risk the lagoon in the dark."

Ally nodded.

Sven and Mark walked ahead. Simmo and Ally stopped by the pedalo. There was something bright in the sand. Ally scraped away at the grains with his foot. It was the bloody cocktail sign, still faintly lit. Ally brought his heel down hard. There was a splintering of glass, and an electrical hiss: its death throws. Ally brought his boot down hard again, and it was dead.

Simmo looked at Ally, tears in his eyes. "What are we going to do Ally?" he asked.

Wiping his streaming eyes with the back of his hand, Ally put his big arm around his friend's shoulders.

"I nae know, wee man, but I've heard that they're looking for welders in Aberdeen."

Printed in Great Britain
by Amazon